THE SHADOW KILLER

CATHERINE YAFFE

First published June 2025
Copyright © Catherine Yaffe 2025

ISBN13: 978-1-8384486-5-3

Cover by BookCoverArt

READER NOTE

The Shadow Killer explores dark themes including violence and trauma. Please take care while reading.

PROLOGUE

Saturday, 4 October 2003

As shadows threw obscure shapes over the ground, he looked at her sweet face. Innocent, beautiful, peaceful in repose. He wasn't religious, but if a higher power did exist, he was envious. This exquisite creation was now in the arms of someone, or something, else.

He'd followed her, studied her day and night, tracking her movements. She was so predictable. It had made his job easy; he'd been doing it long enough to know when someone was gullible, and boy, was she. He'd kept it simple in the end, used the oldest trick in the book – dark alley just a stone's throw from Leeds Central Library, a broken shopping bag spewing its contents across the damp road, faking the need for help. Easy peasy, lemon squeezy.

He enjoyed this part of the process as much as the planning and preparation. The creativity that went into the execution. He laughed at his own joke. He never knew beforehand what he was going to be left with, but he was never disappointed.

By now it was a well-rehearsed routine, and a well-practised routine at that. He'd taken a risk with this one, changed his MO slightly and moved the body from its original place, simply for the thrill of it. From the outside, no one would guess what was taking place right there in his living room. The elevation helped. Being on the third floor of the plush apartment block meant there were very few lines of sight. It had been advertised as being a prime location for the city-living lifestyle, and how right they had been. And he should know – his architectural plans had won the contract. His firm, or rather the architectural firm he worked for, had resurrected most of Leeds city centre. As these thoughts ran through his head, he removed his knife from its sheath and watched as the blade glistened in the moonlight that reflected through the window.

He started to carve into the soft, delicate flesh of the eyelids. What was he going to do? This was the last one, he knew that. He knew he couldn't keep pushing his luck, getting away with it. There were too many moving parts these days. That heightened the risk, which he did enjoy but couldn't always control.

As he collected his mason jar from the bench, he jiggled it slightly and watched as the severed eyeballs glooped around in the formalin.

At least she hadn't seen what he had done. None of them had.

The tension in the control room was the most palpable that DI Ziggy Thornes had ever experienced. Alongside his boss,

Chief Superintendent Hastings, and his colleague DS Sadie Bates, they waited and watched remotely through a mounted screen as the armed unit broke into their target's premises. For the last twelve months, women had been disappearing across the country, and in recent months the situation had escalated, with six missing women from within the Yorkshire region alone, all feared to have fallen into the clutches of a serial killer. Ziggy and his team, along with a dedicated nationwide task force, had tracked and traced every single lead. Frustrated, and facing pressure from above, Ziggy had dedicated the last eight months to covert operations and led from the front as they had painstakingly edged closer to finding the killer.

All that work had culminated in this moment.

'Go, go, go,' Ziggy gave the command and watched as the Armed Response team broke down the door of the flat and called out their warnings. They lost visuals, as the CCTV of the apartment building didn't cover the interior. Ziggy had to wait an agonising three minutes, which felt like three hours, until he heard the words, 'One male detained.'

'Is it Hawthorne?' he asked.

'We believe so,' said the unit commander. 'Cuffed and being transferred.'

Ziggy kept the line open on the radio and could hear in the background until a laugh that could cut through glass echoed down the radio channel. Sickened, he turned off the line and turned to Sadie.

'Got the bastard,' he said, leaving the room to head to the custody suite, waiting for evil to enter the building.

1

———

YORKSHIRE POST

Saturday 4th October 2003

THE SHADOW KILLER CAUGHT!

Tonight, the man who has been terrorising the streets of Yorkshire and beyond for the last twelve months is spending his first of many nights behind bars at HMP Wakefield, known locally as Monster Mansion.

James Hawthorne, a 54-year-old architect from North Yorkshire, was finally arrested at his home in Gipton, Leeds after a lengthy police investigation. He is suspected in the disappearance of five women over the past year — and now, with the discovery of Belinda Riley's body, investigators fear the others met the same fate. The anguished parents of Madeline Wadham, Janine Morley, Julia Newbry, Isobel Harmer and the most recent missing woman, Claire Strickland are still awaiting updates on their loved ones.

At a brief press conference, Detective Inspector Andrew 'Ziggy' Thornes, who has been leading the investigation, said that the residents of Yorkshire could sleep easy tonight, knowing that the sadistic killer is safely behind bars. He asked for the public to remain patient as they gathered all the evidence to ensure that James Hawthorne is never allowed to walk the streets again. He reminded the gathered press that there are still missing women, and that all efforts are now focused on the search and that every available resource is being deployed to find them.

Appearing at Leeds Crown Court, Hawthorne, who didn't speak during a five-minute hearing, has carried out his reign of terror in the alleyways throughout the country, leaving devasted families looking for answers as to the disappearance of their loved one.

Sunday, 5 October 2003

Dr Evelyn Shaw read the news report and placed the newspaper down on her desk. Sitting behind the desk in her office at HMP Leeds, she tapped her pen on the pad next to her and thought through the headline. Along with the rest of the region, she was relieved that she no longer needed to watch her back as she walked from her city-centre office to her canal-side apartment.

When the arrest of the Yorkshire Ripper had been made in 1981, she had been midway through qualifying as a forensic psychologist. She could remember the conversations and speculation between inmates, staff and ancillary workers as to where Peter Sutcliffe would be taken and held. Sutcliffe had declared that he did what he did to satisfy the voice of God and had self-claimed 'diminished responsibility'. After the confession there was no other facility secure enough or equipped enough to deal with such a sadistic killer than the notorious Broadmoor Psychiatric hospital.

Evelyn wondered whether Hawthorne would take a similar stance. Would he opt for the diminished responsibility route? As she had worked with the Met Police on the recent case of Anthony Hardy – the Camden Ripper – building a profile that had allowed them to narrow down their search, she'd been approached by various media outlets to speculate on the kind of man the Shadow Killer might be, but she'd declined all requests. It wasn't in her nature to speculate without concrete facts behind it. Of course, Evelyn had her own opinions, her own thoughts about the Shadow Killer. His profile was already of 'celebrity status', which was exactly what he would want. His trial would become a media circus, and he would gain the notoriety he craved.

She sighed and ran her fingers through her long auburn hair before scooping it up into the hair tie that she kept around her wrist. She had two sessions with long-term prisoners this morning that she had been working with on a long term basis.

Right on cue, there was a tap on the office door, followed by a prison guard leading her first patient in. She stood to greet him, adjusted her pencil skirt as she sat back down and waited for the guard to leave.

After checking on his welfare and making sure he was comfortable, she picked up from where they had left off in their previous session.

'How old were you when these thoughts started, Thomas?' She poised her pen to make notes as the prisoner began his journey into the start of the darkness that had ultimately led to the brutal murder of his wife.

Her office at HMP Leeds was small and poky, with two tiny windows. One window faced the courtyard and had bars across it, while the other looked out onto the corridor, where a prisoner officer stood guard. She had a panic button on her desk, should it be necessary though thankfully she'd never had to use it. As she continued to listen, making the appropriate noises and acknowledging the feelings of the killer in front of her, her thoughts returned to the internal conflict she'd been having with herself far too often of late.

She was tired.

She'd been a psychologist for almost thirty years – thirty years of dealing with the worse that society had to offer – and as she entered her late fifties, she felt each one of those years. It was starting to really wear her down. Each case, each person blurring into the next. Was this really what she wanted? Was it where she had wanted to be at this time of her life? Back in her twenties, when she was newly qualified, she had thought she could change the system. That she could make an impact, change people's lives, stop those she could help from re-offending.

But in recent weeks she found herself asking, had she had enough of the profession she once loved? She had felt disillusioned for a while and working on the Hardy case had drained her.

She was oh so very tired, not just from lack of sleep but physically, emotionally and mentally.

Her focused shifted back to the man sat in front of her. They'd had five consultations so far, where he talked and she listened, and they still hadn't reached the source of his trauma. The trigger for his behaviour. Hearing voices was something she was told over and over by her patients. Most of them were lying. It was a common defence, and offenders often felt compelled to stick to it in the hopes of a reduced sentence. She estimated it would be around session eight or nine that the truth would reveal itself. Childhood trauma. Abuse. The abused becomes the abuser. She should know.

Evelyn shuddered and forced herself to focus on the killer in front of her.

Evelyn checked her watch, feeling guilty when she realised their time together was about to end. 'That's all we have time for today, Thomas. I'd like you to continue with your journal. Bring it with you next week.' She stood and knocked on the window, alerting the guard to open the door.

'Thank you, Doc,' said Thomas as he shuffled forward, hands cuffed.

She closed her office door and sat neatly behind her desk. She'd nudged her desk pad slightly, dislodging the carefully laid out pen, pencil and ruler. She meticulously rearranged everything. Order gave her peace of mind, a sense of composure in the darkness that filled her working life. Despite feeling tired, she still had a glimmer of love for her job. She had always thrived on the unpicking of the mind, peeling back the layers. She felt sure that would never change. It was a part of her psyche.

She collected her leather-bound notebook and pen, dropped them into her briefcase and headed for the door. She checked her watch; she had twenty minutes to get to her next appointment, and she wasn't looking forward to it at all. Already the familiar knot of dread had formed in her stomach, and she felt the tension creeping into her jaw. Forcing herself to drop her shoulders, she walked out of the prison with leaden footsteps, every ounce of her slight frame wishing that she could just go home.

2

MISSING
Claire Strickland
22 years old. Single parent to Sam
Last seen leaving Leeds Central Library

Ziggy crossed out the word *Missing* on the whiteboard and replaced it with *Suspected Murder*.

He stood at the front of the conference room and looked around at the weary eyes of his colleagues, who had worked tirelessly to bring James Hawthorne into custody. Whilst Hawthorne was being held on remand, they now had the dual task of preparing for court whilst still searching for Claire and the other missing women. The announcement that they were no longer searching for a missing woman, but her body, had hit the team hard, but they still had a long way to go.

Hours would be spent pouring over the interview transcripts – not that Hawthorne had given anything away. On top of this, Ziggy and his team were still following up on further lines of enquiry and cross-referencing historic cases of missing women against the profile of the Shadow Killer. The fear was that the true total number of deaths that Hawthorne was responsible for would never be known.

As he left the briefing, Ziggy's team followed him.

'That was tough, boss,' DS Sadie Bates said as they all walked back into the MIT office.

'It never gets any easier. It's taking its toll on all of us, but we have to keep pushing. I'm preaching to the converted I know. Look, would you mind making us all a brew and I'll be along in a minute? I'm busting for the loo.'

Sadie laughed. 'No problem. Old-man bladder got the better of you?'

'Cheeky sod,' he replied, smiling as he pushed open the door to the men's room.

Sadie wasn't wrong, though. This case had taken it out of all of them, and the strain was showing in various ways. His old-man bladder was the least of his problems.

Looking in the mirror after relieving himself and washing his hands, he noted that his usually closely shaved head was longer than usual, and he needed a shave. Dark circles under his eyes reflected the very little sleep he'd had these past few months. He'd promised himself a holiday once the case had gone to court and the verdict had been delivered, but Ziggy was well aware that there was still a long way to go between now and that day. He drew himself up to his full six-foot-two height and pulled his shoulders back. He had a job to do.

He joined the team back at their quadrant in the bullpen. DS Nick 'Wilko' Wilkinson was fumbling with his computer whilst DC Angela Dove finished a phone call. Sadie arrived from the kitchen and set down four steaming mugs. The four of them had worked together for over five years and they each knew their role in any investigation, and Ziggy had complete confidence in each of them. Wilko was close to retirement and happy to bash the phones or help with door-to-door enquiries. Not a fan of technology, Nick relied on Angela to keep him up to date with the latest online practices, insisting she speak to him like he was a five-year-old, the same age as his twins. In sharp contradiction, Angela loved nothing more than data entry and was a trained exhibits officer, which required the high level of attention to detail that she excelled at.

Sadie was a career detective and had been Ziggy's right-hand person for the last six years. He had come to rely on her to keep the wider team moving forward as he found himself tied up more and more with meetings and paperwork, something he loathed. But it also gave Ziggy the opportunity to follow his own instincts from time to time without too many questions from his team.

Nick admitted defeat with his keyboard, sat back in his chair and crossed his arms over his burgeoning stomach. 'Have you seen the latest "expert profile" in the *Sun*?' He used air quotes and gave a disparaging shake of his head. 'Utter bollocks, all of it.'

'I haven't, thankfully. Where are we with forensics from the Hawthorne raid?' asked Ziggy, looking around the team. It was Angela that answered. 'Just started to come through. As you would imagine, Hawthorne's DNA is abundant. There are a few latent prints that aren't on record, so that's something of a lead. Maybe another victim?' She leaned back, folded her arms across her chest and shook her head. 'It's all just so desperately sad, isn't it? I do worry about my girls going to and from college I have to say.' As a mother of two girls in their early twenties, Angela was feeling it more than any other case they had worked on.

'But we've caught him, Ang. We have to stay focused on that at least,' Ziggy said. He turned to Sadie. 'Have you read the interview transcripts?'

'Yeah, for all that's worth,' Sadie replied disparagingly.

Hawthorne had chosen to go 'no comment' throughout the initial interviews. His solicitor had read a prepared statement in which he denied all responsibility, despite being caught – literally – in the act. Ziggy had viewed the interviews and was glad that he hadn't been in the room; patience was not his strongest point.

'Where next?' asked Sadie.

Ziggy slurped the last of his coffee. 'I'm planning on meeting with Doctor Shaw, the psychologist. I'm hoping to convince her to speak with Hawthorne.'

'Didn't she work on the Anthony Hardy case?' Sadie asked. 'She's got a formidable reputation.'

'Yes, that's the one. I figure if she can't break him, then no one can. He's not offered any kind of defence as of yet, though I'm fully expecting diminished responsibility.'

3

___

Evelyn's nose wrinkled as she forced open the front door of the house where her brother lived. Vernon dwelt in abject squalor, but that wasn't the only reason she detested visiting him.

Their childhood had been one of poverty, ridicule and isolation. Raised on a neglected smallholding on the outskirts of the North Yorkshire market village of Helmsley, Evelyn had worked laboriously to leave it all behind her. She had studied hard when she had the chance and moved away as soon as she had scraped together enough to get the bus ticket to Leeds.

For three decades, she'd lost all contact with her given family, creating her own background or avoiding the question altogether if asked. She'd always known a day of reckoning would come, though, and after she read the death announcement of her parents in the *Yorkshire Evening Post* obituary section, she knew it wouldn't be much longer before he came looking.

Vernon walked back into her life after a particularly intense day at the prison. All she'd wanted to do was kick off her shoes, take a hot bath and submerge herself until the tension left her body. Instead, she had found the hulk-like figure of her older brother lying nonchalantly on her cream leather settee, eating crisps and opening what appeared to be his third can of Stella Artois. He had clearly been there a while if the detritus littered around him was anything to go by.

Years of torment had come flooding back, and she'd had to cling to the door frame to stop herself from falling to the floor.

Now, three years later, she was still caught in his world, and she abhorred every second she had to spend in his company.

As she navigated down the narrow stairs to his basement flat, she picked her way through the discarded pizza boxes and takeaway cartons that had fallen from the split black bin liner at the top of the barely carpeted stairs. Lingering black mould patches on the walls added to the general smell and feeling of decay.

'Vernon,' she called, fumbling for the hallway light switch.

'In here,' came the gruff reply.

Evelyn tensed. Just from the deep-throated grunt, she knew her brother had probably been on his computer all day, doing God knows what.

She hefted the bag of shopping into the kitchenette, ignoring him as he turned in his La-Z-Boy chair to watch her. She hadn't had time to go home and get changed, so she was painfully aware of her pencil skirt as it rose above her knee whilst she raised the bag onto the counter. Vernon didn't need any encouragement to look at her lasciviously, sister or not. It turned her stomach. She flicked on the light for the extractor fan in the otherwise darkened room.

'You're late,' he snapped. A host of computer screens flickered in the background. He'd blacked out the windows a long time ago and the only light in the room aside from the blue-screen glow was the light from the kitchen.

'I know, I'm sorry. Traffic was horrendous and I couldn't get parked outside.' She could have kicked herself for apologising to him, but it was behaviour learnt long ago that she had struggled to break, despite the promises to herself. His control of her ran deep, but her shame at failing to counsel herself had stopped her from sharing it with anyone. Delivering him a bag of shopping every other week and paying his rent was a small price to pay to keep her past hidden.

'You should plan better then,' he snapped as he pushed hard on the arms of the chair to leverage himself upwards. 'Help me.' He glowered.

Placing the box of tea bags onto the counter, she sighed and crossed over to him. She hooked her hand under his forearm, which was already moist with sweat, and pulled. She steeled herself to not recoil as rolls of flesh squeezed through her fingers. She tried hard not to dig her filed nails into his flesh, but she accidentally caught his skin as he finally stood upright.

'Bitch!' he yelled, spitting the word at her as he cradled his scratched arm.

Immediately, she apologised again, but it was too late. With the back of his hand, he clipped her around the ear. Her hand immediately flew to where he had struck her and felt the warm ooze of blood as the very top of her ear started to bleed. Stepping backwards, she looked around for a tissue or something to hold against it.

'Clumsy bitch at that,' he said as he shuffled over to inspect the groceries.

Evelyn refused to cry and drew on her inner reserves.

'Don't ever do that again, Vernon,' she said firmly. 'That is not acceptable, and I will not tolerate it.' She held some kitchen roll to her ear and looked at it. It was only a nick, thankfully; no visible cuts that she would struggle to explain.

'Fuck off,' said Vernon as he pulled out a packet of Super Noodles. Although she'd agreed to buy him food, she hadn't promised what kind and often brought him blocks of cheese and foods full of saturated fat. She hoped he would die a horrible death from heart failure with clogged arteries and high blood pressure.

She reminded herself that she still held some of the cards in their bitter sibling war. She paid his rent. Without it, he would be homeless, she was sure. She didn't know what he did for money aside from what she paid for, and she truly didn't care.

Dabbing her ear again, she turned to leave.

'If there's anything else you need, you'll have to get it yourself,' she said as she held open the door that led to the hallway.

'Why? Won't you be here in two weeks?'

'No, Vernon, I won't. I have my own life, and frankly, I'm too busy with work,' she said defiantly. They'd had this conversation so many times.

'Ha! I doubt that. You'll be back,' her brother snorted as he took the multi-bag of crisps and a six-pack of Stella and sloughed his way back over to his chair.

She took one last look at him, wondering how the hell they were ever related, and walked out. As she made her way back into the daylight, she heard his final words, and her earlier repulsion returned with force.

'Bye, bye, Evie.'

As soon as she was home and through her front door, she kicked off her heels, headed straight to the kitchen and retrieved a bottle of Chablis from the fridge. After taking a wine glass from the cupboard, she opened the bottle and poured herself a large glass. Her hand shook slightly as she sipped the golden liquid. Glass empty, she refilled it and headed upstairs to run herself a hot bath. She added plenty of bath salts and lit candles around the tub. She headed into her bedroom and slipped off her clothes. Wrapping herself in her luxury dressing gown, she sat on the edge of the bed as the wine started to kick in. Her head felt woozy, and as the room began to spin, she collapsed back onto the duvet and closed her eyes.

My lungs are about to explode. I need to stop. The alleyway is pitch black – the streetlights didn't extend this far down. He won't come down here. Come on, Evelyn, you can stop when you reach that telegraph pole. I can see my target right in front of me. Past the mist and fine rain. Just a few more steps, then you can stop. Finally, I reach it. It's wet, but I don't care. I cling to the telegraph pole; it smells of tar and feels sticky under my hand. I press my back against it and slide to the concrete pavement, resting my head just for a minute on my knees. My eyes are streaming, though I'm not crying. It must be from all the running, it must be. I sweep back tendrils of wet hair from my face. Some got caught in my mouth earlier and I wonder if I'll cough up a hairball like Mum always says I will. I spit, trying to get some saliva in my mouth. I swallow hard, gasping air into my lungs. My breathing is slowing down, though my chest is hurting and I have a stitch in my side.

I lift my head to see if I can hear anything. There's nothing. Not even the dogs are barking.

I don't know what time it is. It must be past seven cos the streetlights are on.

What was that? I listen carefully. There it is again. He's getting closer. Please don't turn down here. If I scrunch myself up really tight, perhaps he won't see me. He's really close now.

Oh God, he's here. Don't say it, please, please don't say it.

'Oh Evie...'

This was it. This was her unhappy ending.

Evelyn shot upright, alerted by a telephone ringing. Disoriented, she threw herself across the bed and answered her landline. 'Yes,' she said, pushing damp hair away from her forehead, echoes of her nightmare still lingering.

'Evelyn, it's Detective Inspector Ziggy Thornes from West Yorkshire Police.'

She became aware of a dripping sound. Oh, damn, she'd left the bath running. Cursing, she threw the handset onto the bed and hurried into the bathroom. Water had just started to leak over the top.

'No, no, no, no!' she shouted, turning the tap off and delving her hand into the water. She withdrew it immediately as the scolding temperature burnt her skin. 'Holy shit,' she yelled, shaking her hand and grabbing a towel to stem the pain. Swearing and clutching her hand she headed back into the bedroom.

She snatched up the discarded handset. 'Now is not a good time,' she said.

'Are you OK? I heard someone yell?'

'It was me – the bath has overrun. I need to go sort it out.' She replaced the handset and ignored it when it started to ring again.

She went back into the bathroom and slid down the wall, getting her dressing gown even more wet in the puddles that had formed on the floor. Feeling fragile and vulnerable, she placed her arms around her knees, lowered her head and cried.

4

____

Monday, 6 October 2003

Sleep clung to Evelyn as she stood in the cold reception area of the West Yorkshire Police headquarters. She hadn't been surprised to receive the call the previous evening, but she just wished the timing had been better. She dreaded to think what DI Thornes must have thought when she'd finally returned his call this morning. They'd glossed over her abruptness last night with mumbled apologies and moments of awkward silence until Ziggy had just blurted out that he wanted help with the Shadow Killer.

Evelyn knew a little about the detective inspector from her past work with the police, but they had never worked directly together. She'd heard he was a bit of a maverick, and from seeing him on the news, she knew he was handsome, tall, but self-conscious in front of the camera. To her, it seemed that he would rather be working on a case than parading in front of the press. She seemed to recall having read that somewhere along the line he'd had a run-in with the media in the past, but the details escaped her.

Though the reception was chilly, she couldn't stop the hot flush from creeping up from her chest. Fanning herself, she rooted about in her bag for a tissue or a wet wipe when she heard her name called.

'Good to see you, Dr Shaw.' Ziggy walked forward to shake hands.

Hoping it wasn't still sweaty to the touch, Evelyn stuck out her hand and returned the friendly greeting.

'You too, DI Thornes.'

'Ziggy, please. Can I get you a drink? Tea, coffee?' Ziggy asked as they walked through the double doors that led into the main building and down a corridor lined with meeting rooms and offices.

'Could I just have a glass of water, please?'

'Sure,' he said as he pushed open a meeting-room door. 'Take a seat and I'll sort that for you.'

Evelyn did as he asked as he left the room. A large Formica conference table dominated the meeting room, with chairs tucked neatly underneath. A redundant projection screen stood at one end, and in the centre of the table sat a projector. Deciding to sit at the one of the seats on the side rather than at the of the head of the table, she placed her leather tote bag on the seat next to her and retrieved her document folder. She turned to a clean page in a notepad and laid her pen alongside, waiting for the detective to return.

Whilst she hadn't been surprised by the request, she wasn't entirely convinced that she would take the case. It all came down to exactly what was expected of her. She already had a caseload of private clients on top of her work with the prison, and that was her planned exit strategy; she earned more privately, so wasn't in a position to take on underpaid police jobs when the private work added to her pension pot.

The door opened, and Ziggy re-entered with a tray, balancing a jug of water and a cup of coffee. Evelyn briefly regretted her choice at the warming waft of the coffee, but she simply couldn't tolerate any more caffeine if she wanted to sleep tonight.

Once they had both taken a drink, Evelyn cut straight to the chase. 'So, the Shadow Killer?' she said, tapping her Mont Blanc pen against her pad.

'Yes, as the media have helpfully dubbed him.'

'Indeed... What can I do to help?'

Ziggy extracted a few sheets of paper from a folder he had in front of him. 'As you know, he is currently on remand at HMP Wakefield. We haven't managed to get anything out of him, in all honesty, and we need your help. There are still the missing women of course, what does he know about them? There's also Claire Strickland, the most recent Misper. We simply don't have the evidence we need to tie him into all the women that we believe he is also responsible for kidnapping, potentially killing.'

Evelyn blew out her breath noisily. 'And you'd like me to do what?' She hadn't meant to sound so abrupt, but Ziggy didn't seem to notice.

'Talk to him. Interview him. See if you can get under his skin. Anything you can get out of him, to be honest. We have reason to believe that there are more victims out there than we know about. We have a number of other historical cases that we feel we can tie him into, here and nationwide.

Evelyn sipped her water; a bitter taste had developed in her mouth. 'Go on.'

Ziggy shifted his position. 'This is strictly off the record for now.' She nodded, encouraging him to continue. 'Well, whilst he's been on remand, a cell mate has come forward to say Hawthorne has told him of at least one further murder and various other incidents, including rape and sexual assault.'

'Wow, OK. Another inmate? And you believe him?'

'We do. He's told us details that aren't yet in the public domain. Hawthorne's trophy taking, for a start.'

'Trophy taking? That's removing an item from the scene, right?

'Yes, that's right.'

'Tell me about this inmate. Is he waiting to be released? What has he asked for in return?'

'Nothing. He was so disgusted by what Hawthorne told him, he felt compelled to pass the information on.'

Evelyn sat back. 'Huh, a con with a conscience. A rare breed.'

'Exactly,' replied Ziggy. 'Which is why we're taking it seriously, but...'

'How did I know there was a *but*?'

Ziggy smiled again. 'There's always a *but*. The murder he was talking about could relate to the women that haven't been found yet, including Claire Strickland. We need more locations, places to search. We need more indisputable evidence that ties him into the other cases we believe he's responsible for.'

Evelyn stared off into the middle distance for a moment. This was a big ask. It would mean completely clearing her diary and focusing on this one case. Did she want to fully throw herself into it? It would be a demanding case, both emotionally and intellectually, and she wasn't sure she had enough capacity.

She was snapped out of her thoughts as Ziggy stood and started pacing. After a minute or two, he scratched his not-so-closely shaved head and spoke. 'You won't be expected to find all of this out on your own, of course. We have leads that we're working on, but he's been talking in circles, and we can't get a handle on him. What I need – what *we* need – is an insight into his mindset.'

'OK. Tell me what you *do* know.' Evelyn started making notes on her pad as he spoke.

'There are *some* consistencies in the way he *takes* the victims. Always early evening, usually from the city centre or thereabouts. From an alleyway, or somewhere similar. I mean, it's textbook of the routine that offenders will follow but that's about the *only* thing that fits any kind of pattern. Also, let's not forget he was caught with one victim in his flat.'

Evelyn knew all this from the few news reports she had read, but she respected Ziggy going over the main points for her benefit. 'Tell me more about the girls. Where do they work? Are they single? In a relationship? Children? Ethnicity?'

'They've all been single, or in short-term relationships. Live alone or with their parents. Claire was the only woman with a young son. Mixed in relation to ethnicity, with no discernible connection to either Hawthorne or each other.'

'And work?' Evelyn prompted as she made notes.

'Varied. Majority are students, so their jobs are part-time around their studies.'

'Students? College professor, maybe? A tutor?'

'Yes. We've looked at that angle – nothing. Stalking has also been explored. We have no evidence from family or friends that any of the victims had reported or talked about anyone pestering them.'

'You mentioned trophies. What did he take?'

Ziggy sat back down. 'From the victim we arrested him with – Belinda Riley – he'd taken her eyes.' He swallowed and momentarily closed his own eyes, as struggling with the image. 'And he carved numbers into her torso.'

'Now that I didn't know.'

'No, we haven't released that to the press.'

'And this informant, he mentioned both of these details?'

'Yes, which only confirms our belief that he's telling the truth.'

'Has Hawthorne given anything away in interviews?'

Ziggy sighed. 'We've interviewed him for hours, and he either talks in riddles that make no sense to us or goes "no comment".'

'That must be frustrating.'

'We've come to expect it, to be honest, and I think we've prised everything out of him that we can.' He sat back down, placing his hands on his thighs. 'I guess what I'm really asking is if you'll get inside his head, dig deeper than we can in interview?'

Evelyn shrank back in her chair. 'I admit, I'm intrigued, Ziggy.'

'Intrigued enough to help?'

When Evelyn didn't answer, Ziggy leant forward, closing the space between them. 'I understand your hesitancy, but, Evelyn, there are families out there stuck in limbo. They have no idea what's happened to their precious daughters, sisters, aunts. We have to deliver answers for them. We need to serve justice and make sure this piece of scum never sees the light of day again.'

It was an impassioned speech, and Evelyn faltered. She

needed time, time to give herself a chance to really think it through and what it might mean for her personally, the impact on her time and her already depleted energy reserves. 'Can I think about it?' she asked.

Ziggy chewed his bottom lip. 'How long would you need?'

'Just a few hours, I just need to think about the impact on my time.'

'I can't see a problem with that. Will you call me?'

Evelyn collected her belongings and stood up. She was suddenly keen to get out there, as she felt another hot flush starting, and she didn't want to Ziggy to think it was stress or overwhelm. 'Sure, I'll call you tomorrow,' she said and walked towards the door.

As she walked down the long corridor, she could feel Ziggy's eyes on her back. She felt self-conscious; what with the abrupt phone call last night and the swift exit she had just made, he was probably thinking her quite odd.

The desk sergeant buzzed her through to the main reception area, and as she strode out of the building, she took deep breaths as she fought to steady her creeping anxiety.

In amongst everything else, she now had to make a decision that could very likely impact the rest of her career, not to mention her life.

5

Evelyn's Home

Evelyn swallowed hard. No. She couldn't. She wouldn't.

Her hand trembled as she moved to close the laptop, but she hesitated. That old, familiar pull – part curiosity, part obligation – tightened around her like a noose. She had spent years untangling the minds of killers, dissecting their motivations, their patterns, their sickness. And she was good at it. Too good. Good enough that the various agencies still came knocking, even now, when she was supposed to be winding down into a quieter life.

She exhaled and pressed her fingers to her temples. *Quieter.* As if peace had ever been an option for her.

Vernon. Even though she'd told him to back off, she doubted he would. She'd made life too easy for him. She shouldn't have got involved, but he was family – that meant something, didn't it? If she took this case, would she have the mental capacity to juggle the pressure?

And the past – her past – she had spent decades burying

it beneath professionalism, careful distance, and time. With such a high-profile case, there was bound to be scrutiny from the press. She forever lived with the fear that someone would start digging. Someone always did.

Her chest tightened. She could already hear the questions, see the headlines, feel the walls closing in.

Still, she didn't move. Because beneath the fear, beneath the exhaustion and the weight of everything she had worked so hard to escape, there was something else.

The Shadow Killer. A name. A puzzle. A call she wasn't sure she had the strength to ignore.

God help her.

She clicked the email open, replied and went to bed.

Tuesday, 7 October 2003

The following morning, Evelyn studied her face in closely in the bedroom mirror. She noted the deep-set lines on either side of her eyes. Laughter lines, she called them, though she hadn't done much of that in recent months. She gave herself a shake of her shoulders to dismiss the negative self-talk. She'd had yet another night's worth of broken sleep, mulling over her decision to work with West Yorkshire Police. She had liked Ziggy Thornes. He emanated warmth and friendliness, and she suspected he would be easy to work with. She'd emailed him late yesterday and told him that she would work on the case. Not that she really had a choice. It was the biggest case in the UK. Families needed answers. More importantly, victims needed justice. That was a key point for her.

Her first meeting with the notorious killer had been scheduled for later this morning, and she'd hurriedly rearranged her private appointments. Some wouldn't be pleased, but some would no doubt be relieved at the temporary reprieve they'd been offered before their next session of baring their souls.

When sleep had eluded her, she'd spent most of the early hours going over as much as information as she could get her hands on about James Hawthorne. She was mindful that searches were still active for the missing women, and this would be part of her strategy too. If the police interviewers hadn't been able to extract anything from him, she was under no illusion that she had her work cut out for her.

She walked away from the bedroom mirror without looking back.

Same day, HMP Wakefield

Evelyn battled with technology as she entered the secure entrance to HMP Wakefield. Scanners and identity checks. Issuing of swipe cards. Body scanners and physical checks. All time-consuming but compulsory.

After she finally cleared security, the heel of her black patent shoe struck the cold linoleum floor in time with her hurried heartbeat as she followed her allocated guard, who would stay with her for the duration of her visit. She shivered as the bare walls reverted to the cold exposed brick Victorian interior. She was surprised at how clean everything was. Perhaps it was to detract from the plaster that was falling off the walls in places. The floor had just been polished, so she walked carefully to avoiding slipping.

On reaching the interview room, the guard instructed her to sit whilst the prisoner was brought to her.

The allocated room was benign, bland. A simple

Formica table with plastic moulded chairs, one of which was screwed to the floor. An alarm was hidden behind thick white panelling that ran the circumference of the eight-by-ten-foot interview room. Padded walls and insulation dulled the noises from the prison population. Evelyn was used to a certain level of disturbance whenever she went into a prison. The sounds of inmates shouting and, in some cases, screaming.Wakefield was different. Wakefield had an eery silence that unnerved her.

She took her leather-bound notebook from her bag and placed her pen across it. She was grateful for the plastic cup of water she had been given. No hot liquids were allowed. She took a small sip to wet her cotton-filled mouth, relishing the cool sensation. Beads of sweat hung at the back of her neck, and she hoped that it wouldn't develop into the hot flushes she had recently been plagued with. She fanned herself ineffectually with her hand and loosened the top button of her shirt. Thankfully, she'd left her jacket in a locker at the entrance.

Glancing down at the notes she had made about James Hawthorne, Evelyn briefly closed her eyes to order her thoughts.

Judging from the injuries to Belinda Riley's body, his killing was sadistic. The pathology report had macabre details that Evelyn wouldn't ordinarily be privy to, but she had insisted; she needed to know exactly who she was dealing with. Along with Ziggy's revelation about the removal of the eyes and the carving in the stomach she felt she had an insight into his psyche.

In sharp contrast, however, his background presented none of the usual warning signs that would mark him out as one to watch. No animal cruelty or fire setting. No bed wetting. From what Evelyn could tell, his childhood was reasonably settled. Middle-class parents: his father had been a successful businessman, whilst his mother had stayed at home to raise James and older sister Alison. A model student, James had excelled academically before going on to university to study architecture, from which he had built a successful career. He had often appeared in newspaper articles and magazines, cited as a visionary for his brilliant if unconventional designs. He'd won numerous awards for his modern, minimalist creations. Evelyn had read as much as she could about his upbringing and career but could find nothing on his personal life. There was no mention anywhere of a spouse or partner. No reports of any children. No family outside of his sister and now deceased parents.

Evelyn had reached the conclusion that his personal life was pretty much echoed in his artistic creations, barren.

Reviewing the images of the victim, Evelyn believed the motive to be sexual, despite the fact that Belinda Riley hadn't been sexually assaulted – a small blessing in the scheme of things. He had used a knife to stab the breasts, which could be viewed as a form of penetrative sexual assault. He had left the victim naked and had been preparing the graphic display when he was captured. In Evelyn's opinion, for him this was a stage; he wanted what he had done to be viewed, perhaps even admired. It was an indication of his tastes and sexual fantasies. The victim's wrists had been bound, hinting at the inherent sadism in the attack. The poor girl had been through hell.

Ziggy had first mentioned the numbers carved on the body, Evelyn wondered what their significance was. And the gouging of the eyes?

Perhaps that he didn't want to be seen – or he didn't want the victim to see him at his most depraved?

Ego. It all smacked of an overinflated ego.

Narcissist. Almost a given, in her extensive experience.

Evelyn had tried to track down his medical records, but apparently, they had been misfiled in the system somewhere and it was going to take time to locate them. Frustrating but a common enough occurrence.

Her immediate goal was to establish some level of understanding of James Hawthorne. To build trust. A vital element if she was to work with him.

As she turned to a clean page in her notebook, the door opened with a creak and the prison guard walked in.

She'd been in the presence of nasty people in her life, but absolute evil oozed from the pores of the man who followed behind. The air crackled with tension as Evelyn looked at James Hawthorne in the flesh for the first time.

6

———

At six foot two, Hawthorne was lean and athletic, with the posture of someone who took pride in their physical appearance. His hair, which could have been considered unkempt – long enough to verge on scruffy – was instead tousled. Evelyn sensed it was deliberate; *I could look neat, but I choose not to.*

It was his eyes that unnerved her the most. In the photographs she had viewed, she had noted their unusual shade of green. Gemstone green. Seeing them without the sheen of photographic paper, they were even more startling. Piercing. Cold. Calculating. His eyelashes were dark and overly long, making it look like he was wearing mascara. She gave an involuntary shudder and rose from her seat.

'The prisoner must remain handcuffed, miss,' said the guard unnecessarily as he placed his hand on Hawthorne's shoulder and pushed him into the seat opposite her. He adjusted the chain that separated the cuffs and fastened it securely to the bolt that was protruding from the table.

Evelyn nodded and retook her seat.

An uneasy silence fell in the room. She coughed and took another sip of water.

'Can I get you a drink of water, Mr Hawthorne?' she asked.

'No, but thank you,' came the polite reply.

Hearing his voice was a surprise. He was softly spoken, barely moving his lips. She had expected him to be loud, deep, gravelly. Husky, almost. She silently chided herself for stereotyping.

'Mr Hawthorne, my name is Doctor Evelyn Shaw, and I'm a forensic psychologist. I'm here today—' Hawthorne raised his chained hands as far as he could. 'Yes?'

'Please, call me James,' he said, smiling and revealing a set of perfectly white teeth.

'OK, if that's what you would prefer.'

'And you? What do I call you? Doctor? Doc? Evelyn?' He paused, and as much as Evelyn wanted to look away, she couldn't break his intimidating stare. 'Or is it Evie?'

She stared at him, momentarily blindsided. Evie was a name she despised, echoes of a life she had tried so desperately to leave behind. Pulling herself back into the room, she hoped her hesitancy hadn't shown.

'Dr Shaw is fine.' She shifted and pulled her notebook closer.

'No first names then?'

She paused again before answering.

'Fine, if you would prefer to call me Evelyn, that's fine.'

'Evelyn then. Definitely not Evie, though?' He raised one eyebrow and smiled.

She ignored his attempt to intimidate her but was equally intrigued. 'Why does it matter to you?'

'Me? Oh, it matters nothing to me. I just wanted to be

clear.' He sat back in his chair as another smile crept into the corner of his mouth.

Evelyn mirrored his movements and continued.

'James. Thank you for agreeing to meet with me today. I'm here at the request of West Yorkshire Police. I am working closely with them to offer insights into your case.'

'My case?'

'Yes. Do you have an issue with that? You will have signed consent forms...'

Hawthorne shifted abruptly in his seat, crossing his legs. The sudden movement made Evelyn flinch slightly. She hadn't realised how tightly wound she was. Perhaps it was the weight of the atmosphere, or the mention of her childhood name.

Hawthorne looked around the room. 'Is this being recorded? Are there cameras filming us?'

She saw his smile broaden; he would be enjoying the idea that he might have an audience other than her to play to. It would be hard to deny with the red light blinking away in the corner of the room.

'Does that bother you?' she ventured.

He turned back to the table. 'Does it bother *you*?'

'No. It's for your safety and mine.'

'Do you feel unsafe, Evelyn?' He leant forward, tenting his fingers and resting his chin on them.

Did she feel unsafe? Unnerved, unsettled in a way she hadn't before with prisoners, perhaps. But she wasn't about to tell Hawthorne that. 'No. Should I?'

He laughed and sat back, recrossing his legs. 'You tell me.'

'I'd like you to feel comfortable talking with me, James. The video is non-negotiable.' She turned over her notes. 'Are you happy to answer my questions?'

'Will they be used in court? The videos?'

He was going to make me work hard for this, isn't he?

'It's unlikely. This is more of a get-to-know-each-other session.' She hesitated to see if there was any response. He simply continued to stare at her. Her skin prickled under the intense scrutiny, but she absolutely refused to show any response.

Ordinarily, she would use a structured and ordered evaluation in these interviews, but in Hawthorne's case, she had already figured that format wouldn't work. She decided to take a different approach. 'I'd like you to tell me something about yourself. Maybe a childhood memory, or a food you like.'

'Will you do the same?'

'Of course.'

'Hmm. Now let me see.' Hawthorne turned to his side. 'My fifth birthday party.'

Evelyn made notes as Hawthorne spoke. She was wary of his apparent eagerness to talk when Ziggy had told her they had found it so hard to prise anything out of him.

'Is that a happy memory?' she probed.

He ignored her question and spoke in a monotonous tone, not quite bored but one of utter indifference. It occurred to Evelyn that this might have been a well-rehearsed routine. 'We had a party in the back garden. All my friends were invited. My sister was ten. My mother had gone to a lot of trouble, prepared all the food, decorated the living room and garden. Arranged all the party games.'

'How did that make you feel?'

'It rained. All day. It didn't stop.'

Hawthorne closed his eyes in reflection as he spoke.

Evelyn maintained her silence, watching him closely.

After a long moment where time seemed to stand still,

his eyes flashed open, and he looked at her with a penetrating stare, as though he could see into her soul. 'Your turn,' he said, the reappearing smile now seeming haunting, teasing.

She faltered momentarily under his scrutiny. 'I, I, well, I like walks in the countryside.'

Hawthorne laughed. A guttural chuckle that sounded inappropriate in the drab walls of the bland room. He looked up at her through his eyelashes flirtatiously. 'Of course you do.'

Despite herself, Evelyn felt her cheeks redden; not quite the hot flushes she'd been experiencing, but she was conscious of her colour changing. Hoping Hawthorne hadn't noticed, she cleared her throat and continued on. 'Tell me more about your birthday party.'

His face immediately closed down again and looked away. 'It was ruined. The rain ruined everything. No one came.'

'Because of the rain?'

His mouth turned down and he wrinkled his nose in disgust. 'Yes, because of the rain!' He raised his voice, and Evelyn was taken aback at the swift change in his demeanour. His eyes were wide open, and he looked at her with contempt. He tried to stand, the metal cuffs clinking sharply against the table, but they kept him in place.

The guard was at the door in an instant. 'Everything all right in here?'

Evelyn's pulse hammered in her ears. The pressure in the room was suffocating now, like the air had thickened into something solid.

Hawthorne exhaled a slow, rattling breath as he sat down again, his cuffed wrists twitching against the metal bindings.

Then he laughed. A low, wet chuckle that crawled up her spine like a spider.

The overhead light flickered. The guard took a cautious step forward, one hand drifting toward the baton at his hip. "Hawthorne, I need you to—"

Hawthorne snapped his head up. His eyes – wrong, empty, too wide – locked onto Evelyn's. The pressure in the room surged, a deafening silence swallowing every other sound.

7

———

Evelyn, shaken but determined to carry on, dismissed the guard and took a few minutes to let her heartbeat to settle. Hawthorne's expression remained unchanged; although he appeared calmer, his stare was no less intense. As though he were assessing her, not the other way round.

She took a deep breath.

Evelyn had tested the ground with her previous question, but she realised now that, if she allowed him any room, he would redirect the focus of the conversation. Equally, direct interrogation wouldn't work. She had to be subtle, leading – she had to feed his ego.

Sitting back in her chair, she folded her hands in her lap and continued. 'Are you happy to continue, James?' she asked. When he nodded his consent, she continued in a different direction. 'You don't seem like someone who just reacts. You plan, don't you?'

Hawthorne mirrored her movements, leaning back in his chair and letting his hands relax as much as the cuffs allowed. When he spoke, it was deliberate, every word carefully pronounced. 'It's all about the moment before, the pause between thought and action. That's where the real power lies. The difference between a masterpiece and a mess is knowing when to wait... and when to strike.'

'I see. What you're saying is, it's not the act – it's the anticipation. Is that why you changed your routine?' She was deliberately evasive about who they were talking about, hoping he would slip and give something away about where Claire Strickland was.

She watched as he paused, his eyes flickering with what she construed to be amusement. *He was enjoying this*. He exhaled and looked at her down his nose with an air of superiority.

'Now that's an interesting assumption, Dr Shaw. But tell me – why do you think it took longer? Do you believe I hesitated? That I lost control?' He tilted his head, watching her closely. He continued before she had a chance to reply. 'No, no... You should know by now, Dr Shaw – I only prolong things when they deserve to be prolonged.'

'*Deserve*... that's an interesting word. Do your victims deserve the treatment you inflicted upon them?'

'Perhaps.'

'You changed your tactic with the last one, didn't you? Why?'

She saw a subtle change in his facial expression. He thought she was questioning his modus operandi. Maybe she was. Silence fell and she used it to her advantage, not breaking his stare.

'Perhaps the situation demanded it,' he said eventually.

Claire Strickland had been taken from a busy walkway that ran alongside Leeds Central Library. Now that she had his attention, she wanted to pin down some specifics.

'The situation, you say. Were there too many people around? Too public perhaps?'

'Yes, too busy, too messy.'

So, they *were* talking about Claire. Belinda had been taken from a secluded country lane.

She watched as the realisation dawned on Hawthorne's face that she had tripped him up. She tensed, wondering how he would respond.

A slow smile crept across his face, and he lifted his chin. 'If only life was that simple, eh, Evie?'

She jolted at the utterance of the name she detested. 'I've asked you not to refer to me as that.' She regretted her tone but wouldn't be bullied.

Hawthorne continued. 'Who called you that, Evie? Someone you ended up hating? Did they torment you, Evie? Did their bullying get the better of you?'

Evelyn fought to remain calm and studied him like a specimen under glass. When she finally spoke, she deliberately kept her tone neutral and even.

'You want me to say something emotional, don't you? To react? Maybe even to lash out. You're hoping to steer the conversation away from Claire because I was getting too close. That's it, isn't it?' She paused, watching his expression carefully. 'You're better than this, James. Or at least, I thought you were.'

It was a strong statement. She had edged her bets on how he would respond, but she wouldn't be sidelined. It was also the first time she'd used the name of the missing girl, so she waited to see if he'd acknowledge it. He skipped over it, shrugging his shoulders and letting her words wash over him, but she knew she had reached him on some level. Evelyn couldn't let Hawthorne dictate the tempo of the conversation. She needed to either invalidate his tactic, turn it back on him, or push the conversation toward something useful.

Because this wasn't about *her* past.

It was about finding Claire.

And Evelyn refused to let James win.

'Tell me where she is, James,' she asked, leaning forward to emphasise the urgency.

'Closer than you think, Doctor.'

Hawthorne banged on the table and the guard rushed in. Evelyn let him be led away, confident that she had cracked his shell.

8

He hadn't always been this way.

There was a time when he was normal – whatever *normal* meant.

As he threw the tennis ball against the wall of his cell, Hawthorne thought back to Dr Evelyn's question. Why had he brought up his birthday party? When he'd been asked that question in the past – this wasn't his first rodeo with a psychologist, after all – he usually came out with something banal, like how he hated his father. He knew that would send them down the 'daddy issues' route, as he'd heard it referred. If anyone wanted to get pedantic about it, Freud called it the 'Oedipus complex.'

He threw the ball and caught it in one hand.

Fact of the matter was, it was all bullshit.

He'd loved his dad. Not his mum.

He still loved his sister Alison.

But there had been lies, hadn't there? Serious lies with consequences. Not just 'Oh sorry, we forget to tell you.'

He considered family to be important. Everyone needed family. Everyone comes from a family, don't they? Family can be a source of good. It can offer stability, foundations, roots. Somewhere to say that's where you came from. That's who I am.

Until it isn't.

He'd read a lot about nature versus nurture.

He had his own opinions.

He recognised he was an anomaly.

He didn't fit any stereotype.

He had none of his father's traits – well, maybe some.

He sure as hell didn't take after his mother.

He thought differently to everyone he knew.

So, he'd created an alternate being.

Throw.

Carefully.

Throw.

Slowly.

Throw.

Deliberately.

These were no random acts of violence.

These were (are) creative projects. Each one carefully executed – he laughed at his own pun – and slowly carried out. But each one was deliberate. Chosen for a particular reason.

But *she'd* upset him. Made him slip. He must remain sharp, focused. He'd dropped his guard. It wouldn't happen again. His thoughts drifted to Alternate's last victim. Not the unfinished one – the one before. He'd had fun with her, but he could see where he'd gone wrong. He'd – perhaps – grown complacent. He felt he was immune from detection. Boldness had stopped him from being rational, but he had been driven by a desire. An overwhelming, all-encompassing desire. It wasn't entirely his fault. Alternate must have slipped up somewhere. They had led the force on a merry dance for months, especially that Detective Inspector Ziggy, something or other.

Throw.

Ziggy! What kind of name was that?

Throw.

Probably a Bowie fan.

Throw.

Not very original, though.

One of the greatest thrills, he wouldn't lie, had been to watch from the sidelines as Ziggy and his team puzzled over the murders, the victims. It was so flaming obvious, surely? He'd left enough clues, hadn't he?

Hawthorne felt his stomach clench as he considered if the game was over? Would he get a chance to complete the puzzle?

Thinking about it made his anxiety levels rise.

Alternate and he still had work to do.

He dwelt on Alternate for a while, remembering their creation. Initially, it had been to get him through the tedium of school and college. Having Alternate allowed him to play mind games. To compete against his own psyche. He soon learnt that Alternate had a particular sexual preference, which had been exhilarating to explore and something he would never have done on his own. With Alternate, he could experiment. They began trawling the neighbourhood late at night, peeping through windows. It became an obsession. He'd moved out of his parents' home at this point and was living in halls at the University of Leeds. It opened up a whole new avenue of voyeurism.

Dating became a game of cat and mouse. He could be himself on the date; charming, charismatic, romantic, but once it was over and he'd walked her back to her digs, Alternate came out. They'd hover by the window, watching her undress. Often returning the next day to steal the panties from the washing line.

And he'd been this way for years, with Alternate a constant companion. Honing skills, defining its purpose and characteristics.

Planning. He needed plans. He thrived on them through his working life, and he needed one now.

They had set to work, him and Alternate.

They had created a game plan, with the emphasis on *game.*

It was all fantasy, of course.

He could never act it out.

It would never reach a point between them where the compulsion to physically hurt or attack someone would override their sense of morality.

He, James Hawthorne, could never confront someone, take possession of someone, a woman, against their will.

Eventually, the pressure, the tension, the constant battle became too much. He was exhausted. He needed a release. Alternate needed a release. They needed a release.

And then he became aware of Doctor Evelyn Shaw, and the rules of the game changed.

9

Ziggy sat across from Evelyn in the HQ conference room. She had updated him on her first encounter with Hawthorne. When she had finished, Ziggy sat back, taking it all in.

'It's too early to draw any firm conclusions, but I do think that next time I meet with him, you should listen in.'

Ziggy nodded. 'Good idea. It will be interesting to hear how he is with someone else. He's always been very... I don't know how to describe it... Wooden? Not even defensive, just a solid unemotional block of wood.'

'That doesn't surprise me. There's a level of dissociation going on, but that's so he can extract himself from the horrors he inflicted.'

'Have you approached the subject of Claire? Has he given you anything?'

'I have, and he was closed, as you would expect. We have a fair way to go, and I'm hoping my session with him tomorrow will reveal more – hence why you should be there.'

'I agree, anything is useful. We have search teams on standby and, of course, the parents are hanging on a knife edge for news.'

'It all adds to the urgency, and I promise you I'm doing my best.' She knew she didn't need to say that, but she wanted Ziggy to know it was important to her too.

'I don't doubt it for a second. Come and meet the wider team, and I'll give you a guided tour of the incident room.'

Evelyn followed him out and they headed upstairs to the MIT office and incident room. As was to be expected, it was a hive of activity. Ziggy explained that they had been receiving forensic results from the search of Hawthorne's apartment throughout the day and these were being updated on the various boards around the room.

As they wandered through the desks to the front of the office, Ziggy spoke. 'We've found an obsessive number of lists, along with numerous makes and models of cameras, over sixty external hard drives, hundreds of floppy disks, and an unnerving number of gratuitous photographs.' He picked up and passed the list across for Evelyn to study.

'An organised killer then, in more ways than one,' she commented.

'Definitely that. I mean, the photographs were category A, the worst possible. I'll spare you from viewing them, but this is equally disturbing.' He handed over photocopies of pages from a notebook.

At first glance, it meant nothing at all to Evelyn. Ziggy began to explain, but she silenced him with her hand as recognition hit of what they were. The blood drained from her face. Goosebumps developed on her arms as the hairs on the back of her neck stood on end. 'It's a series of preparation lists.'

Ziggy spoke quietly. 'It is. Turn it over.'

Evelyn turned over the pages. She could see that some of the lists were written in the Hawthorne's version of shorthand, but it didn't take a genius to work out the code.

A prep list that included headings such as *Pre-prep*, *Prep* and *Post Event*. Detailed coded plans.

Engage T-1 (engage target one),

Recon DS-1 (reconnaissance of dump site 1),

Locate DS-2 (locate dump site 2).

Further 'to-do' lists including 'set up stage', 'build table', 'destroy files', 'change tyres', 'burn gloves' and 'have story straight' were more evidence that this was an organised killer in both the planning and execution of his victims.

Evelyn looked around the room. She was dumbfounded. She didn't have enough words in her extensive vocabulary to communicate how vile, how evil this sadistic killer was.

Collecting herself, she turned to Ziggy. 'We have to nail him, Ziggy. This man can never be allowed to walk in the presence of any human being again, let alone with women.'

'Couldn't agree more,' Ziggy said.

They left the incident room and Ziggy ushered Evelyn over to a quadrant where three officers were arduously working. 'This is the beating heart of the Murder Investigation Team,' he said, half joking.

'Ha, you'd be nothing without us,' joked the tall, fair-haired woman as she stood. 'I'm Sadie, DS Bates.' Evelyn and Sadie shook hands. 'And this is Nick, DS Wilkinson, and over there is DC Angela Dove.'

Once everyone had shaken hands, Ziggy pulled a seat over and Evelyn sat at the corner of Ziggy's desk, throwing her bag on the floor and her coat over the back of the chair.

The team were all looking at her, waiting for her to speak. She took a breath.

'So, tell me. I've spoken to the man himself, as Ziggy will have told you, but tell me, what are your views on the so-called Shadow Killer?' she asked.

'That the media shouldn't have given him any name at all, frankly. It just feeds his ego,' Nick said, straightening out a paperclip as he spoke.

'Sign of the times, unfortunately,' Angela said, leaning forward, arms crossed on the desk in front of her. 'As for my view, I think he's up there with the Yorkshire Ripper and Ted Bundy. I'm just glad he's off the streets. My daughters are at Leeds college, and everyone had been warned not to walk alone at night. I can sleep a little easier now.'

'Huh,' Sadie grunted. 'Not that sick individuals should stop killing, but that people shouldn't walk home on their own.' That received knowing nods from around the group. 'I agree with Angela, though, and I'll work to the end of time to make sure that bastard gets a whole-life tariff.'

There were more nods as everyone agreed.

Evelyn looked around at the small group. 'I was just saying to Ziggy that it's far too soon for me to make a judgement on his mindset or the game he's trying to play, though I witnessed first-hand how manipulative he can be at my first meeting with him. At this stage, I can only reiterate what you probably already know. He's organised and has a well-established modus operandi, so I would say he's been doing this, at least to some degree, for years and has scaled up at some point. That may be due to an incident, a life event or other catalyst for this, but perhaps not. Perhaps he'd just waited in the shadows for long enough and grew tired of not getting the notoriety he felt he deserved. Main thing is, now he can't hurt anyone else.'

The moment's hiatus that the team had afforded her was over as phones started ringing. Aware that she was delaying them, Evelyn stood, gathering her coat and bag.

'I'd better let you get on.'

'Come on, I'll show you out,' said Ziggy, leading the way.

As they reached the foyer, Ziggy held the outside door open for her.

'Tomorrow, then?' he asked.

'Yes, I'll see you there,' she replied as she exited the building. She hoped tomorrow that Hawthorne would be as talkative as he had been today, but there was no real way of knowing. At least she had introduced the subject of Claire.

Tomorrow, she would push harder.

10

———

Wednesday, 8 October 2003

'How do you want to do this?' Evelyn asked as she and Ziggy cleared security at HMP Wakefield.

Ziggy retrieved his wallet from the x-ray tray and stuffed it into the back pocket of his trousers, following Evelyn through the body scanner. On receiving the green light, he caught up with her.

'He doesn't need to know that I'm watching. Priority of course is anything that will lead us to Claire. After that, we need places to search that can solidly link Hawthorne to the victims we suspect he's responsible for. Places in particular where we might find CCTV, trace evidence though of course if it's outside then the chances of recovery are minimal.'

'What did the search of his flat uncover?'

'Aside from the lists and the digital stuff that is still being looked at, there's very little. It wasn't the main kill site, despite us finding Belinda there,' Ziggy replied.

They walked side by side with the prison guard leading

the way. 'Right. I'll focus on Claire and see if I can narrow down where she might be. Bear with me, though – some of the questions may not seem relevant, but just trust me.'

'You're the expert. I guess it's a case of trying to get into his mindset, isn't it?'

The guard held open the interview-room door. Evelyn walked in, followed by Ziggy, and dropped her bag on the floor.

'I believe I made a good start yesterday. Let's see how it goes today.' Evelyn pulled her notebook out as she spoke and poured herself a cup of water. She noted that the strip light above was still insistently buzzing, as though it would explode any second.

'Did he talk about any other murders yesterday?' Ziggy asked.

'Not in direct terms. I asked him a straightforward question, and unbeknownst to him, his answer gave me an insight into how he thinks.'

'OK?'

'On the surface, it was quite innocuous. I asked him to recall a childhood memory, which he did, without any further prompting.'

'What did he say?'

'He talked about his fifth birthday party. He complained that it had been ruined by the rain.'

'Right...' Confusion crossed Ziggy's face.

'No one turned up, and he blamed it on the rain.'

'Seems perfectly reasonable.'

Evelyn smiled. 'No one went to his party because no one liked him, including the parents. He must have given off weird vibes, even at that age. He had no friends. It was easier for him to blame the weather, externalise the blame, than look to himself and his own behaviour.'

'How do you know he had no friends?'

'It's just a hunch, to be honest. Any true friend would have insisted on being taken there. The party was *inside* his parents' house. The weather made no difference.'

'Ah, clever.'

'He was also very open in his posture and with his hand gestures. He wants to talk, just not necessarily about what he's done wrong.'

There was a light tap on the door. 'We're ready next door for you, Inspector,' a guard said through the open doorway.

Ziggy nodded. 'Good luck,' he said, and Evelyn started to re-arrange the seating.

Not that there was much in the room that Evelyn could move. The grey Formica table was a given, as that's what Hawthorne would be attached to via his handcuffs. It was unusual for a UK prison, but such was the danger posed by the inmates of HMP Wakefield, it was deemed necessary. Ideally, she wouldn't have any barriers between them, and the chairs would be closer. To compromise, she placed her chair on the short edge of the desk, but to the rear and closer to the door. There was still an element of personal space, but a respectful distance.

Evelyn pulled her chair further under the table and waited for Hawthorne to be brought in. She'd worked late into the night, build on the collage of his family background, education, medical history, she'd already done, but there were gaps. There were always gaps.

As the door opened again, a chill ran down her spine.

James Hawthorne shuffled his way in and stared at Evelyn. She noted he didn't appear to be as confident in his posture as he had yesterday. She smiled with what she hoped was showed warmth and friendliness, not the dread in the pit of her stomach. She discretely wiped her damp palms on her skirt, then brought her hands to rest on the top of the table.

Hawthorne never took his eyes off her face.

'James how are you?' she asked.

'Evelyn. How nice to see you again.'

Interesting that he didn't answer her question. Deciding not to make a point of it, Evelyn ran through the wellbeing checks that had to be done before each session. When Hawthorne had confirmed he was well and reasonably comfortable, she chose to dive straight in, aware of the time pressure.

'James, today I'd like you to consider working out an agreement with me.'

She noted that his eyes moved from her face for the first time and flashed briefly to the notebook and paperwork in front of her, but she kept it closed.

'Nothing formal you understand, just something between you and me that will keep us within the boundaries of what we agree to discuss.' She paused.

'How does that sound?'

Hawthorne crossed one leg over the other and bounced his free leg. 'Go on.'

She took a deep breath. She'd only tried this technique once before with very mixed results, but she was willing to give anything a try. Having seen his need for order and the lists he had used in his own preparation, she was hopeful that he would agree. She coughed and pulled a blank sheet of paper in front of her.

'I'd like to work out maybe five key areas – that we both agree on – that we can talk about freely and openly. No lies, no games, no misleading. Just open, frank discussions about the subject matter. What do you think?'

She watched Hawthorne's face as he digested the information. If his skull were made of glass, she was certain she'd see the words *What's in it for me?* looping endlessly inside.

He rattled his handcuffs. The loud noise made her jump slightly.

A twinkle of amusement flashed in his eye before he looked away.

She didn't speak, waiting for Hawthorne to respond to her question. Outside, in the corridor, she could hear the hum of a television and a low indistinct murmur of a conversation; a reminder that prison life continued outside the room. After waiting for what felt like several minutes, she was about to repeat her request when his gaze returned to her face.

'An agreement?' he said.

'Yes.' She divided the sheet of paper in front of her into sections.

Hawthorne coughed loudly, interrupting her flow.

It occurred to her that she was feeding his need for voyeurism. He was enjoying watching her, and in a more assertive tone, she continued. 'I was thinking we could break it into key moments in your life. Your childhood, for example.' She wrote *Childhood* in the first box.

When Hawthorne didn't respond, she continued. 'Then we can move on to your teenage and young adult years.' She continued writing.

'And also explore your university year – perhaps your hobbies at that time? Then we can also discuss you as you are today. How does that sound?'

Hawthorne leant forward and scratched the tip of his nose. 'This works with your clients, does it, Evelyn? This organised-list approach?'

'It has in the past.'

'Why do you think it will work with me?'

She smiled, having anticipated some resistance. 'All I am doing is creating an agreement between us.'

She made a mental note that when something was bothering Hawthorne, he closed his eyes. Whether this was to self-soothe or because he was irritated, only time would tell, but he did it frequently when she challenged his reasoning or thought patterns. She remained silent, waiting for him to respond.

He returned her smile, his lip curling up over his top teeth – the kind a predator might wear while pretending to be a lover. When he spoke, his words were loaded.

'Do you know that you lean in when I speak, Evelyn? That's trust. Dangerous thing, trust. People like you should know better.'

Aware that she was about to enter into a dangerous game, she pushed on. 'The agreement, James?'

'We agree.' When he smiled next, it was almost a mischievous, childish grin of glee.

Evelyn slowly untwisted the lid from her fountain pen and turned to a clean page in her notebook. With her heart beating a tattoo, she began with the second part of her game plan.

'I've been reading through the transcripts of your interviews,' she began, looking up from the empty page.

'You won't find anything about my childhood in there.' Hawthorne scoffed.

'I wasn't looking for it. I'm more interested in you *now*.'

She saw Hawthorne's shoulders drop momentarily as he realised what she had done. But it had been a risky strategy. She had played on his need for order, and it could very swiftly backfire. She watched as he narrowed his eyes, studying her face, possibly calculating her next move. She stayed silent for a couple of minutes. The room felt tight, the tension stretching between them like a wire ready to snap.

When he broke her gaze, she finally spoke again. 'How do you feel about the name that the media given you? The Shadow Killer?'

He didn't reply, just continued to stare hard into her eyes.

'There's a story here, and currently the media are the narrators. They're creating a killer. They've given him a name, and every day they are relaying the story in their own words.'

Hawthorne tilted his head. 'True.' She had his attention.

'But it occurred to me that perhaps you know the story of the Shadow Killer better than anyone.' She waited a minute or two and took a sip of water. 'These murders, the missing girls, let's say the Shadow Killer is responsible for them.'

Hawthorne shifted in his seat and swapped legs. Evelyn quickly continued before he could break her flow.

'The Shadow Killer must have a personality and motives that perhaps you could infer from the evidence.'

'Interesting,' Hawthorne mused, nodding his head slowly. 'So, what you're saying is that you want me to tell you what and how this Shadow Killer operates?'

'Not quite. I don't want you to tell me his psychological profile. I want you to tell me his story. I want to hear it from you is who he is, and what he's like.'

11

———

'The Shadow Killer?' Hawthorne queried – as Evelyn knew he would. She had learnt over time that psychopaths could maintain a certain level of denial, particularly when the stakes were all still to play for. And with Claire Strickland still missing, Hawthorne retained some of the power. By reframing the murders, working with him to develop a 'character' with its own thoughts, feelings, motivations, she hoped it would be fuelled by the inner recesses of Hawthorne's mind. They would both know who they were talking about – James Hawthorne – but under the guise of the Shadow Killer, he might – just might – be more willing to share. It was sometimes referred to as 'doubling' or the creation of a shadow self.

It was a risk, but an educated one.

She watched as Hawthorne picked over what she was asking him to do. He removed an imaginary piece of dust from the Formica desk.

'I suppose you could say he's a sadist,' came the chilling response in a voice that Evelyn would have been hard pushed to recognise as coming from the same man she had just spoken with. It was deep, laced with bitterness. The *S* was exaggerated, spat out instead of spoken.

Evelyn took a deep breath. 'A sexual sadist?'

'Is there any other?'

'What else can you tell me about him?' She let him continue talking in third person, once removed from the violent acts.

'He's been around for a long time,' Hawthorne answered. 'Longer than he's given credit for.'

Did that mean more murders and missing girls?

'How did he start? What brought him to this idea of sadism?'

Hawthorne broke eye contact and looked over her shoulder. It took all her will not to follow his stare and look behind her.

'That's an interesting question.' His cuffs clanked as he twisted his body to one side, moving against his restraints. 'I suppose he saw temptation in front of him from an early age, say seven or eight. It wasn't until later that it started to inconvenience him.'

Evelyn made a note of her pad.

'I saw you write that down, and yes, it was an inconvenience. Once he became aware, he couldn't help but see it. Then he began to look for it. Away from home. Through windows mostly. I imagine this would have satisfied him somewhat for a while.'

'The voyeurism? The watching?' asked Evelyn. 'When did he start to act on it?'

'When? That's a good question. That makes it sound like he had a choice.'

'Didn't he? Couldn't he choose to remain distant, watching?'

Evelyn saw Hawthorne's knuckles turn white as he

curled his fingers into tight fists. 'There was no choice. There never is.'

'What was it that made the Shadow Killer take it further?'

There was a moment's hesitation. 'A compulsion. An almost involuntary act. A need that had to be fulfilled regardless of the consequences.' He uncurled his fists.

'He was aware there would be consequences?'

Hawthorne completely ignored her; lost as he was in the world of his own creation. 'It came from deep within his soul. Like that was his life's purpose. That was why he had been brought into the world. To watch, explore, examine, enjoy.'

'And his victims? What made them stand out from each other?'

'Ha, nothing. Wrong place, wrong time – for them, anyway.'

'I've seen the lists that were made by you, or the Shadow Killer. There was very little left to chance.'

Hawthorne sat back in his chair, and Evelyn tried to judge where his mind and thoughts were at. His eyes still stared off into the distance, and she wondered if he was watching his actions replay in his mind's eye. She maintained her silence, knowing that it could be more powerful than words on occasion.

'You ask what made them stand out, his victims. The real answer is their neediness. They were all needy. The love of a mother, the thirst for attention, the desperation for a lover.'

'Did you feel you were able to meet their needs?'

'No! Absolutely not.' His eyebrow knitted together. 'It was their attention-seeking behaviour that had to be stopped.'

Victim blaming. Deflection, Evelyn thought. 'And it was the work of the shadow self to stop this, was it?'

If Hawthorne heard her, he didn't display any acknowledgement. 'Of course, it's a fundamental human drive to want to be liked, to be seen, but to be so *needy*.' He shouted and exaggerated the last word, making Evelyn flinch again.

'Our work wasn't done. We had more to do,' Hawthorne continued, regret in his tone.

Evelyn noted the sudden change to a collective term. Unconsciously, her breathing had shallowed. The atmosphere intensified, and she barely moved for fear of disturbing Hawthorne. She wondered if Ziggy had picked up on it from behind the Perspex screen.

'Whose work wasn't done, James?'

'My work, mine. My work isn't done.'

She tried a direct approach. 'Can we talk about Claire?'

'Who's Claire?' He was staring at her again, a smile dancing across his lips. He knew exactly who Claire was.

'We spoke about her yesterday. You mentioned that you had taken Claire from a busy walkway, which wasn't your usual routine.'

Hawthorne continued to stare.

'Once you had Claire, where did you go? Do you have a special place or a preferred location?'

He closed his eyes. Was he replaying Claire's abduction in his mind, possibly even her murder?

'A special place?' he asked, opening his eyes slowly and raising his chin so that he was looking down his nose at her.

'Yes, somewhere quiet, maybe? Away from the noise and bustle of the city?' She had to be careful not to put words in his mouth whilst also gently leading him into a false sense of security.

'Do *you* have a special place, Evelyn? Somewhere away from the crowds and busyness of every day?'

'I have my own home, yes.'

'But no husband? Or wife?'

It was unethical of her to talk about her home life, so she didn't answer.

Hawthorne pointed his index finger at her hand. 'No ring, and no mark either.'

Again, she didn't speak.

'You don't have the look of a married woman. Not quite so many crow's feet. Actually, you're quite well put together, aren't you?'

'We're not here to talk about me, James.'

'That's a shame – I think we have a lot in common, you and I.'

'Do you? Like what, do you think?'

'We both like questions, don't we? Asking, not answering.' He tilted his head to one side.

'You were telling me about Claire,' she suggested.

'No, I wasn't. You were asking, but I didn't answer.'

'OK, let's try again, shall we?'

'Claire, Claire, Claire,' he said in a sing-song voice. 'It's a pretty name, isn't it? A pretty name for a pretty girl.'

'Can you tell me where Claire is?'

He continued, his voice rising to a frantic pitch. 'Where's Claire? Where's Claire?'

Then, suddenly, his head slammed against the table with a dull thud. Evelyn froze. A low growl rumbled from deep in his throat. She shot to her feet, hand hovering over the emergency button. But before she could press it, Hawthorne slumped back, arms hanging limply at his sides.

Spittle gathered at the corners of his mouth. The wild,

angry glint had vanished from his eyes, replaced by something far worse.

Emptiness.

His black pupils, blown wide, swallowed the light. And then, as if awakening from a trance, his face twisted. His upper lip curled, his nostrils flared, revulsion flickered across his features. A look of pure disgust. 'Yes, I can tell you where Claire is.' That monotone was back. Even, measured words delivered forcefully. 'She's where all the needy people go.'

Evelyn had to hide her revulsion as she sought more information. 'And where would that be?'

'Ha-ha, closer than you think,' he said.

'Close to where? Your apartment? Leeds?'

'Too many questions, Evie, not enough time.'

The tension had ratcheted up to almost an unbearable level, and Evelyn felt the familiar prickle of a hot flush surging across her face. She was filled with an overwhelming desire to get out of the claustrophobic room. She pushed her chair back as the walls suddenly felt like they were closing in on her. She wasn't sure how much longer she could keep her composure when the door opened, and the prison officer walked in. He released Hawthorne from his handcuffs and escorted him out of the room.

As soon as the door shut, she leant over to try to get some blood to her head. As she leant over, drawing deep breaths with her hands on her knees, she could hear that sing-song voice echoing down the corridor.

'I'm the king of the castle. You're the dirty rascal.'

Behind the Perspex glass, Ziggy threw down the headphones and urged the guard to open the door. He rushed along the corridor, brushing past Hawthorne as he found the interview room. Evelyn was standing behind the door, face pale, hands shaking as she straightened up. He took hold of one and led her to a chair.

'Jesus are you OK?' he asked.

She sat heavily and breathed out. 'I'm fine, just a little shaken.'

Ziggy could completely relate, though he'd had the grace of a separate room and Perspex glass. He was also human, a dad, a husband, a son. He felt the urge to protect, to comfort, though a line of professionalism had to remain in place. He sat in the chair that had recently been vacated by what Ziggy could only describe as pure evil.

'I was certain that he would give us something more concrete,' Evelyn said as she found a tissue in her bag.

Ziggy nodded, though he had a few questions of his own.

'We need to escort you out if you've finished?' a guard said, poking his head around the door.

'Sure,' Ziggy replied.

Evelyn nodded as she threw her notebook and pen into her bag.

They made their way out of the prison and walked along Back Lane. HMP Wakefield was set right in the centre of the Merrie City, surrounded by a busy railway station and various cafes and coffee shops. Ziggy wasn't familiar with the town, so they headed to the station and grabbed a couple of seats in the café bar. Once they were both served and sat with a coffee, he watched Evelyn slowly relax. She rolled her shoulders and rubbed the back of her neck.

'That was some conversation,' Ziggy commented as he

added a sachet of sugar to what had turned out to be an overly strong coffee. He had to lean close to Evelyn to be heard above the sudden rush of commuters grabbing take-aways and snacks for their journeys. They decided to wait a few minutes until the noise died down with the departure of a train bound for Leeds. It gave Ziggy the time to collect his thoughts and check his new Nokia mobile phone for voice messages.

Once relative quiet had descended, he began again. 'What did you make of what he said?'

Evelyn leant forward, elbow resting on the table as she continued to stir her drink. 'It was interesting. There's quite a lot to pick over, but primarily, I'm not sure if we're any closer to finding Claire.'

'He's quite cryptic, isn't he? Like, everything he says has a different meaning?'

'Yes, exactly that, which is why we have to listen closely to what he says.'

'I couldn't help but notice that he almost sang Claire's name. What do you think that meant?'

Evelyn hesitated. 'I'm not sure it meant anything. The one thing that stuck out for me was what he was saying as he was led away.'

Ziggy frowned. He hadn't heard that from his position in the other room.

'He was singing the old nursery rhyme, "I'm the king of the castle".'

Chills went down Ziggy's spine. Though the song was innocuous, he knew there would be a deeper meaning. This was James Hawthorne, after all. 'What's the significance, do you think?'

Evelyn sat upright while licking the foam from her cappuccino away from her lips and nursing the mug in both hands. 'It could have multiple meanings, to be honest. It could be a regression to childhood – a play for power and control, perhaps. When you look at it in the context of Claire, it could be metaphorical – he sees himself as the one who controlled or dominated her fate.'

'But that doesn't take us any closer to finding her?'

'At least he's talking.'

'Yes, and honestly, at this stage, anything is welcome.' Ziggy went quiet for a moment, thinking over Hawthorne's last words. 'Is there a slim chance that he meant it literally? I mean, why would he mention a castle? I get that he could believe himself to be *the* king or *a* king – he has such an overinflated ego – but why a castle?'

Evelyn's head tilted just a fraction, her lips parting as if a thought had almost surfaced. 'It's possible.'

Ziggy felt a tingle of excitement as his thoughts ran at a hundred miles an hour. 'Could a castle be a location?'

'Potentially—' Evelyn was interrupted by the next train announcement, but rather than continuing her thought once the speaker had silenced, she downed her coffee. 'I need to get a move on. I'll be back at the prison tomorrow, if you can make it?'

They rose together and exited the café. At the entrance, they went their separate ways, Evelyn heading back to the prison car park, whilst Ziggy took his phone from his jacket pocket and called into HQ, letting the team know he was on his way for the afternoon briefing.

Sadie was standing at the incident board as Ziggy walked in.

'How did it go?' she asked as she noticed her boss entering before continuing to pin a photograph on the board. It was a map of Hawthorne's movements around the time of Claire's disappearance, though they had very little to go on.

'It was good, I think.' Though, perhaps that was a bit weak considering he'd just watched a serial killer deliver a chilling account. He was distracted, still chewing over the castle connection.

Sadie picked up on it straightaway. Five years of working closely together would do that. 'Go on, what's bugging you?'

Ziggy walked towards the wall that was dominated by pinboards and whiteboards. There was nothing as far as he could see that mentioned a castle or anything even remotely related. 'Just something that Hawthorne said that's stuck with me.'

He relayed the conversation to Sadie, who wrote *Castle?* on the whiteboard in a red marker.

Before Sadie could say anything, Ziggy continued. 'What castles are in the local area?'

Nick had wandered over, and despite not knowing the context, he still contributed. 'There's Sandal Castle in Wakefield,' he said.

Sadie let out her breath and placed her hands on her hips. 'Hell, take your pick. On top of Sandal, there's Scarborough, Bolton, Richmond, Knaresborough. I mean, I could go on?'

'Potentially, they all need searching,' Ziggy stated, though he was hesitant.

'It would mean pulling resources from elsewhere,' Sadie said. 'And it's a bit of a wide brief.' She filled Nick in on what Ziggy had heard at the prison.

'Let's do the briefing and see if we have anything else from forensics,' Ziggy said.

It was 4 p.m. and the wider team had started to filter in

with their notebooks and folders. As they all took a seat around the conference table, Ziggy invited each team leader to share the latest updates. He listened intently, making notes, but his mind was already working out where they should look next.

[Evelyn's home]

Evelyn unlocked the door to her apartment and stepped inside, the silence greeting her like a weight. She kicked off her shoes, shedding the day's clothes in a trail to the bedroom and replacing them with leggings, a hoodie, and the soft cotton of a well-worn T-shirt – comfort clothes.

She climbed the stairs to the mezzanine, but the familiar space of her home office offered no comfort tonight. Hawthorne's words clung to her skin like smoke. She picked up a dry-wipe pen and scrawled bullet points across the whiteboard, fast and messy, as if writing them down might drain the meaning from them.

But it didn't.

She let the pen drop, slumped onto the small sofa in the corner, and closed her eyes.

'I'm the king of the castle...'

The sing-song rhythm echoed in her skull. She clenched her jaw.

Coincidence? Maybe. But it didn't feel like one.

How could he know?

12

Thursday, 9 October 2003

Evelyn had tossed and turned all night, unable to close her eyes with images of Hawthorne and her past intertwining. She had alternately thrown the covers off in a flush as her body temperature rose, only to shiver minutes later when the cold October air seeped through the open window of her bedroom. A sense of fear had lodged in her stomach, and try as she might, she couldn't shake it. She gave up the pretence of sleep just before dawn, moving to sit in front of her desk and computer, forcing herself to concentrate. Scraping her hair back from her face, she tied it back and looked at the notes in front of her.

It was basic stuff, taught in her first year of university. Serial killers don't just pop up one day and decide to murder. It's an escalation of earlier behaviour. Perhaps around the age of seven or eight, the clues would be there. It could be petty theft, or animal cruelty. They could – and probably – would fly under the radar. Dealt with by their parents or peers, dismissed as troubled teens.

With a loving and stable home environment, perhaps they would grow out of the behaviour. Certainly, the justice system couldn't be depended upon for reform. A rare few would continue and become career criminals. An even smaller percentage would escalate their practices.

James Hawthorne seemed to buck that trend. Or perhaps they hadn't gone back far enough or looked deep enough.

Evelyn sighed. Her office floor was scattered with papers and files. She'd spent most of the early morning on the telephone trying to trace Hawthorne's medical records. Finally, after being passed through to various departments she had got somewhere and a helpful lady at the NHS had promised to send copies of the files over to her. She picked up another sheet of paper and looked through it. It was from his employer, an emergency contact form.

James had listed his sister as his next of kin. Evelyn was debating contacting her. She figured it could only advance the investigation if she could get an insight into Hawthorne's childhood.

Deciding it was better to ask for forgiveness than to seek permission, she reached for the handset and dialled the number. The dial tone rang over and over, and she was about to hang up when the call connected.

'Oh hello, is that Alison? Alison Hawthorne?'

'I'm Alison, yes. Who is this?'

'Alison, you don't know me, but my name is Dr Evelyn Shaw. I'm working alongside DI Thornes of West Yorkshire Police.' She waited a heartbeat to see if there was any rebuke. When none was forthcoming, she continued. 'I'd like to talk with you about your brother, James.'

'I've already told the police everything I know,' came the curt reply.

'I know you've already been very helpful, but I'd like to talk to you about James's early life. Your shared childhood.'

'Why?'

Evelyn paused. How should she answer? She wanted to understand when he'd turned bad. But how do you say that to someone's sister?

'I think it might be better if we spoke face to face. Would you be available for a coffee?' It would have to be this morning, as she was due at Wakefield later that day.

Silence filled the phone line. Evelyn wondered for a second if Alison had hung up when she heard her clear her throat.

'I can, but it would need to be today,' came the reply, full of hesitation.

'Great. I can be there in' – Evelyn looked at her watch. Alison lived in Helmsley, the very town where Evelyn had been raised – 'around forty minutes, traffic depending?' She confirmed it was still the same address and promised she would be there as quickly as could. Grabbing her notes, Evelyn shoved everything into her tote bag before she had a chance to think about what a trip back 'home' would mean.

It was a little over forty minutes later that Evelyn arrived in the village that had been the centre of her childhood. Outwardly, shop fronts had changed, as market towns tend to do, to keep pace with modern life. She parked opposite the cottage she thought to be where Alison lived and took a look around. The statue dedicated to Baron Feversham with its neo-Gothic spire stood proudly in the marketplace. She knew that on market day, the square would be busy with traders and shoppers. Today, the chill of autumn was in the air, and she had forgotten how the damp seemed to creep under coats and crawl down the back of your neck, sending shivers through to your fingertips.

Shaking the cold from her shoulders, she crossed the road and double-checked the address. Number twenty-six was a pretty mid-terrace cottage dating from around the seventeenth century. The stone boundary wall that faced the road was worn, the mortar missing in places, with stones that looked as though they would fall with the lightest push. The pathway was in a similar state, riddled with moss and weeds. Evelyn lifted her hand to knock on the UPVC door, but it opened before she had a chance.

A woman in her late fifties stood before her. Evelyn took in the tattered housecoat that Alison clutched close to her like a security blanket. Her dark hair was straggly, unwashed and streaked with grey. Her skin showed signs of a poor diet, pale and paper thin. A few unsightly coarse, black hairs poked out of a large mole that sat at the side of her mouth.

'Alison Hawthorne?' Evelyn asked.

The lady looked at her. 'Yes? Are you Dr Shaw?'

'Yes, please call me Evelyn.' They shook hands. 'Thank you for agreeing to meet,' Evelyn said as Alison stood back and held the door open for her.

Inside the cottage was as dilapidated as the outside. It reminded Evelyn of her own childhood home. A garish flowery brown-and-ochre-patterned wallpaper pulsed in the dim light, like a fingerprint stretched over the walls. In places, it peeled back like flaking skin, revealing years of damp stains beneath. She had to close her eyes temporarily to shift the memories that came racing back unbidden.

Alison invited Evelyn to sit on a settee that came from

the same era as the dated wallpaper. She guessed it had been velvet or cord at some point, but it was worn and bare in areas. Crude stitches showed that someone had tried to repair it with patches of different-coloured fabric. In contrast, the house itself seemed to be spotlessly clean. As she looked around the walls above the fireplace, she saw a collection of family photographs. The typical 2.4-children kind. School photographs, holidays, summer in the garden. She was about to comment when Alison spoke.

'You're a forensic psychologist, aren't you?'

'I am, that's right.'

'And you work with the police?'

'Yes, I do. I have done for a number of years.'

'You work in prisons as well?'

'Yes, I do.'

'Have you met my brother, James?'

'Yes, I have. I—'

'What did he say to you?'

Evelyn wasn't sure where Alison was taking the conversation. 'Um, before we get to that, I'd like to tell you a bit about why I wanted to meet you.'

'Are you selling your story? Well, not *your* story. James' story. Our family story?'

The words came out in a hurry, and a tsunami of emotion rolling behind them. Alison was clearly scared – no, terrified.

'Shall we start again, Alison? I'm not a threat. I'm simply helping the police build a picture of your brother, and to do that, I'd like to find out a little more, as I said on the phone.'

Tears built in the corners of Alison's eyes. Evelyn took a tissue from her bag and passed it to her. Alison dabbed her eyes and took a few deep breaths before speaking.

'I'm sorry. It's just been a horrendous time, as you can imagine.'

'It's OK, you have nothing to apologise for. I can only imagine what you're going through.'

'It's the press. I can't leave the house; I can't answer the phone – they've even turned up outside my work. I've been put on leave by my employers, and I have no idea if they will take me back. And those poor girls and their families. What are they going through?' Alison burrowed her face in her hands.

'Just take your time,' Evelyn said softly. 'I know you're dealing with a lot.'

Blowing her nose and dabbing her eyes, Alison pulled herself together. 'I'm sorry. It's been so isolating. Nobody wants anything to do with me. My friends won't answer my calls, and we don't have any family to speak of. Perhaps distant cousins, but we lost contact when our parents died.'

'The police are working every possible lead and I'm sure you've spoken to them on several occasions?'

Alison nodded through her tears.

'The information I need is a little different.' She went on to explain. 'You know, I was brought up not far from here.'

At that, Alison seemed to relax a little. 'Did you really? Where?'

Evelyn smiled. 'Just over the way there.' She pointed vaguely out of the window. Have you lived here long?'

'Around ten years or so. It's nice and quiet with good transport links. Has it changed much since you lived here?'

'Not really. On the surface it may have but it's still the sleepy market town, I remember.'

Silence fell between them as Evelyn shook off the past and focused on the present.

'Why did he do it, Evelyn?'

Evelyn sighed. 'That's a key question, isn't it? Perhaps it's something you can help me with. Fill in the gaps, so to speak?'

'I don't have any answers, believe me. I have spent every night since his arrest going over and over everything. Nothing adds up. Everything I thought I knew about my baby brother has been shattered. How did we miss it?'

'By "we", do you mean your parents?'

'Yes. We were a close family unit.'

'You can't blame yourself. It isn't anything you have or haven't done.'

'Is it nature or nurture? That question has tormented me.'

'No one truly knows. Perhaps a little of both.'

'But we were brought up with exactly the same privileges. We went to the same school, had the same family holidays.'

'Your parents, were they loving? Did they regularly express their love for you both?'

Alison was quiet for a minute. 'Neither were overly demonstrative. We didn't say "I love you" to each other very often. It was just assumed that the love was there. We never wanted for anything materially.'

Materially. Interesting choice of word, Evelyn thought. 'How did they show their love, then?'

Alison stared off into the distance. 'In small ways, I guess. Dad travelled a lot, but Mum was always there to tuck us in at night. We were never latchkey children – she always picked us up from school. We ate meals at the table, went on family holidays. The usual, I guess.'

Evelyn noted that rather than listing demonstrations of love and emotional support, Alison had listed further practicalities. Delving deeper she asked, 'You mentioned your father travelled a lot. Was that with work?'

'Yes, he was an engineer. It took him all over the world.'

'And when he was home, how was he with you?'

Alison turned to Evelyn with tears in her eyes. 'Fun. He was so much fun. He'd play fight with James, and I could always climb on his knee for a cuddle.'

Evelyn raised an eyebrow questioningly.

Alison was quick to defend her father. 'No, not in that way. It was just what we did, right up until I left school. It had become a standing joke by then. He used to complain of me having a "bony bum".' Alison laughed and wiped tears from her face.

'And with James? You mentioned they would play fight?'

'Yes, until James outgrew my dad, really. James took martial arts, and as soon as he could put my dad on the floor, Dad declared he was far too old to still be fighting a young man.'

'What was James's relationship with your mum like?'

'Oh, they were close.'

Evelyn noticed a change in Alison's demeanour. She gripped and released her fists. Her breathing changed very subtly to short breaths. Evelyn doubted Alison was even aware of it.

'Tell me about that?'

'James was the golden child. He couldn't do anything wrong. In her eyes, anyway.'

'That annoyed you?'

Alison let out a small laugh. 'Annoy me? No. I had my dad, albeit he was away for at least a week every month.'

'Did your mum spoil James?'

'With love, maybe, but we were treated exactly the same

materially.' Alison stood and walked over to the window that looked out over the market square.

Evelyn couldn't help thinking that wasn't strictly true, but she was there to uncover issues with James, not Alison.

Something occurred to her, and she took a moment to structure the question before she spoke. She walked over to the window to stand by Alison. 'When did you notice the darkness in James?'

Alison turned away and her voice faltered as she spoke. 'I'm not sure what you mean...' She walked over to the door and hesitated in the entrance. 'I think you should be going—'

'When did it start, Alison?'

'I honestly don't know what you mean,' Alison said.

Evelyn walked over. 'I understand this is hard for you, Alison, but it's possible that you hold the key to our understanding of James. If we can understand him, there's a good chance we can work out where the missing women are.'

Alison turned, her face burning. 'Don't you dare!' she shouted, pointing at Evelyn. 'Don't you dare put that on me.' She physically pushed Evelyn into the hallway. 'You need to leave. I should never have agreed to this. You're just like the rest.'

Evelyn righted herself and shook Alison off, only to receive another hard push in the back. The front door opened, and Evelyn was ungraciously forced out onto the step. The door slammed loudly in her face.

Hurt and embarrassed as neighbours peered out at the commotion, Evelyn briefly debated knocking on the door again but decided against it.

'Damn.' Evelyn kicked the closest thing to her in frustration, which happened to be the precarious wall. Swearing again as pain raced through her toes, she hopped back to her car and started the engine.

13

Ziggy had been summoned by his boss, Superintendent Hastings, as soon as he arrived at the station that morning. He knew why – or at least he thought he did. They wanted answers; top brass needed to see what his team had been doing. Working all hours was the answer. He'd missed numerous weekends with his son, Ben. Rachel, his ex-wife, understood, and he'd tried to squeeze in breakfasts with them as often as time allowed, but everyone was under a mountain of pressure. All leave had been cancelled, and overtime had been granted. He knew a couple members of the team, himself included, would have worked without the overtime bonus just to see justice served.

He sat forward on the hard plastic chair outside Hasting's office. His own thoughts had drifted once again to the prison meeting between Evelyn and James Hawthorne. Aside from the million and one other things he had to do today, the castle angle was something he was keen to pursue. He made a mental note to speak to Evelyn and ask her to push that angle when she met with Hawthorne later.

Another thought randomly occurred to him. What did

they actually know about Dr Evelyn Shaw? Sure, she came with all the right credentials, and her reputation was untarnished, but what did they actually *know*? His thoughts were interrupted by Hastings.

'Thornes, come on in.' Hastings stepped aside to let Ziggy pass.

'Sir,' Ziggy replied, doing as he had been instructed.

'Take a seat. This won't take long. What updates do we have?' retreated behind his desk as he spoke but remained standing.

'The task force are all over it, sir. We are doing everything we can.'

'I know, I know. But you know how it is – shit rolls downhill. Everyone is on this; National Crime Squad, Home Office – hell, even Blair is pushing for information from Downing Street, despite having his plate full with the fallout from the Iraq situation. It's a mess, Ziggy, an utter mess.'

's thoughts pretty much echoed Ziggy's own, so he remained silent.

'Let's get some answers, Thornes. NCS are on standby with their resources – let's utilise them if we need to. How's it going with Dr Shaw?'

'Good, great actually. She's arranged daily visits.'

'And Hawthorne, is he talking?'

'He seems to be. Speaking of Dr Shaw, what do we know about her?'

'Why do you ask?'

'No reason. She's clearly highly qualified. Has she worked on any recent cases?'

'She was the consultant on the Hardy case, the Camden Ripper. Did the initial profile, I believe.'

'Hmm, yes. Sadie mentioned that. Interesting.' Ziggy couldn't put his finger exactly on what was niggling at him about her, and it seemed churlish to be asking his superior for information about a colleague, so he let it drop. 'Is there anything else, sir?'

'Not at the minute. Any updates, et cetera, et cetera.' sat and picked up his phone. 'Always available, Andrew – let's get some answers.'

'Will do,' replied Ziggy as he turned to leave. He closed the door behind him and headed back into the MIT office, where his team were busy following up more leads.

Pulling up a chair at his desk, he turned on his PC and accessed the intranet. It was an internal information system that listed all the approved service providers that were external to the police force. A quick search for Evelyn Shaw brought up various results and a link to her profile page. He clicked the link. Along with the details of her qualifications, of which there were many, there was also a short paragraph about her early life. *Helmsley.* The word jumped out at him. Why was it familiar? He was sure he'd never been there. He knew someone who would have answers.

'Sorry to interrupt, Ang, could I ask a small favour?' Ziggy asked over the desk divider.

She was rapidly typing away at her keyboard.

'As long as it's above board?' she said, only half-jokingly.

'Yes, perfectly,' he replied, showing his teeth as he smiled sincerely.

'Go on, what is it?' She held out her hand, no doubt expecting him to hand her a phone number or IP address that he wanted her to trace. Angela was their go-to IT whizz, and whilst it hadn't been breaking the law exactly, he had taken advantage of her knowledge to help them get information in a more off-the-books capacity from time to time.

'No, nothing like that. I wonder if you could do a little research into Helmsley for me?'

'As in North Yorkshire?'

'Yes. It's come up already in the Hawthorne case, hasn't it?'

'Yes, it's where Hawthorne's sister Alison lives.'

'Is there are castle there?'

'Yes, Helmsley Castle— Ah, a castle!'

Ziggy grinned again. 'Bingo. Can we get a search team organised?' He was about to ask more of Angela when he was interrupted by his mobile phone. 'DI Thornes?' he said, and he gave Angela the thumbs up as he listened to the caller. He stood and headed to the swing doors that led to the stairs he ended the call. 'I'm on my way.'

There was a definite nip in the air as the autumn day brightened. Low mist hung over the river as Evelyn drove through Leeds city centre. She replayed her conversations with Alison over in her mind and wondered about its abrupt end. Had she gone too hard and fast with her questions? Should she have continued to play it more softly? It was no use. She'd been beating herself up on the entire trip back to Leeds, but she could do nothing about it now. She had to shift her focus.

She took the exit to the M1 towards Wakefield and wondered how Hawthorne would be with her today. Her mobile phone buzzed in the centre console, and she reached for it, while not taking her eyes off the road, and pressed to connect to the Wakefield number that flashed on the screen.

'Dr Evelyn Shaw,' she answered.

'Doctor Shaw, it's Governor Davis over at HMP Wakefield.'

'Governor Davis, hello.'

'I see that you're due to visit later with Hawthorne. What time are you expecting to be here?'

'I'm on my way now. I'll be around twenty minutes. Is everything OK?'

'Hawthorne's been moved into segregation.' The static on the line broke the governor's message up.

'Did you say "segregation"? Are you able to tell me why? Actually, I'm about twenty minutes away... Hello?' The line went dead, so she pressed her foot down and sped over to Wakefield as fast as she could.

Governor Davis was standing in HMP Wakefield's reception, waiting for her when she arrived. As they passed through the numerous gates to his office, he went on to explain what had happened.

'After your meeting with him yesterday, he became restless. Pacing his cell, then throwing the one personal possession he's been allowed, a tennis ball, noisily against the adjacent cell.' Governor Davis picked up his pace and Evelyn had to practically run to keep up. 'It went on for hours. He'd been asked to stop several times, as the other inmates were complaining, but he ignored us.' Davis turned a corner and unlocked his office door. 'Then the verbal abuse started.'

'By Hawthorne or at him?'

'Both, it escalated quickly. Control and Response were called in. Hawthorne was apprehended, and I instructed them to place him in segregation.'

'How did Hawthorne take it?'

'He calmed down but was pissed off that we wouldn't give him his ball back.'

Evelyn worked through the implications for their next session in her mind. If he was unsettled or preoccupied, she may not have such a productive session with him – a time delay that neither she nor the police nor Claire Strickland could afford – if they weren't already too late. 'Am I still able to visit today?'

'Absolutely. In fact, he's demanding to speak with you.'

Evelyn looked at her watch. She had twenty minutes to prep herself and the revised strategy she was going to take in light of the situation.

The office door opened, and Ziggy walked in, his imposing frame filling the doorway. 'I got here as quickly as I could.'

'Inspector.' Davis stood to greet him. 'I was just going over the situation with Dr Shaw.'

'Right. Good to see you, Evelyn. Where is he now?' Ziggy asked of Governor Davis.

'Still in segregation. I'm not sure how cooperative he'll be, but we can take him to the interview room?'

'We don't have a choice. Time is critical,' Ziggy said, but he was looking at Evelyn.

As though Evelyn wasn't feeling the pressure already, his intense glare was unnerving. 'Give me a few minutes and I'll see you over there,' she replied.

She stood, smoothed her trousers at the waist and tugged her shirt back into place – small, deliberate movements, as if tidying herself might steady her thoughts. The room emptied while a guard waited outside to escort Evelyn. She had a couple of minutes to compose herself. Reaching into her bag, she took her notebook out and flicked to the page where she had made notes, refreshing her memory. A lot had happened in the space of a few hours, and she was very aware of the ticking clock. There would be no more time for niceties, as Ziggy had unnecessarily pointed out; every minute was critical.

14

———————

Evelyn entered the interview room. Ziggy was already there, waiting for her.

'Does this change your plan for today?' he asked.

'Yes. We need to be direct, but not forceful. He knows we're under pressure, but if we give the slightest hint of how desperate we are, he'll make it difficult for us. And I don't know yet how he feels about being in segregation.'

'Understood. Have you given any more thought to the castle connection?'

Of course she had. It had plagued her in the early hours and was the reason she could feel what she could only describe as grit in her eyes. At this point in her day, she had to focus, and she could hardly share her nightmares with the detective.

When she didn't speak, he jumped in, bringing her back to the present.

'Can we push him on that? See if we can get any closer, any more information?'

'Yes, yes of course,' she replied distractedly.

Ziggy headed off to the viewing room, whilst Evelyn arranged her chair into the same position as the previous day. Once again taking her notes from her bag, she flicked through the pages, mentally and physically preparing herself. She deliberately dropped her shoulders, released her tense jaw and waited for the prisoner to be brought to her.

As Hawthorne entered, escorted by a guard, she took a note of his clothing. He'd shown previously how appearance was important to him, and despite being in segregation, he was still immaculately turned out – as much as any prisoner could be. Clean shaven, uniform unmarked. Quickly glancing at his face, she saw that in direct contradiction to his posture, his jaw was locked solid, teeth grinding hard. Despite trying to look casual, he was wound as tight as a coiled spring.

'How are you, James?' she ventured as the guard bolted him to the table.

'In segregation or in general?' He let out a low laugh. 'I'll lose my privileges, but they were scarce anyway.'

'You were throwing a tennis ball?'

'Yes, it helps me think.'

'What were you thinking about?' she asked.

'You.'

As though someone had switched on a giant vacuum, the air evaporated out of the room. Evelyn stumbled over her words, interrupted by Hawthorne before she could fully form a sentence.

Hawthorne continued. 'Not specifically you. Our conversation.'

Feeling her face flush, she fought to keep it under control. Trying to buy herself some time, she asked him to be more specific. 'We covered a lot of ground last time. Anything in particular?'

'You don't like talking about yourself, do you?'

'Because we're not here to talk about me. We're here to help you.'

'To help me? Help me how?'

'To help you uncover why you are the way you are. What drives you to do the things you do.'

'Kill, you mean?'

She carried on, trying to appear unfazed by the offhand use of the loaded word. 'Yes, but also your motivations. What makes you that way.'

'And to find out where Claire is?'

She stared at him at the casual mention of Claire's name. 'Yes, that as well.'

'What makes you think I need help, or that I want to know why I am the way I am, as you put it?'

'Perhaps you don't want to know, but it will help us to understand the human condition more. And bring some kind of closure to the survivors.'

'Bah, *closure*. I hate that word.' The words spat out of his mouth.

'Why?'

'What does it mean, actually? *Closure*. An act, an ending. Of what? Misery? Need?'

'It can be interpreted in several ways, I guess. In this instance, it's about allowing the surviving family members to know why their loved ones were taken from them so violently. And to locate a missing woman.'

Hawthorne started drumming his fingers on the table and yawned. 'Did you sleep well, Evelyn?'

The quick change in conversation threw Evelyn slightly off, especially as she'd had to stop herself from following Hawthorne's contagious yawn. 'I slept perfectly well, thank you.' She lied.

'Really? Do you have nightmares, Evelyn?'

'No, not as a rule. As you mentioned it, I'd like to talk to you about Claire.'

'I'm sure you would,' Hawthorne replied, a smile crossing his lips. 'What would you like to know?'

A strong sense of déjà vu came over her. She'd been here before, asking these or similar questions.

She shook her head to clear her confusion. 'Is she alive?'

'Why?'

'Because if she's alive, then she needs to be found.'

'Will it bring *you* closure?'

'This isn't about me. A woman's life is at stake. You've taken so much away from so many families. Perhaps you could see this as your chance to make amends. Doesn't that appeal to you? That you can square something off. Put things in the order they are meant to be?'

Hawthorne didn't reply.

There was a shout from the corridor outside, but it did little to change the atmosphere in the room. He continued to stare at Evelyn, but she was reluctant to look away and break the connection. She carried on.

'What's stopping you from sharing, James?'

'I told you all I'm willing to share last time. The clues are there, Evie – you're just not looking hard enough.'

She clasped her hands on the table in front of her. She would have to play his game. If she was going to get anywhere, to get anything meaningful, she needed to step into the darkness that she had fought so hard to leave behind.

'Tell me about the castle,' she asked.

'Ha! So, you were listening.' Hawthorne gave a light-hearted chuckle that was at odds with his usual deep-throated laugh. Like he was playing, enjoying himself. She supposed he was in some warped way.

'Why is a castle significant, James?'

Still no response, just an intense stare.

'Is it any castle or one in particular?'

She wondered what Ziggy was making of this behind the glass. Was he as frustrated as she was?

'What about you, Evie? Were you lonely roaming the moors on your own?'

She felt the blood drain from her face. 'I, I, I... I don't know what you mean,' she stammered, brushing a stray hair back behind her ear.

'Or perhaps you preferred hiding in the ruins?'

All Evelyn could hear was her heart thumping in her ears. The blood that had earlier drained came rushing back to her chest and face. Heat emanated from her cheeks until she could no longer hold his intense glare. Breaking eye contact, she briefly glanced at the Perspex glass behind Hawthorne's head. With her mouth dry, she took a small sip of water and noticed the liquid shaking slightly in her hand.

'Of course, you couldn't do that afterwards, could you?'

'Please, James, we're not here to talk about me.' Her voice was reedy, barely audible.

'You had nowhere to hide then, did you? Did you hate it when he found you, Evie?'

She couldn't stand it any longer. She shot to her feet, spilling water everywhere. Hawthorne did the same, leaning forward as he did so to compensate for the handcuffs. A chill skated down Evelyn's spine. Her throat tightened, dry, and her fingers twitched. She hit the emergency button, and the door burst open. Several guards entered the room and removed Hawthorne.

Still shaking and feeling physically sick, Evelyn sat back down and took several tissues out of her bag to mop up the spill, whilst simultaneously trying to control her emotional state by taking deep breaths.

She was furious with herself. Her grip on control was slipping—fast. Hawthorne had exposed a fracture in her composure, and now the cost of that moment could be everything. With the weight of Ziggy's expectations pressing down and her credibility on the line, she knew she must find a way to regain command of both the investigation and herself. But as the psychological war with Hawthorne deepened, one thing became terrifyingly clear to her: the next move could either save Claire—or destroy Evelyn completely.

15

———

'I guess you're wondering what that was all about?' Evelyn ventured as they left the prison. Ziggy hadn't broached Evelyn's reaction to Hawthorne while they were still inside the prison grounds, and Evelyn had been grateful for the chance to fully compose herself.

'Feeling better?' Ziggy asked as they walked across the car park.

'Yes, thank you,' she said.

'What made you react so strongly?' he asked.

'It was a shock, that's all. I let him get to me.'

'Evelyn, you're not made of steel. Whatever it was, you can't let him get into your head.'

'I did, though, and it was unprofessional of me.'

'I dare say you're not the first and certainly won't be the last.'

'I'm sorry about that, Ziggy. To be honest, it was the mention of castle ruins.' She stopped walking and turned to look at him, clutching her bag like some kind of security blanket. 'I don't know how he knows – and it can't be a lucky guess – but he talked about an event from my past that I thought I would never have to revisit.'

'Something from your childhood?'

Evelyn bit her lip and nodded. 'Yes.'

'What was it?'

She started walking towards the car park. 'We were kids, Ziggy, we didn't know any better. We ran because we were scared.'

'Ran from what? Where?'

Evelyn started to shake at the thought. 'From the old castle, from Helmsley Castle ruins.'

'What happened at the castle?'

'It was an accident.' They had reached her car. She clicked it open and threw her bag on the passenger seat, slamming the door after it. Leaning against the car, she swallowed hard.

'It was during the summer holidays. We were bored. There was nothing for thirteen-year-olds to do around there, so we'd hang out in the ruins of the castle once the early patrol had cleared off. You know the kind of thing – drinking, smoking, fooling around.'

Ziggy nodded.

'It was just one night—the night everything went sideways,' she said, voice thinner now. 'Chris came down. He was older than us. Thought it'd be hilarious to light matches in the basement. Said it would make things more exciting.'

She twisted a ring on her finger. 'We all laughed at first. The air was so dry, the smoke started fast.' She paused. Her eyes flicked around the car park—anywhere but at Ziggy. 'We ran. Nobody said anything. Just bolted up the steps and scattered.'

'Hmm, interesting for sure, but hardly the catastrophe he hinted at.'

'I don't know what else he could have been referring to.'

'But you're from Helmsley, right?'

'My family are, yes, and I lived there for a while when I was younger.' She walked round the front of her car and climbed into the driver's seat. 'I really need to be going, Ziggy.'

'Do you feel OK to drive?

'Yes, I'm fine. Again, I'm sorry.' She drove off, knowing that she had left the detective with more questions than answers.

Ziggy had been back in the incident room for around an hour when the call came in. The brief message was passed along, clearly taken in a hurry judging by the scrawled handwriting. A local unit in Helmsley had made a discovery that needed their immediate attention. He grabbed his jacket and headed to his car. Sadie ran to keep up with him.

'Did they say what it was they had found?' she asked, strapping herself in.

'No. A PCSO had taken a look as requested and called PolSA via the control room. I said we'd meet them there.'

Ziggy sped through the streets of Leeds until he reached the motorway. He picked up the A1M, headed north, then took the Thirsk exit twenty minutes later. He weaved his way along the A170 towards Sutton Bank. The trees lining the route had turned golden, amber and deep red, contrasting with the dark greens of the moorland as autumn extended its presence. Ziggy dropped his BMW down a gear as he climbed the winding incline up Sutton Bank itself.

One of the steepest main roads in England, with sharp bends and tight corners the road demanded his full attention, barely giving him time to consider what lay ahead.

Passing the visitor parking for Sutton Bank National Park – gateway to the North Yorkshire Moors – he dodged day trippers as he sped into Helmsley. The small market square, made up of honey-coloured limestone buildings and cobbled streets was picture-postcard perfect but also packed with day trippers. Ziggy had to beep his horn a few times to get people out of his way. Finally, they reached a side road where he could leave his car. They exited, just as a police van pulled into the main square, causing a crowd to gather.

Ziggy turned to Sadie. 'See if you can find that PCSO. Have them meet me at the entrance. And can you keep that crowd back please?'

Acknowledging his requests, Sadie went off to follow his instructions while Ziggy strode over to the small brick building marked as the visitor centre. Its narrow windows and slate roof and walls that looked to be bowing under the pressure of holding it up seemed very fitting for the surroundings. Glancing over to his right, he saw what looked like the start of a building site. Areas were cordoned off from the public and steel fences ran along the outer edge of a grass banking. What was that about? He took a walk over, trying to figure out who was in charge.

'DI Thornes,' he said in a loud voice over the small crowd that had gathered inside. 'Can someone tell me what's going on?'

A uniformed policeman and a young woman took a step to

one side of the crowd. 'Sir, I'm PC Ken Stipe, North Yorkshire Police, and this is Jane from English Heritage.'

Ziggy asked to be brought up to date on what had been found.

'I think you'd better see for yourself,' PC Stipe said. He went on to explain that he had already called forensics and reconfirmed that PCSO Sam Henley had been the one to make the unfortunate discovery.

'I've asked my colleague to locate him, or her for me.'

'Ah, they won't be able to, I'm afraid. I sent her home.'

Ziggy tipped his head. 'Why?'

'Perhaps you'd better come with me.'

Ziggy looked around for Sadie as they headed towards the grassy bank that Ziggy had seen earlier, just beyond the building works. He waved her over as she finished putting the outer cordon in place.

Stipe led them over a wooden bridge, and as they started to climb the short incline, Jane spoke.

'The building works are set to be complete in 2004. It's a new visitor centre. If it's kids that have been playing on the sand, then it's nothing to do with us. You would have to contact the construction company.'

Stipe turned to her. 'It's not kids, and I think for scene preservation, it would be better if you stayed here.'

Jane looked offended but did as she had been asked.

Peter Beck, the lead search officer from PolSA caught up with them and joined the group as they headed across what had once been the entrance to the west tower of Helmsley Castle.

Ziggy stopped to take in his surroundings and the land-scape. The ruins were stark and striking. Looking up, he could see what remained stood tall and weathered – broken stone walls rising against the sky, jagged at the top where the structure had crumbled over centuries. The outer face still hinted at its former strength, with thick masonry and narrow vertical slits for windows or arrows. Parts of the internal rooms lay open to the elements, their outlines just visible in the rough stonework.

Time had stripped it of decoration, leaving bare walls and scattered rubble. Grass grew where floors once were. From some angles, it was possible to see how it had once loomed over the rest of the castle, but now it appeared more skeletal than solid – haunting, but with presence.

The tower's position gave it a clear view over the surrounding land, as it once did when it guarded the entrance to the moors. Now, it was more about atmosphere than defence – quiet, exposed, and steeped in history. In the glimpses of late-afternoon sunlight, Ziggy could see the texture clearly – the aged stone, lichen and deep shadows where stairs or rooms once were.

'What do we know?' Ziggy asked as they closed in on a set of narrow stone steps that led to some kind of basement. PC Stipe stopped.

'It's grim, I'll warn you now. PCSO Henley was shaken to her core, and I have to confess that in all my years on the force I haven't seen anything like it.'

'Perhaps I should go in first,' Beck proposed, as was protocol.

'It's fine. I'll go,' Ziggy said, never one for standing on the sidelines. He also figured, after all his years in the force, he'd pretty much seen it all. 'Is it down here?'

'Yes, just watch your step, those stones are wet and it's slippery.'

Ziggy had pulled on protective gloves as he'd walked

across. On hearing about the wet steps, he decided to wait before he protected his shoes. His shoe prints could be eliminated later. Gingerly placing one hand on the wall, he carefully stepped down until he was below ground level.

16

———

The smell hit Ziggy's nostrils as he took another step closer. He recoiled, closed his eyes and took a deep breath through his mouth. Being careful where he placed his feet, and wafting away numerous bluebottle flies as he did so, he pulled a face mask from his pocket and hooked it over his ears and pinched the nose band. He looked at the image in front of him, but his brain refused to process what he was seeing.

A wheel of dead women stood before him, silent and inexplicable. It leant against the far window, the bruised light of dusk filtering through the narrow window, landing on the pale edges of skin and bone. The structure was angular, almost ritualistic – some kind of hexagonal frame with spokes that held limbs in a pattern too intricate to follow. Arms and legs overlapped in tangled symmetry, their arrangement deliberate but unreadable, like a language he couldn't translate. It was impossible to tell where one body ended and another began. Faces turned toward him – or perhaps away – mouths slightly open, eyes gone, only dark cavities remained. It had the air of a circus attraction long since abandoned, left to gather dust. No music played. No one laughed.

Ziggy had to turn away, and he took a step back for a few minutes to remind himself that he didn't live in this nightmare. When he stepped back in, he stole himself to look more closely.

He didn't dare to approach anything else. It all looked too precarious, as though it could collapse any minute. He shouted up the steps. 'Have Forensics arrived yet?'

The cheerful face of Irfan Mohammed came into view. 'The cavalry is here.' He started to descend. 'Though, you shouldn't be in here, as you well know, Ziggy.' He admonished good naturedly then stopped in his tracks. 'What in the name—?'

'Yes, it's something...'

'You need to leave, Ziggy. This is my scene now,' said Irfan, pointing him back up the stone steps. Ziggy didn't need telling twice. And he took the steps two at a time as more crime scene investigators started to filter down.

Ziggy reached the outside and sucked in fresh air. 'Let me know when...' He began to call down but couldn't finish his sentence. When what? When you've released them all? When you've sorted the limbs?

Suddenly, Irfan shouted again. 'This one is alive.'

Holy shit. Ziggy shot back inside. 'What?'

'Get the paramedics! This woman is breathing – barely, but she is alive.'

Ziggy peered in closer. It was Claire Strickland. He saw the faintest of movements in the very topmost body. 'Help her,' he urged, trying desperately to figure out a way of removing her.

Thankfully, Stipe had had the foresight to call the fire

service and an ambulance when he'd arrived. A paramedic came rushing in. 'Step back, please— Jesus.'

Ziggy began to loosen the ropes that held the breathing victim's hands in place. Even with the ropes removed, her arms remained stiff as they'd been lashed in place for so long. Ziggy gently moved the woman's head and shoulders. The angle that she was at made it impossible for more than one person at once to attend to her, and as Ziggy was closest, the paramedic passed him the oxygen mask as two others tried to manoeuvre a stretcher down the narrow steps and into the enclosed space.

'No room, I'll carry her,' Ziggy yelled. She was still being kept in place by the bindings on her feet and legs that were lashed to the wooden spoke. Ziggy looked at it for a moment and made a split decision. 'Get me something to break that spoke. An axe, chainsaw, anything.'

Outside the ruin, someone passed along a heavy-duty knife from the fire service.

Being careful not to hit any of the other victims, Ziggy cut through the remaining ropes. The whole structure gave way, and before he knew it, the rudimentarily constructed wheel collapsed and fell onto him. The smell was intense as he pushed and pulled his way from underneath. The slime and stench of rotting flesh hit him full force. Bolting up, he scrambled to his feet and just made it outside as he brought up the contents of his stomach. Paramedics came over and offered him a sheet to wipe the maggots and vomit-inducing fluid that had exploded all over his suit. Thankfully, nothing had gone into his mouth, but that didn't stop him from continually retching for the next ten minutes.

The breathing victim was carried out and whisked away in an ambulance.

Fire officers took over and secured the structure before

paramedics re-entered and continued slowly removing the bodies. Ziggy stripped off down to his underwear in the back of an ambulance and pulled his way into a barrier suit. Feeling the need for fresh air, he sat down heavily on the cold floor of the footpath, damp seeping into his bones. Every time he closed his eyes, the sensation of human bodily gloop touching his skin made him want to puke.

He shook his head to clear the sensation.

'All right, boss? I saw what happened.' Sadie hesitated but offered him a hand up, which he gratefully took. Ziggy saw her trying not to recoil from the smell that oozed off him.

Ziggy shuddered. 'I don't know what's worse. Seeing the bodies or having them all over me.' He gagged at the thought. 'I need a shower.'

'How many were there?'

'I couldn't tell you, to be honest. It was some grotesque structure or display. I'm not sure what the hell you would call it, but I have never seen anything like it.'

'I don't understand why it hasn't been discovered before. I mean, if there were flies and maggots, then it's been what? 3 days? About the length of time that Hawthorne's been in custody.'

'Exactly. Was it his last act?' Ziggy tentatively rubbed his head to make sure nothing was stuck to him. 'Hell, I don't know. It just adds to the complexity, Sadie. And also, this isn't the kill site, it's only the deposition site. There wasn't enough blood.'

'My God, can this case get any more complicated?' She glanced around her as Ziggy adjusted himself in the uncomfortable Tyvek suit.

'Looks like SOCO are going to be a while, so shall we

head back to the station? You can get a shower there,' she said, turning back to him.

They walked side by side away from the chaos at the castle ruins as more units poured in to preserve the scene, recover and record evidence. 'I'll catch a lift with you if that's OK. You can update me on what we know.'

'Sure, I'll even leave the car windows down for you,' he said, heading back towards the side street.

17

———————

'Do you think Evelyn knows more than she's letting on?' Sadie asked as she poked her head out of the car window to allow fresh air to remove the smell. Ziggy had filled Sadie in on the conversations he'd had with Dr Evelyn Shaw and the story she had told him about the fire in the castle ruins as they drove back to the office.

'I'm not sure. I can't find any connection between her and Hawthorne. I've had a brief look into her background, and there doesn't seem to be anything that stands out. I don't know... It's odd that he seems to know so much, that's for sure.'

'I can do some digging if you like?'

Ziggy knew Sadie would take it upon herself to turn up any information that could be found. Sadie was ambitious and currently working through the inspector programme, which Ziggy knew she would pass with flying colours. He'd be sad to lose her if she chose to relocate. She worked incredibly hard on every case and nurtured internal contacts in a way that he had never been able to, even if he had wanted to.

'That would be good, actually. I'm not sure how far back you'd have to go. All I turned up in my preliminary intranet searches were her professional details – I haven't had time to dig deeper.'

The pair were quiet for a while as they battled through the traffic.

'Tell me your thoughts about the discovery of the bodies,' Sadie asked. 'What are your first impressions?'

'Macabre. That's one of the many words I'd use for it. To think that someone was still alive in all that horror doesn't bear thinking about. I dare say that her physical injuries may recover, but the nightmares are unlikely to ever go away.' He knew, personally, that the memory would stay with him for a long time and he'd only been there a few minutes.

He shifted in the Tyvek suit, his skin itching as a scene of maggot-filled cavities flickered in his mind's eye.

Swallowing down bile, he focused on the road.

'I can't even begin to get my head around that,' Sadie said. 'I'll check with the hospital and see how she's getting on. The remaining bodies, they were the other missing women? Did they have the same signatures? The stabbings, the carving on the torso?'

'I've got to be honest, I couldn't take much in. It was sensory and brain overload. Very confusing. I'd like to be at the post-mortems, just to get a closer look.'

'I'll check in with Pathology. It's likely to be in the next twenty-four hours, I think.' Sadie said.

Ziggy agreed, knowing everything for this case was being expedited.

'How the hell did he get, what, four bodies in there? I mean, taking them from one site to the other would be a hell of a lot of movement before we even consider how he... displayed them. He'd have needed a van at least—'

Ziggy jumped in. 'Exactly, which means more of a chance for error. Which means...?'

'More evidence for the prosecution.'

Ziggy gave a wry smile, his earlier thoughts on Sadie's promotion confirmed.

They pulled up at HQ and headed straight up to the MIT office. Nick, Angela, Superintendent and Dr Shaw were all in the incident room, along with the remaining task force that weren't still on site.

Desperate for the feel of hot water washing away the crawling sensation under his skin, Ziggy made his excuses and headed to the locker room. Stripping out of the sweaty suit that stuck to him in the worst places, he peeled it off and placed it into a brown evidence bag. Not the most powerful of showers, but adequate enough to deliver a steady flow of hot water, he stepped under the stream and turned the temperature as hot as it would go. Letting it scold his skin, he reached for the tea-tree shower gel he kept in his locker and poured it into his hands. Rubbing his palms together, he swept his hands over his body, repeating the process until his skin was tingling and he finally felt clean. He dried off, sprayed a significant amount of deodorant and changed into a clean set of clothes that he kept in his locker. He felt a little better, but the smell that clung to his nostrils, he was sure, would leak from his pores forever. Nick came into the changing room just as Ziggy closed his locker.

'All right, boss? That got a bit messy, I hear.'

'Don't. It was gross. I'm trying to put it out of my mind.'

'You're wanted upstairs, anyway. I'll get you a coffee whilst you head up.'

'Nice one, Wilko. Thanks.' Ziggy shrugged into the zip-up hoody and headed upstairs.

The team were all seated around the large conference table, waiting for him. He joined them, followed by Wilko bearing a steaming mug, which he placed down in front of Ziggy.

Ziggy gratefully took a sip of the coffee and relayed to the gathered officers what had been discovered. Once he'd brought everyone up to speed, he took a few minutes to answer questions from the wider team.

'Do you genuinely think it's a copycat?' asked a uniformed PC.

'We'll need the post-mortem results back before we can make any more of that. The PM should give us some kind of timeline to work to. Once we have that, we'll know if we're looking at a copycat... or an accomplice.' A murmur went around the room, and Ziggy held up his hands to silence. 'No speculating or jumping to conclusions. We need hard evidence.' He allowed Sadie to issue actions, whilst he headed over to his desk. He'd just logged in when Evelyn came over to see him.

'Ah,' he said. 'I was just checking something then, I was going to come and find you.'

Evelyn pulled up a chair and sat alongside him. 'It sounded horrendous, Ziggy.' He noted that she shuddered, which is what everyone else had been doing since he got back.

'Yeah, all part of the job, I guess.'

An uneasy silence fell between them. Ziggy wanted to broach the subject of her potential connection to Hawthorne. It seemed more important now that the discovery of five further bodies had been made in the small market town of Helmsley. He didn't believe in coincidences.

But he'd seen her reaction to Hawthorne's question. Would she open up to him more? There was definitely more to the castle story than she'd said so far.

Deciding that directness was the only way, he just came out with it. 'Tell me how you know James Hawthorne.'

She pulled upright in her chair. 'I don't know him...' Her voice rose at the end of the sentence, as though questioning his logic in asking the question. He tried his best to temper his tone as he continued. 'Are you sure you don't know him from some dim and distant past? University perhaps?' Evelyn's face turned not just a rosy glow but a burning, fierce red. 'How does he know these things about you, Evelyn?'

She laughed awkwardly, but Ziggy's eyes never left Evelyn's face.

The red started to creep down her neck.

'I don't know where you're getting your information from Ziggy, but—'

'From you Evelyn. I'm getting my information from you.'

'There is no basis for your... for your suspicion.' She was talking with her hands flapping in the air to emphasise her words.

'I just can't work it out,' replied Ziggy. 'How did he know where you grew up?'

'I honestly don't know. I wish I did, believe me,' she said.

Ziggy could see that Evelyn was getting more defensive. He sat back, watching her face. Was he being unreasonable? There was definitely something there, though, he was convinced.

18

The early start, the stress of the day and the endless questions from Ziggy had all conspired to trigger a headache that started at the base of Evelyn's neck and crept upward, reaching the back of her eyes. She placed one hand on her shoulder and pulled, trying to alleviate the tension. With promises to update Ziggy she made her excuses and left the building. Walking to the car park, she climbed into her car and rested her aching head against the steering wheel. She just wanted to get home. To her safe place. To where she could truly trust that no one was watching, and no one was asking difficult questions. She didn't know how Hawthorne was getting his information, nor why he was using her own insecurities to undermine her. With all her being, she regretted taking on this case, but it was too late now; she was committed. Inhaling deeply, she sat upright and dug deep within herself for some resolve. She wouldn't be beaten by this. She had worked too damn long and too hard to be manipulated.

When she arrived home, she stumbled through her front door, kicked off her shoes and surrendered to the comfort of her sofa. Despite her best intentions, tears started to fall, and she battled to keep her anxiety in check. Taking deep breaths, she closed her eyes and let her mind wander to that fateful night.

Evelyn hated Helmsley. Evelyn had been raised there, and she hated it. It was far from the bright light of York, or even Leeds. There was nothing to do. It was barren, filled with old people, and boring. In the winter, it flooded, and in the summer, it was invaded by tourists, making it impossible to hang out in the market square, where Evelyn and her friends would gather on an evening.

The defining incident that would mark the end of Evelyn's childhood happened during the long, hot summer that she and a group of friends had finished secondary school. The school year was out, and they were desperate for something different to do to celebrate before leaving their sleepy existence and embarking on their chosen career paths. Chris, a couple of years older than Evelyn, had told them that he had found what he described as an 'old underground tunnel'. No one needed any encouragement to investigate it for themselves. Except it wasn't a tunnel, but a basement within the ruins of Helmsley Castle. What had originally been the west tower, its foundations dating back to the twelfth century, was now a visitor attraction during the day, and a place of rebellion during the night. Chris assured them that no one watched the site after sundown and they wouldn't get caught, so the party entered by the stone steps and made it their home for the evening.

'Let's get this party started,' Chris said as he brandished a bottle of his parents' vodka from underneath his coat. The friends cheered as they settled on the old newspapers and plastic bags

they'd brought to sit on. Evelyn hadn't been convinced. She'd seen the devastation that alcohol had on the lives of those she loved, so only pretended to take a sip when it was her turn. As the others passed the bottle around, she sat on the edge of the circle. As the evening went on, and everyone became louder and more boisterous. Evelyn tried to make excuses to leave, but her friends kept her trapped there, blocking the stone steps – the only way in or out.

Then, as the evening temperature started to drop, Chris had the incredibly stupid idea of lighting a fire. She tried to talk them out of it, but her words were in vain. They threw everything they could find onto the tinder they had managed to scrape together. As the flames took hold, Evelyn started to choke on the smoke. Air seemed to take forever to get to her lungs and she frantically looked around her. She wasn't the only one. She scrabbled towards the opening they had already tried to block, pushing the rocks and debris out of the way. Everyone pushed over each other, desperate to get out as thick, black, acrid smoke filled the enclosed space. Finally, after what felt like an age, she felt the damp grass under her hands as she crawled away from the flames that were lapping at her feet. Evelyn's eyes were streaming, whether from the smoke or tears of fright, she had no idea. She wiped her face on her jacket sleeve and looked around her.

'Wait, where's Jan?' she asked the bewildered faces around her.

No one answered. They just looked at each other.

Evelyn stood up. Smoke was pouring out of the tunnel now; there was no way anyone was going back in there.

'Jan!'

'What do we do?' Chris asked.

'Call the fire brigade,' Evelyn screamed as she ran towards the main road.

'We can't!' Chris gasped. 'We're not supposed to be here.'

Evelyn stopped in her tracks. 'What are you saying?'

'We go home – we don't tell anyone.'

'But our friend is stuck in there!'

'And we'll get done for murder.'

Evelyn's tears fell freely and looked around at her so-called friends. Was no one really going to help? She turned back to the tunnel, but orange flames now crept along the side of the steps, eating up the parched ground as it did so.

'We can't just leave.' She sobbed.

Chris stood in front of her. 'Move out of the way.' He pushed her away from the steps. 'Go home.' He spoke to the wider group but held Evelyn by the scruff of her coat. 'We go home. We say nothing. We don't know anything, right?' He glared at the shell-shocked friends, who all stared back, not daring to stand up to him. 'And you' – he twisted Evelyn around to face him – 'if you breathe a word, I will make your life a living hell, do you hear me?'

Terrified, she nodded a meek yes and wriggled free of him.

The friendship ended that night. As far as she was aware, none of them had spoken of it again. Guilt plagued Evelyn for years and still did. The thought of going to prison and the guilt of her friend's death had stuck with her and been a poisoned chalice she silently carried for years.

She hadn't exactly lied to Ziggy, just omitted a key fact.

And now she feared that Hawthorne somehow knew her darkest secret.

19

Friday, 10 October 2003

Hawthorne continued to throw the tennis ball against the ceiling of his cell. He'd been newly returned into a single cell, away from the general population of A Wing. A little gentle persuasion with the prison officer had resulted in his tennis ball being returned.

So, they'd found the bodies. The victims. The human sacrifices. He smiled and threw the ball. He wondered what the great Detective Inspector Thornes would think of the discovery. No doubt he could expect a visit. He idly wondered when Dr Shaw would show her face again. He hoped soon. He enjoyed talking to her, playing with her. Showing her glimpses of himself, his true self. He changed his position and started throwing against the wall of his cell. He rarely missed a catch. He was precise in his throwing. He could single out a spot on the wall as a target and hit it exactly in the centre. It was all about the mind. He'd spent years visualising outcomes; at school, in his buildings, at work – if it could be called *work*. Surely something from which he derived so much pleasure couldn't possibly be called *work*.

The spy hole opened in his cell door.

'Visitor for you, Hawthorne,' a guard called.

He jumped up from his bed and stood by the door.

'Thank you, officer, can I ask who?' He was always polite to the guards in charge. He never knew when he might need them.

'No clue, just been told to take you to the interview room. Come on, get your shoes on.'

Hawthorne followed the guard through the maze of corridors, doors locking at every turn. In the interview room, he was surprised to see DI Thornes seated behind the desk. Hawthorne was cuffed to the table as per. He waited for the detective to break the silence. He didn't have to wait long.

'No doubt your brief will have told you that we found your hiding place.'

Hawthorne didn't reply, unsure if there was a question to answer.

'Except that wasn't where you killed them, was it?'

Ah, now there was a question. But how should he answer? After all, he didn't want to give the game away too early. The good detective would have to work for his answers, just as everyone else had. Apart from Evelyn. Evelyn already knew the answers.

Hawthorne stayed silent and continued to stare at Thornes. He had to admit, albeit silently, he was surprised that the detective hadn't broken eye contact. Yet. He pulled his attention back to what Thornes was saying.

'... carried them some way. So that raises several questions. What vehicle did you use? We've already taken possession of your car and forensically searched it to no avail, so you must have another vehicle somewhere.'

He furrowed his brow. *Oh, Inspector, you're asking all the wrong questions. If only you would push those thoughts a little further. Think a little deeper, a little darker.*

'My guess is that you have a lock-up somewhere. It can't be too far from your house, and it won't be very far from where you supposedly work.'

He gave a slow shake of his head. *Come on. Questions, Inspector. Ask me questions.* Hawthorne sighed deeply.

'Or perhaps in one of your hideous buildings.'

Hawthorne's head snapped up. 'What did you say?'

'Ha, you can hear me then?'

Hawthorne was furious with himself but did this detective really call his beautiful architecture hideous? 'You are a philistine, sir.' He spat the words Thornes. 'How dare you berate something that you have no appreciation for.'

'Is that what you used as your kill site, James? One of the buildings that you created?'

Hawthorne had let Thornes get under his skin, and he needed to pull it back. Regain control. He reverted to staying silent, seething, but silent.

'We can and will search everywhere and everything that you and your sick mind have ever touched. It doesn't matter how far back it goes, or how obscure it may seem. I will ensure that every crime you have ever committed will be uncovered. I will personally see that the evidence we have sends you away for not just this life, but the next one and the one after that.'

James laughed at how irate the detective was becoming. Who knew silence could be so powerful?

'Calm down, Inspector, think of your blood pressure.' Hawthorne continued laughing. He watched as Thornes adjusted his jacket, took a sip of water and appeared to take Hawthorne's advice to calm down.

'Did your brief also tell you that one of your victims survived?'

Hawthorne's eyes widened, his body tense. 'Impossible.'

'You don't deny that they are *your* victims, then?'

'What you say is impossible.'

He watched as Thornes took a photograph from his jacket pocket. 'Really?'

James looked down and saw the pale face of a young woman. She didn't look like she was alive. There was a blue tinge to her skin. Beneath her eyes were dark bruises. She had blood on the corner of her mouth. Unfortunately, he couldn't see the rest of her body, but he could imagine, and his imagination was something else. Still, he didn't speak. He showed no reaction.

'This is Claire,' Ziggy continued. 'Claire is twenty-one. She's a single parent. She's putting herself through college. She's hoping to learn about the beauty industry so that she can work from home whilst taking care of her son.'

James wasn't sure where this was going. Was he supposed to feel something?

'She's fighting life-changing injuries. Horrific injuries she has suffered at your hands.'

Again, was there a question there?

'There's a connection between all of your victims, James, isn't there?'

'I'd love to hear your theory, Inspector,' Hawthorne said, wiping imaginary dust from the edge of the table.

'They're all young, under twenty-five. They mostly work part-time whilst studying at college or university.'

James shrugged his shoulders and held back from slow clapping the detective.

'Tell me about the numbers on the torso.'

James huffed. 'What do you want to know?'

'What's the meaning of them? Why did you do them?'

'Why not?'

'No. It's not that simple. Nothing you do is straightforward. Much like your architectural designs.'

James felt his anger rise slightly at the mention of his designs again, but refused to let it show. 'I'll take that as a compliment.' He smiled.

'Don't,' Ziggy replied. 'Tell me where the kill site is.'

'Why? If you have enough evidence to put me away for the next three lifetimes, why do you need anything from me?' James watched as Ziggy shifted uncomfortably in his chair. Everything snapped into focus. 'Oh... That's it. You don't have enough evidence to connect me to all of them!'

Ziggy snatched the photograph from the table and started to collect his coat.

'You don't have enough evidence, do you? You need more to tie me to all the cases, don't you?' James let out a taunting laugh. 'The good detective is struggling to tie up the loose ends.'

Ziggy summoned the guard with a knock on the window. 'We'll get it, you sick bastard,' Ziggy muttered through gritted teeth as the guard uncuffed Hawthorne from the table and connected himself to the other handcuff.

Still laughing as he was led out of the room, James called after DI Thornes, 'The answers are closer than you think, Inspector.'

20

'Aaarrggh.' Ziggy was furious with himself. What the hell had he been thinking, going in with Hawthorne without any kind of plan? He turned the air blue with self-deprecation as he drove towards his home. He hadn't spent much time there recently, and he was desperate for a few hours' sleep. He was making clumsy decisions, stupid choices that, with the right amount of sleep, would never cross his mind. He'd allowed himself to be manipulated, coerced by a serial killer, no less. Frustration hit him again, and he rubbed his hands through his closely cropped hair.

Justice had always been at the core of everything that Ziggy did, as clichéd as that sounded. Since the loss of both of his parents at an early age, he had strived to deliver justice to families that his own situation had lacked. He had always remained focused, on track, targeted, very rarely letting a suspect unsettle or unnerve him the way that Hawthorne had just done. Ziggy wondered if something similar had happened to Evelyn and idly considered calling her. As he pulled into his drive, he decided against it. He would catch up with her later.

Opening his front door, he collected the mounting pile of mail and threw it on top of the shoe cupboard with every intention of opening it later. Heading to the kitchen, he pulled a beer from the fridge and took a swig directly from the bottle. He headed upstairs to change into something more casual and laid down on the bed, placing the beer bottle on the bedside cabinet.

The next thing he knew, his mobile phone was vibrating at the side of him, threatening to fall off the bedside table. Glancing at the clock, he saw that it was 3 a.m. How long had he nodded off for? He rubbed the sleep from his eyes and answered the call.

'Ziggy? Sorry to wake you, boss.' It was the on-duty sergeant.

'It's OK. What's up?' Ziggy cleared his throat.

'There's been an incident at HMP Wakefield. The governor rang, said to let you know.'

At the mention of HMP Wakefield, Ziggy became instantly more awake. 'Did they say what kind of incident?'

'A suicide.'

Had heard he incorrectly? 'I'm sorry, what?' His brain kicked in. Hawthorne was dead? What would this mean to the case?

'A suicide.'

'Who? How?' Ziggy dragged on yesterday's clothes as he spoke.

'James Hawthorne's neighbouring cell mate.'

'I'm on my way.' Ziggy ended the call and headed to the stairs before realising he was still in his tracksuit bottoms. 'Nah, feck it,' he said, slipping his trainers on by the front door and heading to his car.

Due to the early hour, the journey from Leeds to Wakefield took no time at all. On the way to the prison, he rang Evelyn Shaw, but there was no answer.

Ziggy abandoned his car at the entrance and showed his ID to the security. He was escorted through to Governor Davis's office. Evelyn, also the recipient of an early morning call, was already there, along with a face that Ziggy recognised but couldn't quite place.

'What the hell happened?' Ziggy asked without waiting for introductions.

Governor Davis, Evelyn Shaw, and the mystery man glanced at each other.

'I don't care who tells me, just as long as someone does.'

The mystery man stepped forward. 'My name is Mike Gladstone. I'm from the National Crime Squad.'

Ziggy tried hard not to roll his eyes, but clearly not hard enough, as Gladstone quickly looked away after they had very briefly shaken hands.

'Please, Inspectors, Dr Shaw, take a seat,' Davis instructed, who was actually the only one currently sitting down. The others took him up on the offer and pulled chairs from the edges of the room and sat in front of Davis.

'Earlier on in the evening, we had an incident with an inmate who we believe to have been influenced by James Hawthorne. The incident ended in the suicide of the inmate, Liam McLardy.'

Keen to get to the core of the situation, Ziggy's foot bounced as the governor spoke, silently urging him to get to the point.

'First of all, let me say that whilst Hawthorne wasn't involved in the initial disturbance, we have reason to believe he was instrumental in the reason behind it.'

The governor had a rapt audience as everyone leant in to listen closer.

'Hawthorne was out of segregation, but he was being kept on the close-supervision centre. Interaction with other inmates is minimal, only at mealtimes and the thirty minutes in the exercise yard. We believe it was here that Hawthorne began a conversation with Liam McLardy. McLardy is an Irish prisoner who's serving multiple life sentences for a series of vile rape cases dating back years. We've never had any bother from him. He's doing his time quietly, spends most of his days reading and studying. He's always been very respectful to staff, but his designated prison officer noticed he'd started to get agitated after morning exercise yesterday.'

Davis paused and leant forward on his desk, weaving his fingers together. 'Now, we aim to prisoners separate when they're outside. We try to organise it so it's at different times, of course, but yesterday, Liam was showing serious signs of agitation and asked if he could have extra yard time. The officer on the floor couldn't see an issue, so took him out – supervised, of course. When he tried to return him to his cell, Liam assaulted him. Completely out of character.'

'What has Hawthorne got to do with any of it?' Ziggy asked.

'I'm getting to that. It turns out that Hawthorne was in the next yard. It's enclosed, but the PO said the two of them had been talking through the fence. Hawthorne had told him a pack of lies basically – and had been doing so for a number of days, as they are in neighbouring cells. We don't know how the written messages we found in McLardy's cell were getting between the two of them – that's an internal investigation we'll be conducting, and we've reported ourselves to the relevant authorities—'

Davis's desk phone started ringing, so he paused and took a call. 'Sorry about that. Where was I? Oh, so McLardy was kicking off. The officer had pushed his alert button on his radio, but as other officers were on their way, Hawthorne could be heard shouting encouragement from behind his cell door, and the others joined in. Before we knew it, chaos descended.'

'And so, the riot squad took over and Liam McLardy was taken to the hospital wing for treatment of minor injuries. It would seem a careless medic left a scalpel lying around, and in seconds, Liam grabbed it and slashed his own throat. Though every attempt was made to save him, he bled out.'

Silence descended as the news was taken on board.

'Jesus,' Ziggy muttered. 'Did Hawthorne have anything to say? Has anyone spoken to him?'

'He denied all knowledge,' Governor Davis replied.

'I bet he has,' Ziggy said. 'Where is he?'

'He's back in segregation, where he will stay now until his trial.'

Gladstone stood up. 'I think we should speak to him.'

'Just hold on,' Ziggy said. 'As Evelyn will tell you, you can't just walk in there without a plan. He's a manipulative bastard.'

Evelyn nodded her head in agreement. 'Ziggy's right, this needs some thinking about, which I'm guessing is why I'm here?' She looked at Davis.

'Yes, there is that, and also he's adamant he won't speak to anyone other than Dr Shaw.'

Liam McLardy had wanted to do his time and do it quietly. Originally from County Down, he'd moved over to the mainland aged sixteen at the promise of work. He'd jumped at the chance to put his chequered and troubled past behind him. Having left school at fifteen, he had no longer been able to stand the constant bullying from pupils and teachers alike. Letters and numbers didn't appear the same to him as they did everyone else. They merged into each other, often sloping off the page. He was happier out in the open air, where no one could boss him about or ask him awkward questions. When the job in England hadn't worked out, he'd grown frustrated and his old habits from home started to appear again. He couldn't explain it. He couldn't help it. He had urges, impulses. He'd needed an outlet, and he'd found the worse possible one.

For his own safety in prison, he had been kept in segregation and then, more recently been moved to close supervision. It had made no difference to him. As long as he had access to the books he needed, he was relatively happy. He had been studying for his GCSEs. It was hard. He had a tutor for an hour once a week and he was trying his best.

When he met James Hawthorne for the first time they'd had an interesting conversation about the law, and overall, he'd liked the bloke. Liam wasn't aware of what Hawthorne had done. Only the snippets he'd heard third hand whilst queuing for food on the rare occasions he'd been allowed to mix with others in close supervision.

Hawthorne had told him a few things that Liam hadn't been aware of.

That they shared the same lawyer.

That the lawyer believed McLardy was guilty of recent sexual assault and rape charges against children.

That although the cases McLardy had been charged with weren't in dispute, he was facing additional charges.

Hawthorne had told him it was the way of things. That

rapist's behaviour changed over time. From the sexual assault of women to children. The age of the victims would start to get younger. Hawthorne had told McLardy that he had an inside track with a detective and psychologist.

McLardy had followed his last victim home from school. How would Hawthorne know that if he was lying?

Liam had known he was never getting out of prison. He knew he would die incarcerated and truly, it hadn't bothered him. He had been clean, dry, fed and mostly left alone. He liked the uniformity of the routine. He even liked the officers that looked after him.

The final note from Hawthorne had reached him via a borrowed book. Hawthorne had heard that McLardy was due to be moved that night. He'd told McLardy that they were moving him to a mental hospital.

This had upset Liam. He'd grown angry. When his friendly PO came to take him back to his cell, he'd lost control. He punched and kicked and bitten with everything he had.

All the years of frustration came out in a savage, frenetic attack that had ultimately ended with an opportunity for him to end his own suffering. He finally found peace.

21

____

It was 4 a.m. The meeting had been wound up, and she had been left sitting in the staff canteen.

Evelyn had had very little sleep even before the phone call. Exhaustion, compounded by the scale of Hawthorne's manipulation of Liam McLardy, left her feeling hollowed out, as if some vital part of her had been quietly carved away whilst she wasn't looking. She thought she had managed to get a handle on Hawthorne and his way of thinking. Had she failed? Could she have stopped it from happening? It was pointless being hard on herself, but someone had died, and her patient was likely the reason why.

She knew – or at least she thought she did – why he wanted to speak to her, and she was torn. She wanted to resist his manipulation, but if she did so, she ran the risk of him never speaking with her again. Unable to delay any longer, she asked the prison officer to fetch her a strong cup of coffee and to direct her to a quiet room where she could collect her thoughts.

She envied the police officers that had left for the night – well, morning as it now was. She imagined them returning home to warm beds, safe in the knowledge that their side of the investigation could be continued later.

Sighing deeply, she shook the thoughts from her head and returned to the preliminary report from the prison officer who had been in charge of McLardy. It came as no real surprise to Evelyn that Hawthorne had managed to convince McLardy of the erroneous charges. She had witnessed first-hand how devious he could be. Evelyn felt a degree of sympathy for the young prisoner; he was clearly a vulnerable person and even if she believed that the prison had been at fault to some degree, it didn't negate Hawthorne's sick and twisted antics.

She breathed deeply as she thought about how she wanted this session to run. Although Hawthorne had refused to speak to anyone but her, *she* had to remain in control. She wondered what his thinking had been behind manipulating McLardy. Evelyn knew Hawthorne well enough to understand that he usually only acted in his own interests. He couldn't possibly have done it for his own entertainment, could he? Evelyn felt sick at the thought but had to admit that it was an absolute possibility.

As he entered the room and was once again handcuffed to the table in front of her, Evelyn noted that even at this hour Hawthorne was once again neatly dressed, with his hair – now cut short – combed and even gelled to sit precisely with a side parting. When their eyes met, he seemed to be amused by something, but she was driven by her inner conviction to stick to her strategy. She wouldn't allow herself to be swayed.

'James how are you?' she asked with sincerity.

He reached his forearms up as far as the cuffs would allow and rested his chin on his hands. 'I'm good. Really good, actually.'

She was being invited to enquire why he felt so good when something had gone so wrong, but she kept control and continued with her plan. 'It's good to see you, James. I'm pleased you asked to see me.'

She saw a slight twitch in his posture. When he didn't speak, she continued. 'It can't have been your idea, the incident with McLardy?' she said, giving him a chance to distance himself from the event. To blame others. To let the narcissist in him believe that everyone knew he wouldn't be stupid enough to do something that had his name written all over it.

Evelyn didn't break eye contact with Hawthorne as she watched him processing her subliminal suggestions.

He started gently stroking his chin and neck, as if deep in reflective thought, which she supposed he was. He knew what she was doing, and she hardly dare breathe, wondering if he would take the bait.

An oppressive hush filled the air with anticipation.

He placed the palms of his hands flat on the table. 'You're referring to poor Liam, of course?' He raised a quizzical eyebrow.

Evelyn stayed silent, just lifted her own eyebrows in answer to his question.

'Amateur and problematic from the get-go.'

'Hmm, I can imagine.'

'Can you, Evelyn?' His focus, which had been on the back of his hands, shifted abruptly to Evelyn's face. His tone was loaded with accusation. 'Can you imagine how problematic it was?'

She felt the power balance in the room shift. 'I can *only* imagine, James. I wasn't there.'

She heard his nostrils whistle as he inhaled deeply whilst facing her with a look that came straight out of the evil playbook – should such a thing exist.

'Do you like playing games, Evelyn?'

She didn't reply immediately, trying to work out a measured response to such a loaded question. If she answered his question, would he tell her something new? She took a chance. 'Games? What kind of games?'

'Games that involve the mind.'

Moments passed before she spoke. 'Like chess, for example?'

He tilted his chin and looked at her down his nose. A slow smile crept across his lips. 'Perhaps. It's a game of skill and strategy, I suppose. Do you' – he shifted in his seat again – 'Do you play chess?'

'Not since school.'

'Hmm. What were they called in days gone by? Parlour games, I believe.'

It wasn't a question, so she remained silent, letting him ramble until he reached his point.

'Old maid – I bet you're good at that,' he said pointedly.

Evelyn flushed. Aged forty-eight and unmarried without a partner, she felt as though he'd slapped her cheeks.

'Oh!' he exclaimed. 'Have I hit a nerve?' A sneer dashed across his face.

She refused to be drawn in. She pressed on, hoping the colour in her face had subsided. 'You were telling me about Liam McLardy...'

'Pfft, that.' He wafted his hand as much as he could. 'It

was nothing. The stupid boy. He shouldn't have been so gullible and then we wouldn't be where we are now, would we? No, that's nothing. A minor inconvenience for me to prove a point. I'd much rather talk about you.'

She refused to rise to the bait. Evelyn steeled herself and addressed him directly. 'Tell me what your thinking was behind your messages to Liam McLardy?'

Hawthorne continued, completely ignoring her. 'Ah yes, old maid. Why have you never married, Evie? Does intimacy scare you?' He picked at an imaginary spot on the Formica table, blowing away perceived dust or dirt.

It was now a battle of wills. 'There were no further charges to be brought against McLardy, James. You lied to him.'

'I'm sure I don't know what you mean, Dr Shaw. Please do elaborate.'

'Did you mean for him to take his own life?'

Hawthorne smiled, a tooth-baring grin that sent involuntary shudders down Evelyn's spine. 'If he hadn't done it himself, someone else would have done when he moved to another prison. I did him a favour.'

Utterly repulsed, she broke her gaze and flicked through the pages of her notebook to take her away from his eery, gurning face and changed tack.

'In one of previous conversations, you mentioned the needs of a sadist. I'd like you to elaborate on that. Who is the sadist? Was it the sadist that spoke with Liam?'

Hawthorne's smile faded. His expression became serious, eyebrows knitting together, eyes focusing on a spot behind Evelyn's head. She sensed he had changed character, adopted another persona like before. It was with this version of James Hawthorne that she wanted to speak.

22

Hawthorne tapped on the table with the forefinger of his left hand. A rhythmic tap, as though there was music playing that only Hawthorne could hear.

Evelyn held her position but studied him intently. Was he reliving the scene? If so, which one? She watched as he closed his eyes, which answered her unspoken questions. He arched his back, a slight smirk fleeting across his face.

He's enjoying this, she thought, but still, she didn't speak.

'Yes,' he said finally. 'Temptation. It can be a wonderful thing. It can be heightened, of course, depending on the state of mind of said sadist. Indeed, it – he – doesn't have to be a sadist at all.' He paused, pushing himself deeper into his seat. 'But, for your example involving McLardy, let's assume he is.'

Evelyn noticed the deflection. He was removing himself from the picture, exonerating himself of any blame as she suspected he would.

'And' he continued, 'assuming he is a sadist and that he does face temptation to manipulate, why would he do it with no obvious benefit?'

'You tell me,' Evelyn queried.

'Because he can.'

'But what about the others that fell foul of the sadist? What was the benefit there? They can't all have happened simply "because he could".'

'Oh, absolutely not.' Hawthorne leant forward, bridging his hands, crossing his fingers. He licked his lips and looked down at the floor. 'It had another effect on him.'

Hawthorne looked at her. She had noted that he used the right social cues when he was talking in third person. It could be a clever defence play, but Evelyn didn't think so.

'Such as?'

'It allowed for the shifting of personalities.'

What was he saying, exactly? She remained silent.

'The more dominant thoughts could filter through. Thoughts that might not have occurred to him had he been the "other".'

'Did the thoughts make him brave?'

'Brave? Yes. And along with the bravery was a realisation of his naturalistic needs. His base desires.'

Evelyn's heart was beating out of her chest. 'How did they show themselves, the realisations?'

'It was more like a rupture,' he said, eyes unfocused. 'The watching, the allowing... it split something open inside me. Like a pressure valve finally giving way. Years of silence and holding back—gone in a single moment.'

He'd dodged her question completely, but Evelyn didn't press. Letting him talk was more useful. He was clearly revelling in the sound of his own voice.

'Ha! There was even a time I let one get away,' he added with a dry chuckle. The sound scraped across her nerves, too loud in the empty room, bouncing off the stone walls like it didn't belong there.

'But that moment... it wasn't just curiosity.' He leaned forward, voice low now. 'It was recognition. The realisation that it wasn't a mistake. It was purpose. That was the moment I knew—this wasn't just thought. It was instinct. It was calling.'

Evelyn hoped the disgust wasn't showing on her face. She had sat in front of killers, rapists and serial offenders, but she had never before heard someone deliver such a cold explanation of his needs.

'You said before that they, these thoughts, were an inconvenience. Did that feeling stay?'

'Interesting question, Evelyn,' Hawthorne said quietly. 'I think we've heard enough about sadists and their thoughts for one day, don't you?'

Damn! She knew better than to try to get Hawthorne to talk more. It was obvious from the open-legged position, the relaxing of his hands and the subtle grin on his face that James Hawthorne had done enough reminiscing for one day.

She tried to stifle a yawn, but it got the better of her and her jaw stretched open wide. Her eyes watered, and she quickly pushed the residue away.

'Am I keeping you awake?' Hawthorne smiled a supercilious grin that made Evelyn's skin crawl.

'It is quite early,' Evelyn acknowledged. Wakefield Cathedral bells had just tolled to signify it was 6 a.m. and she had a full day of private clients.

'And yet we've avoided the elephant in the room,' Hawthorne said, pushing himself back from the table.

'Which would be?'

'Oh, I think we both know.'

'The reason behind Liam McLardy's death?' Evelyn queried.

'No! Not that, that was... Well, that's not what I'm referring to.' Hawthorne's shoulders rounded and his chin dropped to his chest. His breathing rate increased, air whistling through his nose as he exhaled.

The change from affable to monster was instant, and Evelyn immediately felt threatened. She banged on the window and summoned the guard.

'I'll think we'll leave that there today, James.'

The guard came and as he released Hawthorne and began to lead him away, Hawthorne turned to Evelyn, and said,

'Think, Evelyn, think. What were we talking about? What are you avoiding? What are your needs? We're not so unalike really, are we, old maid?'

Ziggy and Mike Gladstone walked to the prison car park. Ziggy still wasn't clear as to why Mike was here, so now that he had him on his own, he decided to quiz him further.

'What brings you this far north?' Ziggy asked, assuming Mike had travelled up from Scotland Yard in London.

'I live in Sheffield, actually, so it's not too far,' Gladstone replied.

'OK, I'll put it another way. Why are NCS involved in this case?'

Mike let out a laugh. 'Straight to the point – they did say that about you.'

Ziggy's ear pricked up. 'Well, if I wasn't intrigued before, I am now. Who are "they"?'

Mike gave another low chuckle. 'My bosses, I guess you'd call them. Look –' Mike dangled his car keys in his hand as they approached Ziggy's car – 'let's start on the right note. First of all, I'm not here to take over the case.'

Ziggy stayed silent.

'I've been asked to check in on progress and report back. I answer directly to the Home Office, and as I'm sure you're aware, this case has national interest.'

'I thought you guys covered organised crime and the like.'

'We do, but this is an unusual case. A serial killer in the UK is an unusual thing, and we – meaning my bosses – want to have someone on the ground to learn as much as we can.'

'Why didn't my super say something?'

'He'll find out later this morning.'

Ziggy was amazed. He knew the case would attract attention, and part of him had known it was only a matter of time before higher-ups put pressure on his team.

Mike spoke again. 'There's no need to take you off the case, if that's what you were thinking. In fact, quite the opposite.'

Ziggy tilted his head and smiled. *Mind reader, too.*

'You did an exemplary job with the Jon Winter case in 2002, – we have every confidence in you to handle this the same way.' Gladstone was referring to a case the previous year when young girls had been taken and killed before being deposited around Leeds city centre.

Ziggy flinched at the mention of the name he'd rather leave in the past. He still saw the faces of the girls every time he drove through Hyde Park in Leeds. 'Except that this time, we already know who the killer is.' Ziggy felt like he was stating the obvious.

'But there is still a lot we don't know, and that's what we're interested in. We need to nail this guy.'

Ziggy shrugged his shoulders. 'Fair enough, as long as no one interferes. I have my own way of working.'

'We know. Only difference is, you will report to me. Directly to me.'

'I have a team, I'm SIO. I have a boss.'

'You do – well, you did. I'll be clearing it with Superintendent . You'll work for the National Crime Squad for now, and this is the only case you will work on.'

Ziggy couldn't believe what he was hearing. 'What about Sadie? Nick, the rest of the team?'

'They'll be working on other cases, though DS Sadie Bates will still be your internal contact and keep things ticking over at HQ.'

Ziggy needed a few minutes to process the news. 'What do you want from me, exactly?'

'Keep doing what you're doing. Liaise with Dr Shaw. Look into Hawthorne's background. Speak to any witnesses, multiple times if needed. Find out how Hawthorne operated, where his kill sites were. Let Dr Shaw deal with the *whys* of the case. It's your job to uncover the rest – to get the evidence we need to send this bastard away for a very long time.'

It was a huge undertaking, but – Ziggy couldn't lie – the thought excited him. He'd be away from usual the red tape of police work, and that could give them the edge. Not wanting to appear too eager, he chewed his bottom lip as though he was thinking it over.

'And don't forget we have a survivor,' Mike added. 'When the young lady is able to talk, she will be a key witness.'

Ziggy didn't need any more time. 'OK, I'm in. What next?'

Mike smiled, as he turned to head towards his own car.

'That's for you to decide. Just a word of warning, a heads-up. This case will consume you. Your feet won't touch the ground. It will take up every waking hour and probably most of your sleeping ones, too.'

'No change there,' Ziggy huffed.

23

Monday, 13 October 2003

Despite having numerous meeting rooms at West Yorkshire Police HQ available to him, Ziggy had decided to keep away from his team for now. Not his team specifically, but more the general populace at the station. There would be endless questions, and perhaps a hint of jealousy from those not on his team, and he was in no mood to have to deal with naysayers and nosy parkers. He wanted to get his own head around what working for NCS meant before dealing with anyone else's input.

Instead, he had agreed to meet Evelyn at her offices on Park Row. He parked in the railway-station car park and headed across City Square. The street unashamedly displayed the wealth of it tenants and owners. Glass-fronted banks loomed on either side, their brass plaques proudly displaying the occupants' names. Offices above high-end restaurants buzzed with the lunchtime crowd of solicitors, stockbrokers and hedge-fund managers. Checking he had the right building, Ziggy read down the list of office suites and pushed the buzzer when he saw Evelyn's name. The door clicked open, and he went inside.

The interior was oppressively warm in contrast to the cold autumn day outside. He removed his coat and unfastened his jacket. Evelyn came downstairs personally to meet him just as he was looking for somewhere to hang his coat.

'Bring that upstairs with you,' she said briskly, before turning and retracing her steps. He threw it over his arm and followed. Two flights later, and Ziggy was puffing his breath.

'Jeez, they're steep,' he said as they finally reached the office.

'Victorian building dragged reluctantly into the twenty-first century,' Evelyn replied, pushing the door open and allowing Ziggy to step through. It was much bigger than Ziggy had expected. A receptionist sat behind a broad corner desk, wearing a headset and clearly busy with incoming calls.

'There are four practices here,' she said as they walked through to what must have been Evelyn's office. 'Myself and three colleagues work together, though I specialise in criminal psychology. We often say we cover every area of life, from birth to death. Coffee?'

He gave a half smile. 'Coffee would be great, thank you.'

Evelyn pushed a buzzer on her desk, ordering refreshments. The desk was stacked with files and papers, and it all looked very disorganised for someone that Ziggy had noted to be a neat freak. She must have caught him looking at the untidy piles.

'I haven't spent much time in the office lately.' She pulled a pile from her desk and dumped it on the floor. 'Actually, shall we sit over there?'

She walked over to the arrangement of four chairs and a coffee table that were on the other side of the room.

Ziggy joined her and sat on one of the high-backed lounge chairs.

'Why do I feel as though I'm about to talk about my childhood?' he jested.

'You can if you like.' replied Evelyn as she sat in a chair opposite, though Ziggy noticed she perched on the edge as if she was ready to jump up and run at any point. He fought the urge to tell her to relax as the moment was broken with a knock on the door.

'Ah, that will be the coffee.' Evelyn retrieved a tray ladened with a cafetière and cups from her assistant at the door and put it on the coffee table.

'A mug would have been fine,' Ziggy said as Evelyn pushed the plunger on the coffee pot and poured the black liquid into cups.

'I didn't tell the receptionist who you were, so she will have taken it that you're a client, hence the paraphernalia,' Evelyn said.

'Was there a reason you didn't tell her?'

'Ha! Who's the psychologist here?' She passed him his cup, which he took gratefully, realising he still hadn't eaten that day.

Once they had both had a drink, Ziggy placed his cup on the coffee table and looked at Evelyn. 'How are you holding up?'

She seemed taken aback by his question. 'I'm good, at least better now I've had a chance to catch up with every-thing over the weekend.'

'That's good. I imagine sitting face to face with a killer takes it out of you?'

'Don't you feel the same?' Evelyn said.

'I suppose,' Ziggy replied, 'but my job is to prove they did it. We have a team of specialists that enables that. I think that must be somewhat easier than uncovering the why?'

'Isn't the why part of your job as well?'

Why did he feel like he was being judged? 'In a way, but I'm looking for a motive, whereas you're looking for a psychological reason, right?'

'That's true. With Hawthorne, it's a little different. I thought if I brought you up to date with where my thoughts are, it would help you in your investigation into him.'

'Absolutely,' Ziggy agreed, though he sensed a defensiveness to Evelyn that hadn't been apparent in their previous meetings.

She stood and took one of the files from her messy desk. 'I won't go through the basics; I think we've been over that before. What I'd like to do is give you a glimpse into his way of thinking – as I interpret it, anyway. I thought that might help you uncover clues that perhaps he hinted at but that I missed for whatever reason.'

'Sounds fair enough. Did much of this come from your conversation with him after McLardy's death?'

'About that actually, it's a good place to start.' She walked over to her desk, picked up a file and sat back down. Ziggy glanced over at the pages and pages of handwritten notes she was flicking through. It looked unformatted, not in paragraphs or even sentences, just bullet points and scribbles.

'I don't think Hawthorne influenced the suicide,' she said.

Ziggy's brow creased and he couldn't keep the surprise from his voice. 'Really?'

'If James Hawthorne had wanted someone dead, it would have been at his own hand. I believe that without a shadow of doubt.'

Ziggy scratched his head and nodded slowly in agreement. 'But he did talk McLardy into a state of agitation?'

'Yes, I believe he did that deliberately.'

'But why?'

'Attention. Ego. Calculated manipulation. Thrill-seeking.'

Ziggy sat back and blew out a breath. 'Wow, that's a lot.'

'If we take each one in turn, it sums up Hawthorne in a nutshell. He wanted the media attention back on him – that feeds his ego. It was mass manipulation, if anything, of me, you, the entire force and, of course, the whole of the prison service. Where is he now?'

'What do you mean?'

'He talked a usually quiet man into taking his own life, albeit indirectly. Where is he now?'

The penny dropped. 'He's in isolation,' said Ziggy.

'Which is exactly what he wanted. And I'll tell you why.'

24

'It suits him,' Evelyn said matter-of-factly.

'He likes to be alone?' Ziggy replied.

'He does. Being alone, in isolation, is a game to him. He can and will create mind games. He'll plan how he can further manipulate his situation.'

'But he's in a high-security prison. He doesn't have a "situation",' Ziggy queried.

'He has both of us visiting him, asking him questions, trying to uncover who he is. That, to him, is a situation. It's one of his making. He's in control.'

'Is there like a medical name, or condition, or something that explains his behaviour?'

Evelyn paused. 'He shows strong traits consistent with antisocial personality disorder – what some might colloquially call psychopathy, though that's not a clinical term we use lightly. It's just one aspect of a much broader picture.'

'Antisocial is right, that's for sure. Can he be treated, cured even?'

'There's no simple fix. People with this diagnosis can learn to manage their behaviour, especially with the right support, but a full "cure" isn't how we frame it. He might learn to mimic empathy, even pass for rehabilitated. But change? Real, lasting change? That's rare.'

'Should he be in Broadmoor, then?'

'Perhaps, but the judge will decide that when he's sentenced.'

'What did he say to you on your last visit?'

Evelyn took a sip of her coffee. She shuffled through more of her notes and pulled a few sheets out. As she read through them, Ziggy watched her closely.

Her eyes seemed to skim over the words, like she was faking reading them. Her expression was impassive, and he couldn't tell what she was thinking. He was about to ask if she was OK when she spoke.

'He was organised with his thoughts. Despite the early hour and the circumstances, he was calm and in control. He knew exactly what he was doing. As I said before, he orchestrated the whole thing.'

Ziggy had glanced at the morning papers as he passed through City Square and all the headlines had covered the prison disturbance and subsequent death. He had no idea how they had gotten a hold of the information, but they had most of the facts right, which was close enough to the truth for the media to publish a story. He nodded, and Evelyn continued.

'He said something that grabbed that my attention, though. He talks about the events in the third person, another trick to remove himself from the blame, but today he mentioned the possibility of another personality.'

'Interesting,' Ziggy said. 'Is that legitimate, do you think?'

'That he has dissociative personality disorder? No. I've

thought about this, but I just don't think he fits the rest of the criteria required to class someone as having DID.'

'So, you're convinced it's antisocial personality disorder?'

'I don't think there is a one-type-fits-all for James Hawthorne. I believe he suggested another personality in preparation for his defence.'

'Master manipulator at play,' Ziggy added.

'Exactly. Now consider what we've uncovered so far, and my own research. His work as an architect relates to how the victims were found. He sees them as art, objects to be used to fulfil his own creations.' Evelyn stood, straightening her skirt. 'The rest of it, finding the victims at a heritage site, for example, it's an area of beauty – the castle, the gardens, the surroundings. They're all iconic, well-known local structures and buildings. His frustration at still being a mid-level architect at his time of life is fuelling his narcissistic need for notoriety.' She turned to Ziggy. 'My guess would be there are more discoveries to be made at other local sites similar to those in Helmsley; Temple Newsam, Roundhay Park, perhaps even Fountains Abbey, though that might be too close to Helmsley. As for the kill site, no idea. Over to you on that one.'

Ziggy sat back and let Evelyn's assessment wash over him. It certainly gave him plenty to think about. He began to break down his next actions and consider his next steps. 'When are you speaking with him again?'

Evelyn was sat back behind her desk. 'Tomorrow. I'll let you know what, if anything, I uncover.'

Ziggy had the sense that Evelyn was keen to bring the conversation to a close. 'The stuff you mentioned before, about the castle ruins. Do you still think that was aimed at you?'

Her head snapped up. 'No!' she exclaimed, glaring at

Ziggy. 'I think I was over emotional at the time and should never have mentioned it.'

'OK, OK – I'm not looking to upset you here, Evelyn—'

'If there's nothing else?' Evelyn stood and moved to her desk and began typing away at her laptop.

Ziggy turned and left without saying goodbye.

Dr Evelyn Shaw was hiding something. If she truly didn't know Hawthorne, then the question was what exactly was it?

25

Ziggy liked being part of the National Crime Squad, even it was only temporary. Several requests for information and permission to access to files that were usually slow to get responses were suddenly actioned at record speed and sent, without query, to his laptop over a secure IP address. He could get used to this.

As he climbed the steps to his attic home office, his mobile phone rang – Sadie.

'Now then,' Ziggy answered and sat down in his office chair.

'Boss – if I can still call you that,' she said, not without a hint of sarcasm.

Clearly word had spread that he had been seconded to the NCS. 'Ha-ha, always DS Bates,' he replied. 'What's the latest?'

'Great news. We've found something. Or rather, uniform have,' Sadie rattled off, barely stopping for breath.

Ziggy sat forward. 'Bloody brilliant, what have they found?'

'Here, I'll put you on speaker so they can tell you themselves.'

Ziggy heard the phone click and the noise of the room filtered into the enclosed attic room.

'Sir, we've worked through the night and finally managed to spot something on the CCTV footage from the off-licence.' There was a pause and a shuffling of something. 'A red transit van was seen circling the market square at Helmsley at various different times and dates. It stood out because of the colour, but we also suspected it was a decommissioned Royal Mail postal van.'

'The livery removed, though?' asked Ziggy.

'Yes,' said the voice.

Sadie took over. 'The number plates have been changed, but we've checked with local businesses and traders. No one recognises it, and the house-to-house hasn't turned up anything, but it's a positive lead.'

'Definitely sounds that way. What's the plan?'

'We're going to continue tracking it, see if ANPR can pick it up anywhere.'

'Good stuff. Check local auction houses too – it might have gone through them.'

'We're on it,' Sadie said.

Ziggy ended the call. It was something at least.

His next step was to catch up with Pathology. He rang the number and was put on hold for what seemed like an eternity. As he waited, his thoughts turned to what Evelyn had said about the iconic places. He'd instructed search teams to start looking for any other potential deposition sites at Helmsley Castle and other historic sites further afield—

'DI Thornes?' a soft female voice finally said on the other end of the line.

'Yes, hi, and please call me Ziggy,' he said.

'Ziggy, then, I'm Gabby. I'm the Home Office pathologist working on the case.'

'Great to meet you. I was hoping I could call in and go over the results of the post-mortems from the Helmsley Castle scene?'

'Certainly. We've finished with our first one and I have the report and notes here, so if you don't mind them being informal, I can share our findings, so you don't have to wait until I get around to writing them up.'

'That's fine. I'll make my way over.' The call ended, and Ziggy stood to leave his house. He like the sound of Gabby; her efficient tone filled him with confidence that they had found more leads for him to follow. After the loss of his best friend, Lolly who had also been a pathologist, he had stayed away from the morgue where Lolly had spent so much of her time, but he figured it was time he overcame his reluctance and faced his fear.

The morgue sat in the bowels of Leeds General Infirmary and as he made his way through the ancient building, familiar smells began to waft over him. The hint of bleach, mixed with a lemony scent. Memories of Lolly came flooding back and his step faltered slightly as the familiar surge of loss touched his heart. Closing his eyes momentarily, he took a deep breath and coached himself into taking the next step forward, forcing his emotions back down into the space where he kept them hidden.

As he approached the outer door, an underlying base note of decay joined the olfactory assault – whether from the morgue or the hallowed walls of the ancient hospital, he was never quite sure. Perhaps, it was a hint of both. The coded entry door to the office of the morgue was being opened as he approached. A tall, slim Asian woman beckoned him forward.

'Ziggy?'

'Yes, are you Gabby?'

'I am. Gabriella, if you want my full name, but Gabby to friends.'

They walked through the corridor into Gabby's office. It was tidy, with a few family pictures around and a low-level desk light that highlighted a stack of reports. The two office chairs were empty, so they each took one.

'I'm sure you're eager to find out what we've learnt from the poor victims, so I'll get straight into it, if that's all right with you?'

'That's fine by me. Carry on.' He appreciated her no-nonsense attitude, and she seemed to understand the urgency.

Gabby pulled a file onto her knee and turned towards him. 'I just want to preface this by saying that these are probably the most complex post-mortems I have ever had to conduct.' She passed Ziggy a report. 'This is from the first victim, Madeline Wadham. She wasn't the first victim to be killed, but she was the first body that we extracted after Claire Strickland.'

'We now have confirmed identities for all the bodies found at Helmsley?'

'Yes, so at least that's something. Madeline had ligature marks around her neck, and she'd also been tied to some form of rack and a piece of equipment that was capable of holding her spreadeagle, star-fished in other words.'

'How did you get to that conclusion?'

'Her limbs were dislocated from the torso,' Gabby said with a hint of sympathy in her voice.

'Was it done when she was alive?'

Gabby nodded. 'I'm afraid so. All injuries occurred pre-mortem. I believe, ultimately, she bled out. It would have been a very slow and painful death.'

'That's horrific.' Ziggy grimaced, thinking that now he had heard it all.

'She had fifty-three stab wounds across her body, and the number carving on her torso,' Gabby continued.

'My God.'

'And, of course, her eyes had been removed.' Gabby shook her head.

'That seems to be his signature. How long do you think she had been dead?'

'Hard to say. The injuries were caused over a period of around two weeks.'

'So, he held them somewhere,' Ziggy pondered, thinking back to what Evelyn had said that morning. *Objects to be used to fulfil his own creations.'*

'Exactly, which brings me to this.' Gabby pulled a picture from the folder on her lap. It showed the back of someone's head, with long hair hanging down. She pulled a second image, which showed a pile of dried leaves and twigs. 'When we brushed Madeline's hair, all kinds of debris fell out. The soles of her feet were also covered in woodland detritus.'

'She was kept outside?'

'Potentially. We've sent samples off for testing, and ento-mologist Professor Sue Grey has been drafted in to help identify any specific plants or foliage that may be able to pinpoint an area. She's working on them at her lab as we speak.'

That filled Ziggy with hope. He said so, and added, 'Have you managed to assess any of the other bodies yet?'

'Not as completely as Madeline, but my initial assessment suggests your killer followed a similar – if not the same routine – with all of them.'

Ziggy thanked Gabby profusely, and they parted with promises that she would contact him as soon as anything else came to light.

As he exited the building, his mobile phone started to vibrate in his pocket. The signal had been non-existent in the hospital and was barely connecting now. He hurried over the road back to his car, hoping to get at least a couple of bars of signal. His phone started ringing just as he closed his car door.

'Sadie,' he said, recognising the number.

'Couple of updates, Ziggy. The news has been delivered to the families.'

'Yes, I've just been with Gabby, the pathologist. She said they had identified them, so that's a bit of closure for the families. What else?'

'We have the registration for the decommissioned Royal Mail van. Following your suggestion, we discovered that the registered owner sold it to Motor Auctions a couple of years ago, but it was actually stolen from the auction yard last year.'

'Damn!' said Ziggy.

'It's not all bad news. One of the constables has continued to follow the van on CCTV as promised. He's spotted a potential storage space.'

Ziggy punched the air. 'That's fantastic. Is it local? How soon can we get a search term there?'

'We're liaising with them now, so we should get a team across in the next hour. As for location, it's in Selby, so not a million miles away.'

'Selby? Do we have any other connections to the Selby area?'

'Not that I'm aware of, but it would make sense. It's all in the North Yorkshire region.'

'Look, I'll head up there now. Could you tell SOCO and the search advisors I'll meet them there?' Ziggy ended the call and put his key in the ignition.

For a man who had had very little sleep, he felt dangerously alive.

26

Ziggy pulled up outside the storage facility in Selby just as the search team arrived. He waited by his car as the units parked up and unloaded. He looked around the forecourt, noting the size and condition of the various units. A bald-headed man in work overalls was walking in their direction.

'Hello there,' the man called out. 'I'm Jack. I own this facility. I've just had a call from your lot telling me you were on your way, but not much else.'

Ziggy shook the man's hand and introduced him to Irfan Mohammed, who had just turned up with his team of SOCOs, and Peter Beck, the search officer, who had joined the small crowd.

'I'll get to that in a second, but so we don't delay things further, can we get access to unit C please?' Ziggy said, using the information that Sadie had phoned through to him on the journey over.

'Yes, that's right. I have the spare padlock key here.' Jack handed it over to Peter's extended hand, who took it, turned and walked over to his team. Irfan followed him and stood in a closed circle with his own team a few feet away.

'Can someone please explain to me what the hell is going on?' Jack asked.

'Is there somewhere we can talk?' Ziggy said, aware that a small crowd of passersby had built up, and along with the required officers, there was already quite the scene.

'You can talk to me here. What are they doing?' Jack was getting more irate, and Ziggy wanted to placate him to allow the searches to go ahead.

'We have reason to believe these premises have been used for storing a vehicle that may have been involved in the act of a crime. We need to search to see if we can find any evidence.'

'What crime? Not bloody MOT certificates again? We vet our customers very thoroughly now. I can assure you—'

Ziggy cut in. 'No, nothing to do with that, sir. I can ask an officer to explain everything in more detail, but right now, I need to supervise the searches. Rest assured, you're not in any trouble.'

This seemed to take some of the bluster out of the business owner. 'Well, we have nothing to hide, so go ahead. But I do want an explanation.'

Ziggy assured the man he would get one in due course, then turned and joined the group of SOCOs and search officers. He listened in as Irfan outlined his plan. PolSA picked up where Irfan left off, and with a detailed strategy in place, the operation could begin.

The key to the locking bar at the foot of the steel roller-shutter door was unlocked, removed, photographed and bagged as evidence. Ziggy held his breath as the up-and-over door rumbled along its tracks.

He wasn't sure what he had been expecting to see, but Ziggy was bitterly disappointed to see an empty unit.

'Wasn't expecting that,' Peter said, who sounded as disappointed as Ziggy felt.

'No, me neither.'

Without pause, SOCOs slowly stepped forward, being careful where they stepped, photographing the seemingly empty interior as they went, but all Ziggy could see was a dusty floor. There were very few cabinets or shelving for evidence to be hidden in or behind. A few loose containers were strewn around, but no obvious doorways to secret rooms for bodies to be secreted. Ziggy scratched his head. He should have known nothing would be straightforward in this case.

An hour later and Irfan declared the scene 'clean' – the technical term for 'no dead bodies here'.

'Over to your team, Peter,' Ziggy said.

The PolSA team would now lift and remove any fixture and fittings, again photographing and documenting everything they found – or potentially didn't, in this case.

Leaving them to it, Ziggy walked over to the main entrance of the facility. The light was starting to fade, and he dreaded next week when the clocks would go back. Autumn was well and truly here. He was thankful that it wasn't raining at least, but he was starting to feel the cold despite his heavy winter coat. Tiredness would do that to you, he thought as he bought another coffee from the vending machine in the reception area. He'd felt the adrenaline leave him when unit C was revealed as empty and the tiredness was starting to become overwhelming.

He'd just taken a sip of what could have only been liquid cardboard when he heard a cry from the yard. The reception door flew open, and Peter Beck stood there smiling.

'Come and see this,' he said breathlessly.

Ziggy left his polystyrene cup on the counter and

hurried outside. One of the search team thrust a barrier suit towards him, which he hastily dragged on along with over-shoe booties. He walked over to the unit and could hardly believe what he saw.

Three search officers were supporting a huge cut-out area of the floor. As he walked inside, he leant over and a huge black pit opened up below him, with a flight of stairs leading down into the depths of the darkness.

'What the hell?' Ziggy asked no one in particular.

All searching had stopped, and any unnecessary staff were asked to step outside. SOCOs entered the unit, and Irfan took a torch to peer into the pit. Once he was certain the stairs were attached to something, he descended. Ziggy stood at the top, shining his own Maglite. As Ziggy leant over the hole in the floor, a familiar, unwelcome smell hit his nostrils. The scent of rotting flesh and human waste. He fought back his heaving stomach and waited for Irfan.

'Anything?' He shouted down after a few moments, hearing his own voice echo back.

'Yes,' came the reply, 'but I need more powerful light to see clearly. We definitely have a crime scene down here.'

'Yes,' Ziggy muttered under his breath, standing back to let the SOCOs do their job.

He stepped outside, stripped off his barrier suit and sanitised his hands. He spotted Peter talking to his team and headed over.

'That's quite the find, well done,' Ziggy said.

'We almost missed it. If it wasn't for the sure footing of Meghan here, we probably would have missed it.'

A shy girl stepped forward. 'It was the undulation in the floor. It just didn't feel right. When I brushed some of the dirt away, I spotted a break in the concrete.'

'She called me over and, using a crowbar, we managed

to wedge underneath the false slab and revealed the hatch that Irfan has just gone down.'

SOCOs filtered past Ziggy, carrying all kinds of forensic equipment. Though he was keen to get down there and see what Irfan had uncovered, he was mindful of disturbing evidence, so he stayed put.

He'd been updating Mike at the NCS and Sadie at HQ of the latest when Irfan resurfaced. Ziggy ended his calls and went over to the inner cordon that had been erected.

'It's a mess down there,' Irfan said, removing his face mask and inhaling clean air. 'It's going to take a while to process.'

'Can you give me an idea of what you've found?'

'It's a crudely constructed laboratory.' Irfan's grim face told Ziggy all he needed to know.

'I'm afraid to ask, but anything stand out to you, anything at all?'

Irfan looked at Ziggy, and he could see that the usual jovial crime scene manager was trying desperately to hold his emotions together. 'Eyes, Ziggy, there are eyes everywhere.'

27

———

The deep-rooted headache that had started a day ago behind Evelyn's eyes had grown progressively worse as the day wore on. She saw her last client at 4 p.m., and then finally left the office an hour after that. Her city-centre apartment was within walking distance and there were numerous bars and restaurants she could call into on her way home. She had a favourite Italian that she would ordinarily phone ahead and place an order to collect, but she had forgotten to do so. Frustrated with herself, her day and her life in general, she headed home to beans on stale toast with a glass of water.

Prison fodder. Her mind automatically went to James Hawthorne, as it did so often these days. Did she really believe his declarations had anything to do with her? And the location, Helmsley Castle? It was too close to the truth, surely? He had never really answered her questions about it, and she'd been caught up in hearing something – anything – new from him that she hadn't pushed it. In other words, he'd manipulated her.

Sighing at the repetitive nature of her own thoughts she

let herself into the apartment. While throwing her bag and coat over the kitchen counter, she kicked off her shoes, not caring where they landed, and headed straight into her bedroom. Stripping out of her clothes, she ran a hot shower and stepped in.

There was no way this case could relate to her. James Hawthorne had made lucky guesses, and they had all fallen for it – Ziggy included.

Rinsing shampoo out of her hair, she slipped into comfortable clothes and headed to the kitchen. She found half a bottle of white wine in the fridge and poured most of it into a tumbler. She climbed up to the mezzanine floor and sat at her computer. She had checked her emails sporadically throughout the day and had set a reminder to chase the NHS reports that had been promised last week she still hadn't received. She refreshed her emails and waited for her inbox to update.

Leaning back in her chair, she sipped her wine and looked at the wall in front of her. Once upon a time, it had held a myriad of photographs from before. Before she'd dedicated her life to helping the seemingly helpless.

A ping brought her out of her memories, and she rattled the mouse to waken her screen. Her inbox pinged. Sitting there was the long-awaited email.

Sorry for the delay, they took a while to track down, but attached are the records you requested.

Evelyn scrolled to the attachment and clicked, waiting for it to download. Eventually, a PDF document revealed itself in its own folder. The size of the file was huge. The pages and pages of notes had been crudely scanned in by hand, some missing the top or bottom where the page had been hastily removed to allow for the next one to be scanned. It was a jumble of doctors' notes, along with more official-looking reports. She strained her eyes, looking for the dates to see if she could assemble the information into some kind of order, but as she scrolled, she saw it would be impossible. There were too many pages. She closed her eyes, tiredness rearing its head again. They felt scratchy and ached along with her throbbing head. She took another sip of wine and debated what to do.

She was bone tired. The words on screen were blurring into one after only two sips of wine. Deciding to honour her body's needs, she left everything exactly where it was and headed to bed. She had barely touched the pillow when sleep descended.

The only living beings out in the driving snow were sheep who hadn't yet been called in by the shepherd. Evelyn pulled her coat tighter around her and huddled further into the corner of the ruined shepherd's hut. The wind was howling over her head, and a mixture of snow and ice battered her back. Her hood was up, but she was still chilled to the bone.

She wasn't sure how long she had been there. Maybe two hours. It had been light when she had left the cottage, and it was now pitch black, though the stars were trying to light the sky as she peeped out from her hiding position. She couldn't hear him shouting her name anymore, but she supposed it could be drowned out by the wind. Did she dare to stand up? Forcing herself, she pulled her hands from her coat sleeves where she had been hiding them to try to keep warm. Her fingers were still frozen as she felt along the drystone wall. It was wet with snow and moss, but she needed to lean against something as she struggled to a standing position. Though only ten years old, she felt her knees creaking as she stood up, blood trying to circulate its way once again into her limbs.

Pushing her hood backwards, she looked around her. Through the milky light created by the moon and scant stars, she could see maybe a hundred yards in front and to the side of her. She listened carefully but couldn't hear anything other than the wind cutting across the top of the weather-beaten landscape. She was still wearing her school shoes, which were now sodden, but she didn't care. She wanted to be back in the cottage, in front of the open fire, warming bread on a toasting fork whilst her mother plaited her hair. She would pull the family dog, a border collie named Timmy, onto her lap and watch the flames of the fire until she felt tired enough to fall asleep. Her mother would then help her to bed, read her another chapter of Famous Five, before kissing her gently on the forehead, pulling the warm blankets over her and blessing her as she drifted into a dreamless sleep.

The reality was very different. In reality, she would race home, hoping that her mother was passed out drunk as usual and that her father was either still in the pub or had taken himself off for an early night. Her brother would be hanging around the market square to see what mischief he could cause as the pubs emptied. If he couldn't find any outside the house, then he would bring his bad mood home, and it was that she feared above all else.

Taking a deep breath, she braced herself against the weather and ran as fast as she could towards the village and home. When he'd chased her out earlier, he had threatened to catch her when he returned. As she pelted around the corner that led to the front door, she heard the singsong call that made the blood freeze in her veins.

'Oh, Evie.'

28

Tuesday, 14th October 2003

Ziggy stood and looked around at the overwhelming evidence that surrounded him. Space was at a premium on the MIT floor, so Ziggy had commandeered a large conference room on the second floor and instructed that everything unnecessary that wasn't nailed down to be relocated. Even then, the sheer volume of evidence seemed to swamp the floor, conference table and walls. At least in here he could see everything clearly laid out. The discovery of the underground chamber the previous day had added an almost insurmountable amount of forensic evidence to the case against Hawthorne. It was currently still being processed and would continue to be for the next few days, but the key evidence, the eyeballs of the victims, had already been taken to the forensics lab in Wakefield, and Ziggy was scheduled to catch up with Irfan later that day to go over the rest of the discoveries.

For now, Ziggy had the preliminary post-mortem results

for the bodies removed from the ruins in Helmsley. The poor girl that had survived the brutal attack, Claire Strickland, was still medically sedated as they waited for the swelling in her brain to subside. Her bedside was being monitored twenty-four seven.

In the extended space, each of the victims had been allocated their own area on the wall, with evidence that linked them to the Shadow Killer displayed in chronological order as far as they understood the timeline.

Madeline Wadham
Janine Morley
Julia Newbury
Isobel Harmer
Belinda Riley

Each name had a family attached, a mum, dad, siblings.

Each name required a death-notification visit, thankfully something that had been handled by the local constabulary, though Ziggy wanted to meet with the families over time.

The MO was the same on all of them. They'd been tortured, held captive and mutilated before dying a slow, excruciatingly painful death. And each victim had a six-digit number carved into their torso. They didn't seem to make any sense, but if Ziggy knew anything about the Shadow Killer, there would be some explanation behind it.

He looked through the carefully numbered evidence bags that contained the video cassettes that had been found in the initial search of Hawthorne's home after his arrest. They had been viewed and categorised in order of how graphic they were in their levels of violence and abuse. Ranging from the lowest rating of D to the most violent and horrific rating of A. Ziggy shuddered when he thought of the poor victims that had had to endure such hideous treatment at the hands of such a sadist. Pulling up a chair and inserting the first video into the video player, he braced himself.

The scene was black at first, then a tiny chink of light that expanded from the room above and threw slim, eery shadows across the walls. He peered closer to the screen, but it was too dark to make anything out. Making a note to have someone look into cleaning up the shot, he hit the volume on the television, as there was no sound, but then he realised why. The victim, the young woman in the video was unconscious. The person that had entered the room wasn't speaking. They were dressed in some kind of a rubber gimp suit, complete with hood and zippered mouth. They were carrying something that Ziggy couldn't quite make out, so again he moved closer to the screen. In one hand were a pair of pliers, in the other was a bladed weapon – what appeared to be a cyclone knife. An evil knife capable of inflicting the most horrific wounds with its twisted blade.

His attention moved to the victim. She was held on what he could only describe as some kind of medieval rack, with arms and legs tied to the four corners. He could see the working mechanism, the axles near the head and foot. When the axles turned, the poles would pull the boards that were inserted periodically along the rack, widening the gaps in-between, taking the victim's limbs with it. He shuddered, appalled by the barbaric nature of what he saw, but dreading what the person in the gimp suit was about to do.

Taking the tip of the knife, the rubber-suited figure lifted the head of the victim. He had no idea if they spoke. The victim's eyes flicked open, and the look of terror mixed with horror was plain to see.

Ziggy didn't have to – couldn't – watch the rest; he had a general idea of the heinous crimes that would unfold. He leant over and switched off the television.

He needed fresh air. And coffee.

'All right, boss.' Sadie walked past the conference-room door just as he was exiting. 'You're a bit pale.'

Grateful to see a familiar, friendly face, he smiled. 'I need a brew. Are you heading that way?'

'Can do.' They fell into step together as they headed for the canteen. 'I was just coming to find you, actually.'

'Dare I ask why?'

'Let's get a coffee first.'

They joined the queue and waited in silence. Sadie directed Ziggy to a quiet table in the far corner.

Ziggy poured two sugars into his cup of coffee. He didn't usually take any, but felt he needed the rush. He stirred slowly as Sadie squeezed the tea bag in her own brew.

'I've been doing some more digging into our revered Doctor Shaw.'

'Anything interesting?' asked Ziggy.

'Born and raised in Helmsley, as we know. Both parents passed away when Evelyn was quite young – well, she was sixteen. She has an older brother, but I think the parents were quite elderly, and that maybe she was a later-life gift as there is an age gap between them.'

'What kind of age gap?'

'Five years. She's registered for state education in local schools from age five to eleven, when she attends the local comprehensive until she's sixteen.'

'The brother, Vernon, followed a similar path, but he left school at fifteen. By the time he was eighteen, he'd been in and out of remand centres and local boys' homes, as they were called then.'

'What for?'

'Just minor offences, really. House burglary, pickpocketing, stealing cars as he got older.'

'What about Evelyn?'

'Interestingly, I can't find anything about her until she turns eighteen.'

Ziggy frowned. 'So, there's what? Two years missing?'

'Hmm,' Sadie replied, taking a drink of her tea. 'Once she enrolled at college in Leeds, she follows her studies in psychology all the way to leaving university at twenty-four.'

'I wonder what happened in those missing two years?'

'Me too, Boss. I'm working on it, though.'

They both finished their drinks but remained seated. Ziggy shared with Sadie his difficulty with getting a reading into Evelyn's personality.

'You would think someone who studies human behaviour for a living would be better at hiding their emotions?' Sadie suggested.

'That's what I thought, too,' Ziggy said, 'but it would seem our Evelyn wears her emotions on her sleeve.'

29

———

Evelyn pored over Hawthorne's health records she'd abandoned the previous night, hoping for an insight into a medical condition that would hint or directly point towards his evil behaviour. She had started with the early-childhood vaccines and worked her way through past his TB jab at school and a rudimentary health check with an earlier employer.

There was nothing that would point to the monster he would become. No history of mental illness. No childhood brain injuries. No signs of abuse in the home. Just a very 'normal' history for a man who turned out to be anything but.

She had hoped to find some record of him having been sectioned, or some violent outbreaks that required therapy or treatment, but there was nothing.

'A psychopath doesn't simply start killing in their mid-forties,' she mused to herself. Where was the gradual build up? The slow start? He had mentioned voyeurism in an earlier chat. He had talked about watching through windows. Were there no arrests made that needed psychiatric help? Had he really been operating in secret for all these years?

She took a sip of her lukewarm warm coffee, screwed up her face, and threw the remainder in the sink. Closing her laptop and stuffing it in her bag, she grabbed her coat and headed for the door.

She had a meeting that she just couldn't miss.

As she faced Hawthorne in the same interview room as before, she noticed that, in contrast to all her previous visits, his appearance was a little dishevelled. In anyone else, the misaligned buttonholes and untucked shirt would look casual, normal even, but this was James Hawthorne. A man who, even at 4 a.m. the other morning, had presented himself impeccably.

She started as she always did. 'How are you, James?'

James sat back in his chair, and looked at Evelyn. He looked pensive, hesitant, not at all his usual forthcoming self. His eyes looked puffed up, baggy, dark.

When he didn't answer, she asked if he was tired. 'Didn't you sleep well?' She knew better than to criticise his appearance.

Still, he didn't speak.

She carried on with her strategy, silently wondering if this was once again one of his attempts to manipulate her, tailor the conversation to his advantage. She also had an ethical stance to take, that of his wellbeing. The prison officer hadn't mentioned anything she should be aware of, and the warden was instructed to advise her ahead of time if there were any incidents she needed to know about before she spoke with him.

As the silence remained, the intensity in the room increased. It was like sitting in a pressure cooker with the lid about to blow any second. Regardless, Evelyn pushed on with her questions.

'James, picking up from where we left off last time, in what way did the lifestyle of the sadist become an inconvenience?'

'It entirely depends on which lifestyle you're referring to.'

An imperceptible sigh of relief left Evelyn's lips, grateful that he had chosen to speak.

'If it's the day to day you're referring to, the minutiae of living, of working, of participating in the rat-race, then all of that became a necessity, a means to an end.'

'In what way?'

'It interrupted the... real work.'

The pause hadn't gone unnoticed by Evelyn. 'That being?'

'To satisfy,' Hawthorne replied as if it were the most natural urge in the world. He shifted in his seat and tucked his chin into his chest. Evelyn recognised this change. The monster had appeared.

When he next spoke, the pitch had changed, becoming deeper with words spoken with careful consideration.

'It's simple really,' Hawthorne said. 'Once the urges could no longer be fought – and God knows, he tried – there was an acceptance of the behaviour. The only outcome was to satisfy.'

'To satisfy what exactly?'

'That's an interesting question, and one he pondered on in his quieter times.'

'Did he reach a conclusion?'

A wry smile crept across Hawthorne's face as he raised

his head and looked at her. For a moment, she thought maybe she had lost him. But when he spoke again, the monster was still very much there. His eyes flashed dark, and the supercilious smirk was daubed upon his face.

'It couldn't be stopped, but he always knew that,' he said, ignoring her question. 'After a few false starts, he created a plan. One that he refined over time.'

'What was the plan for? To control?'

'To kill.'

The word was dropped so casually that it caused Evelyn to take a sharp, audible gasp of breath. She saw a flicker in Hawthorne's eye, and she stopped breathing.

'Death wasn't the ultimate goal. Well, not initially, but as I said, after a few mishaps, he realised that in order to avoid being discovered, to kill was the only option.'

Evelyn's mouth was dry. She swallowed hard to generate saliva. 'The mishaps, these were women?'

'Subjects. No longer individuals but objects, threats to his existence.'

Evelyn felt herself recoiling. She closed her eyes and tried to mentally reset, taking deep breaths. 'When you refer to "mishaps"' – she assumed by this he meant the ones that had 'got away' – 'were there many?'

'Seven, perhaps eight until he refined the process.' His chin had once again tucked into his chest, his eyes blank as he reminisced. 'Sex stopped being the driver. Yes, I know we've danced around the word, but that's what it was initially, until he could no longer control his overwhelming desire to control.'

There were potentially further victims out there that hadn't had the justice they deserved. Evelyn made a note to pass the information on to Ziggy.

'Once that desire had manifested itself, it brought about further issues.'

'Such as?'

'Where to hold them, where to test their resilience.'

Swallowing her disgust, she pushed him further. 'Resilience?'

'Why, yes,' he answered, as if it were obvious. 'Just holding them in place. Once he'd had carnal knowledge of them, he had to watch what they were made of.'

'Made of?'

He laughed. 'Oh, not in the way you're thinking. No, this was the... the intangible.' He laughed again. 'How much could a body stand.'

Evelyn felt utterly repulsed by the inconsequential way Hawthorne spoke of these women. They were or had been living, breathing, functioning adults. Someone's daughter, mother, sister. But she couldn't let her emotions show or get involved. Wouldn't make that mistake again. She had to stick to her strategy. She had to get to the truth.

'During all of this... testing, so to speak' – she couldn't bring herself to use his terminology – 'did he consider stopping?'

There was a pause. 'No.' The word was definitive and final.

She swallowed, glanced at her notes and ploughed on. 'You mentioned holding the victims? Where did you hold them?'

'Oh, you would love that, wouldn't you? It would be so simple, wouldn't it? Everything tied up in neat little boxes.'

'That's not what—'

'Don't say that's not what you meant.' His tone rose in volume, and he slammed the table with his thigh as he shot from his seat. 'It doesn't work that way, old maid. You should know that. This is my game. We play by my rules!'

He pulled violently at his handcuffs and lifted the entire table from the floor. Just as swiftly, he let out an almighty roar and thrust himself and the table towards Evelyn. Unable to extract herself in time, the table and full weight of James Hawthorne collapsed onto her. His mouth landed adjacent to her ear, and she could feel the wetness of his tongue as he whispered.

'You had your chance, Evie, but you can't escape your past.'

The commotion prompted the waiting guard into action in a matter of moments.

Riot-suited officers stormed into the room and untangled the mess in front of them, restraining Hawthorne as they did so.

As the door slammed behind the retreating prisoner and his guards, Evelyn crunched up on the floor in the foetal position, shaking uncontrollably. Hawthorne's words played on a loop in her head. 'I'm the king of the castle...'

30

———————

Ziggy scratched his shaved head for the umpteenth time. The number sequences that each victim had on their torso had been covertly passed around team and beyond. More than once, a reference was made to the Zodiac Killer, who had famously plagued law enforcement and the media in the US with coded letters about his victims. Except these codes were carved *into* the unfortunate victims. Ziggy was convinced that the key to the whole mystery was held in these numbers.

As he stared at the sheet of paper in front of him, the numbers started to blur into one. He immediately sat bolt upright.

'References,' he said to the empty room. He dragged the paper in front of him and folded it in half lengthwise. Tearing it down the middle, he then folded over each number until he had six sets of numbers. After slotting a couple of the pieces together, the realisation came to him that they could possibly be map coordinates.

He practically ran into the main office and headed

straight to the large map of the UK that stood proudly on the wall. But it had no grid.

'Damn!' he muttered, turning round to face the general office. 'Does anyone have an Ordnance Survey map?' He looked around but saw a sea of blank faces. 'Come on, team, an Ordnance Survey map that covers North Yorkshire?' He repeated in a much louder voice that couldn't be ignored.

'I have, sir,' replied a face that Ziggy didn't recognise.

'Go get it then,' he snapped, immediately regretting his tone. The young officer dashed out of the office and came back a few minutes later, clutching a rather tatty-looking object.

'I mean, it's a book, sir, but will it do?' he stammered as he offered it over to Ziggy.

Ziggy took it from him and headed back to the conference room. 'Come with me,' he instructed as he walked.

'What's going on?' Sadie asked, peering over Ziggy's shoulder as she joined them.

Ziggy pulled the pieces of paper towards him. 'Could these be map coordinates to the kill sites?' he blurted out, his enthusiasm spilling over as he rattled the paper and tapped his pen on the desk.

Sadie dragged a chair alongside. 'Hell, it's possible, I suppose. We've exhausted every other possibility.'

'What's your name, son?' Ziggy asked.

'Fyre, sir. PC Danny Fyre.'

'Do you know how to read one of these maps?'

'Yes, sir,' came the nervous reply.

'Great, and no need to call me *sir*. Danny, can you take a

look at these numbers and see if they match any locations on this map?'

'Or any map,' Sadie suggested.

'Sure,' Danny said as he sat down and flicked to the index. 'Do you want me to explain how it works?'

Sadie glanced at Ziggy. 'Don't you know how a map works, boss?'

'Never had a reason to need one. Growing up on the streets of Liverpool, there was hardly a need.'

'Were you never in the Scouts, then?'

Ziggy laughed. 'Ha, we couldn't afford the uniform, and if it didn't involve football, it wouldn't have held my interest.'

Their chatter was interrupted by Danny asking for a red pen.

'Have you found something?' Ziggy asked, leaning over in his chair to see what the young PC was pointing at.

'Potentially, but I'd like to cross-reference it before I'm certain.'

'Get the lad a red pen.' Ziggy grinned at Sadie. 'We might just have a breakthrough.'

If Ziggy had been hoping for a quick solution, he was sadly out of luck. Danny Fyre spent the rest of the day and into the early evening plotting the references onto a large Ordnance Survey map that Ziggy sent Angela out to buy. By 9 p.m., they had six locations that were as far apart as the ideas that the team had been throwing at them. By 10 p.m., Ziggy called it a day.

'Let's all get some rest. A break might bring fresh ideas. Go home, team, sleep on it, and I'll see you back here bright and early tomorrow.'

When Ziggy and Sadie were on their own, Ziggy confided his fears.

'Do you think we're making a colossal mistake here? Is Hawthorne manipulating us? Is this what he wanted?'

'Oh, God knows. I never thought of that, to be honest.'

Ziggy picked up on her downbeat tone. 'No, I'm just thinking out loud. I believe we're on to something, but I don't think we should focus all our energy on solving this. We need to keep on top of the other lines of enquiry, too.'

Sadie smiled. 'Of course you're right.' She yawned and stretched.

'Go home, Sadie. I'll see you here in the morning.'

For once, she didn't complain, and as he watched her tired walk to the exit, he figured he needed to head home too.

Everything will look different in the morning, he thought as he turned off the office lights.

Except it didn't. He'd had a restless night, unable to switch his mind off from the damn number sequences that kept running through his head. As he opened the door to the conference room that morning, he glanced around. Unfortunately, no magic elves had solved the mystery overnight.

More's the pity, he thought. As he turned the lights on and started to open the blinds, the door burst open and PC Danny Fyre came barging through.

'Where's the fire?' Ziggy said, then realised what he'd said. 'Bet you've not heard that before.'

'What? Oh, yeah right.' Danny was slipping off his coat. 'I think I've got something.'

'Really?' Ziggy said, hope underpinning his tone.

'Yeah, we've been looking at it wrong.' Danny pulled a copy of the numbers from his notebook.

'In what way?'

'Well, they are all OS numbers. We were right about that. I think so, anyway.' He shuffled the numbers around. 'I think these are…'

The door behind them opened, and Sadie walked in carrying a tray of coffees. 'Morning. Your local caffeine dealer is here,' she said as she handed out the mugs.

'Fyre here thinks he's got something,' Ziggy said, gratefully taking the cup from Sadie. He turned back to the constable. 'Go on.'

Fyre separated out three of the number sets. 'As I was saying, I think they are all OS references.' He pushed the remaining three numbers together. Reaching down into the satchel he had brought with him, he pulled out an OS map of Malton and Pickering. Standing, he walked to the other end of the table and cleared away the detritus from yesterday's brainstorming. Unfolding the map, Ziggy spotted three areas highlighted in pink.

'What are those?' he asked, adrenaline starting to kick in.

'They are locations in and around Helmsley,' said Danny proudly.

Ziggy and Sadie looked at each other. 'How sure are you?' Ziggy asked.

'As sure as I can be. I hope you don't mind, but I asked my dad to take a look. He's a geography teacher and uses this map when he's out walking so—'

Ziggy cut him off as he spotted one of the locations. 'That's close to where the bodies were found. It can't be a kill site. We would have spotted it. Those woods have been searched thoroughly.'

'But it's not exactly the castle, is it? It's slightly off to the side,' Sadie pointed out. 'What about the next one?'

Fyre moved his finger to the next location. 'From what I can make out, it's an old farmhouse. Dad seems to think it's partly ruins now. He's walked that way for years and can't remember when it was last lived in.'

'And the third one?'

'It's a cemetery.'

'Hmm.' Ziggy rubbed his head and screwed his face up. 'Let's organise searches, see if it turns anything up. Let's just plot them on the map anyway and see where it leads us.'

Danny reached for his red pen and started marking out the other three locations.

'Do you want me with the search teams?' Sadie asked.

'Let's leave it to PolSA for the time being. Peter can let us know if anything comes up. I'm going to see Evelyn. She was interviewing Hawthorne again. Can you chase the results about the debris in Madeline Wadham's hair? And speak to Gabby about the remaining post-mortems?'

'Sure thing,' Sadie said, taking her brew and heading out into the general office to hold the morning briefing.

Ziggy turned to Danny Fyre. 'That's great work, Danny. Well done.'

'You're welcome, sir— I mean, boss.'

Ziggy laughed. 'If you have any more breakthroughs, call me direct.' He gave him a business card.

'Will do, boss.'

31

Wednesday, 15th October 2003

Ziggy left the office feeling a tad more optimistic than he had when he'd arrived a couple of hours ago. He tried Evelyn's mobile, but it went straight to voicemail. Leaving a message, he was about to climb into his car when he heard his name being called across the car park. Mike Gladstone was trying to get his attention. Ziggy turned and walked over to meet him.

'How's it going?' Gladstone asked as they shook hands.

'I was just about to ask you the same.' Ziggy hadn't caught up with the NCS agent in a day or two. He hadn't seen any need. They were still waiting for various results to come back, and the latest breakthrough with the maps hadn't been thoroughly processed. Until he had definite answers and results, he was reluctant to share information. It was the way he worked, had always worked his cases.

Wasn't that one of the reasons why they'd seconded him, anyway?

Mike ignored Ziggy's comment. 'I just meant in general, Ziggy, I'm not on your back. I don't expect a daily briefing.'

'Yeah, sorry I was just expecting...'

'I know what you were expecting. Relax, unless I hear otherwise, I know you're working your arse off for results.'

'We've had a semi-breakthrough, if you can call it that.' Ziggy briefly explained the map coordinates. 'I've left it with the team to update me as soon as they hear anything. I'm just on my way to find Evelyn Shaw.'

'Great, well, let me know what she has to say,' Mike pivoted on his heel and headed towards the glass-fronted West Yorkshire Police building, throwing a casual wave as he crossed the car park.

Ziggy turned back to his car, opened the door, but before he could get in, he felt his phone vibrate in his pocket. Fishing it out, he saw Evelyn's name on the screen.

'Dr Shaw, I've been trying to get a hold of you,' he said.

'I know. I've just seen the missed calls and the voicemail. Is it urgent?'

'I wanted to catch up, see how your interviews with Hawthorne are going? Has he revealed anything else?'

The sound of traffic in the background made Evelyn's voice a little hard to hear. 'I'm just heading into the office. Do you want to meet me there and I'll update you?'

Thirty minutes later, and Ziggy was sat facing Evelyn in the same lounge chair he'd sat in only a few days so. He'd declined the coffee in favour of a glass of water.

'It was challenging to say the least.' Evelyn said, casting her eyes down as she recalled the whisper in her ear and the weight of him on her. She shuddered, not yet willing to share what had happened in her last visit. She coughed to cover her pause. 'Manipulative as ever, revealing very little details about his victims. I approached him about motive, but he was as vague as ever.'

'Do you think he will reveal anything further about the potential rape cases he mentioned?'

'Potentially, maybe in time, but he wants to work at his own pace. It's a game, isn't it? For him, anyway. His final act of control.'

Ziggy felt his phone vibrating in his pocket. He pulled it out to check the screen: Sadie. 'Excuse me, Evelyn – I'm sorry, but I really need to take this.'

Evelyn lifted her hand in acknowledgement, waving him away. Ziggy stood and left the office.

'Sadie?'

'Boss, are you nearby? Could do with you taking a looking at something.' Sadie's tone suggested she'd uncovered something.

'I can talk. What is it?'

'It's a bit hard to explain over the phone. I've looked at each of the potential places from the coordinates on the victims' bodies and searched through historical records to see if there was any criminal activity related to it, and in all three instances there's at least something.'

'Right. But is it relevant to our case?'

'That's where I need you, boss.'

Ziggy debated for a minute or two. He knew Sadie wouldn't waste his time, and he wasn't convinced he was going to get anything else from Evelyn that would be as useful. Mind made up, he told Sadie he'd be back within the hour and ended the call.

'Everything all right?' Evelyn asked as Ziggy walked back into the room.

'Yeah, I'm going to have to cut this short, I'm afraid. Is there a chance you can send me the transcript of the meeting with Hawthorne? Or just your notes, if that's quicker?'

'Has something changed? New evidence?' Evelyn stood and approached Ziggy.

Ziggy stepped back. 'I really can't say – it might be nothing.' He turned and opened the door. 'If it's relevant, I'll let you know,' he said, heading to the exit.

He hurried down the steps, wondering not for the first time about Evelyn's change in mood. She'd hardly seemed engaged before he'd taken the call from Sadie, but then appeared animated, hyper even as he'd re-entered the room. With no chance to dwell on his passing thoughts, he unlocked his car and headed straight back to HQ.

As he entered the office, Sadie almost dragged him to the conference room.

'What the hell?' He had to practically shake himself free from his sergeant's surprisingly strong grip. 'I haven't seen you this excited since Nick bought us all pizzas.'

'Now that was a once-in-a-lifetime occurrence.' Sadie laughed. 'But come and look at this.'

Spurred along by her excitement, Ziggy dumped his jacket and followed her to the side of the conference table that had now been commandeered by a huge OS map, replacing PC Fyre's handbook. Several Post-it notes had been added close to the locations that Danny Fyre had high-lighted.

'First of all, this is the first location that I looked into, as I knew we'd searched here already. Going through old records from around that time, I discovered that there had once been a fire in the basement of that tower resulting in a girl's death. At the time, it was ruled an accident.'

'OK. Evelyn told me about that, but she never mentioned someone had died,' said Ziggy, scratching his chin.

'Secondly, I looked at the old farmhouse that Danny mentioned. It did used to be a working farm – well, smallholding – but it fell into ruin when the last family abandoned it.'

'Go on.'

'Thirdly' – Sadie moved around the table – 'these coordinates point towards a cemetery. Helmsley Church's cemetery, to be precise.'

'Great work, but what's the pattern?'

'The pattern, my dear Watson, is that they all link back to our dear friend Doctor Evelyn Shaw,' Sadie said triumphantly.

'All of them?'

She moved back to the first point. 'The young girl was called Janette Smith. She lived and grew up around Helmsley. She went to the same school as Evelyn Shaw.'

'Yes, Evelyn already told me that she was there with friends.' Ziggy knew Sadie wouldn't mind her theory being challenged.

'But Jan and Evelyn were *best* friends. They went everywhere together. Did everything together. *Everything.*'

'How do you know?'

'I spoke to Jan's sister. I told her we were looking at cold cases. I'd seen Evelyn's name on a school photograph that was in the original case archives, so dug a little deeper and Jan's sister volunteered the information.'

'That's great work, Sadie. Well done. What about the rest?'

'I looked up old property-ownership maps. Guess who owned the smallholding?'

'A Mr and Mrs Shaw, by any chance?'

'Bingo.'

'And the cemetery?'

'I was just about to go take a look, if you care to join me, Mr National Crime Squad.'

32

———

The weather had closed in by the time Ziggy and Sadie had driven the forty minutes to reach the cemetery in Helmsley. The air was damp, and a thick fog was developing, rolling in from the moors above them.

As they fastened their coats and headed down the long entranceway, they stopped at the gates and looked around them.

'Do you have the coordinates?' asked Ziggy.

'Yes, but it won't take us directly to the grave, will it?'

'If it's a grave we're looking for,' Ziggy said. 'We don't actually know what the coordinates mean.'

'This is true.'

Ziggy spotted a tree-lined building off to the side of the cemetery that looked like some kind of reception area. He made his way over. He rang the old-fashioned bell on the desk and waited for someone to answer. Just as he was about to walk away, an elderly woman approached from behind a closed door.

'Can I help you?' she asked, pulling her cardigan tighter. Her face was drawn, with the cold pinching her cheeks. Her hands looked frail, the skin tissue-paper thin. He noticed a slight tremor in one hand.

He introduced himself and Sadie. 'I'm not sure if this is the right place to ask, but we're looking for a possible grave or burial site, but we're not sure where in the cemetery it will be.'

The old lady squinted at their ID badges and called for someone in the back. 'Albert will be able to help you, if you have a name, that is. Or a surname at the very least?'

An equally frail-looking chap appeared around the corner. 'What is it, Alice?' he asked.

'These officers are looking for someone,' Alice replied before she turned and retraced her steps deeper into the building.

'Do you have a date?' Albert asked as he walked towards them with surprisingly light steps.

'Not a date, but we do have a name, potentially.'

'And what would that be?'

'Shaw.'

Albert inhaled and lifted his chin. 'Any first names?'

'No,' Sadie replied. 'Just the family name.'

'We have the name Evelyn, if that helps? She may be the daughter or granddaughter perhaps,' Ziggy offered, hoping it didn't seem as though they were stabbing in the dark.

'Now, let me see.' Albert walked through another door, mumbling to himself as he went. He turned back. 'Are you coming then?'

Ziggy and Sadie obediently followed him into a large room that was lined with thick ledgers.

'No idea of date, you say?' Albert said as he scanned the shelves.

'No, unfortunately. It's part of an ongoing investigation,

so we're not one hundred per cent on the full details,' Ziggy said.

'To do with that case at the castle ruins, I expect. Your lot have been everywhere.' Albert said as he pulled a ledger from the shelf. 'Not been archived by English Heritage yet, this lot, but it will be done in a year or two.' He opened the pages, and Ziggy saw rows and rows of names, along with the date that they had died and the cause of death. Ziggy watched as Albert ran an arthritic finger down the page, and glanced over at Sadie and shrugged his shoulders.

Without looking up, Albert said, 'If it's the Shaw that I'm thinking of, then it will be William and Harriet Shaw. Bill and Hattie as they were known in the village.'

'Did you know the Shaw family?' Ziggy asked, intrigued, though he supposed in a small village like Helmsley, everyone knew everyone.

'Aye, if it's who I think it is.'

'Can you tell us about them?'

Albert looked up. His eyes were milky with visible cataracts, but Ziggy had the sense that behind them was a whole world of knowledge. 'What do you want to know?'

Ziggy blew out his cheeks and let the air leak from his lips. 'Pretty much everything, but shall we start with their burial site?'

Albert scribbled a reference number on a piece of paper, handed it to Ziggy, then led them back into the grounds of the cemetery.

'Follow this path along, take the first right and you'll see the headstone on the fifth site along.'

The detectives thanked the old man and made their way through the graveyard. The plots were all immaculately kept, some with artificial flowers, others with small ornaments or pictures. Many were shared graves, sometimes with whole families buried in one plot. Sadie pointed out the site of a baby that had been stillborn back in the thirties but that was still lovingly maintained.

She shivered. 'These places give me the creeps. Look at that one there?' She pointed to a headstone that once would have been a beautiful angel memorial, but time had ruined its shape, and it now looked like a ghost hovering over a fenced-off grave site.

'Here,' Ziggy said, stopping abruptly. He looked down and, sure enough, the names William and Harriet Shaw were listed alongside the dates of their births and deaths.

'It's definitely them, then,' Sadie commented as she read further down the inscription.

"Loving parents to Evelyn and Vernon".'

'That's pretty definitive, isn't it?'

'Unless there's another Shaw family?'

'That would be too much of a coincidence, and we both know there's no such thing.'

Ziggy took photographs with the disposable camera he'd brought with him, making sure he took in the inscription in his shots. 'Let's go speak to Albert again. See if we can get any more information from him.'

They trudged back the way they came, but as they approached the reception building, they noticed that all the blinds had been pulled down and a *Closed* sign hung over the window.

'Strange... You would have thought he'd have mentioned they were closing,' Ziggy mused.

A tinny ringing sound came from his pocket, so he fished out his phone and pressed it to his ear.

'Ah, Professor Grey... Yes, I've been waiting for your call.'

33

Ziggy's visit to the office had played on Evelyn's mind from the moment he'd stepped out of the door. What had the phone call been about? Why did he have to leave suddenly? What had the caller said to him? She sighed and shook her head. What difference did it make? If it was anything relevant to the case, he'd tell her, wouldn't he?

What was she so scared of anyway? Hawthorne was safely behind bars. He'd taken a few lucky guesses. He was an intelligent man, perceptive. He'd made assumptions based on what he could see in front of him, that's all. Annoyed with herself, Evelyn briefly wondered where this level of paranoia had emerged from. This case was clearly getting to her more than she dared to admit.

She unlocked the door to her flat and felt something bump against the skirting board, stopping the door from opening fully. She sighed. The postman knew to leave any bulky post with her neighbour to stop this from happening. Struggling to push the door further to allow her inside, as well as balance her satchel and handbag, she dropped everything in frustration.

'For goodness' sake!' she exclaimed through gritted teeth, pushing her shoulder against the door. She finally opened it wide enough to squeeze through and removed the bulky envelope that was trapped behind the door.

It was a large brown package, and Evelyn was surprised it had even fit through the letterbox in the first place. Retrieving everything she'd dropped, she turned the envelope over in her hands and looked for the postmark but couldn't see one.

Her name and apartment number had been handwritten, but no address. It hadn't gone through the postal system. There was no stamp and no indication who had sent it.

A cold wave of uncertainty swept through her. She threw her coat and bags into a corner and headed to the kitchen. After pausing for second to allow her racing heart to slow down, she took a knife from the block and slid it underneath the flap. She carefully tipped the contents out onto the worktop.

Paper scattered everywhere. She picked up the sheets that had fallen onto the floor and glanced at them. The paper was old, yellowing. Faded black letters from a typewriter headed the sheet she held.

HOPEGOOD CHILDREN'S HOME

Evelyn's stomach took a dive. What the hell was this? Hands shaking, she scooped everything up and took it over to the coffee table, where she had more room to spread everything out.

There were reams and reams of notes, index cards and old, faded photographs. It took a while for her brain to process what she was looking at. She knew Hopegood Children's Home. When she was training to become a psychologist, she had undertaken voluntary work there to explore the possibility of working with children. After eight weeks of speaking with some of the most disturbed young people she had ever encountered, she had opted out. She had been young herself, only in her mid-twenties. She thought that perhaps she could help young people, relate to them on some level, but she had soon been disabused of that notion. That she could just swoop in and solve the problems of children who had seen more horror in their short lives than most people ever would was deluded.

The memories had stayed with her for a long time. Though she had chosen to work in the prison system, she was driven to advocate for early intervention. She had championed reform and reducing recidivism. Her efforts had felt small, and on her difficult days, she considered a change of career, but the good days, where she could see a change, spurred her on to do more.

To be jolted back into the challenge of the children's home was a physical shock. Her hand trembled more as she picked up a clinical report. The name of the patient wasn't clear, but the notes couldn't have been more chilling.

Behavioural Observations: Highly intelligent but withdrawn. Shows unsettling fixation on symmetry and control.

Incident Reports: Prone to violent outbursts, inc. orchestrating the death of a family cat, claiming it was an experiment when challenged.

Family Background: Temporarily removed from family following allegations of abuse. The father, a controlling figure, reported to have used 'unusual' and cruel punishments.

Evelyn sat back. It was the phrasing that caught her attention. She turned the paper over and looked for the signature. It was faded, but she recognised her own name. Swallowing, she reread the report.

The death of a family cat.

Symmetry and control.

Cruel punishments.

It all rang alarm bells. She grabbed more reports. They were dated the summer months that she had volunteered there. An effort had been made to scratch out the patient's name, but as she held it up to the light, she could just make out *HAWTHORNE*.

She felt the blood leach from her face.

'Oh God, no,' she said. She pushed papers aside to get to the photographs. There was one with the patients and staff stood in front of the home. Her eyes scanned the rows of grubby, faded faces. It was a bad photograph, blurred and on low-quality paper. She couldn't make out any face that she recognised, either staff or patients.

With her heart beating out of her chest, she gathered everything together and started going through each report, one at a time.

She clutched at her throat, desperately trying to prise away the hands that held her so firmly down on the damp peat earth.

'Let me go,' she choked out, trying to use her legs to kick him away. He towered over her, breathing Scotch and stale beer into her face. As the stars started to fade and her struggles lessened, he released his grip and slapped her hard across the tender skin on her face.

'That should teach you a lesson, you little bitch,' he grunted whilst still keeping his hands in place. 'Think you're better than us, don't you?'

'No, no, I don't. I just...'

'Just what? Think you can get away? Think that moving away from here will be any different?'

Finally, he removed his hands and sat back on his haunches. She was still pinned underneath him, but she dug her heels in deep and pushed herself backwards. This time he didn't stop her, so she flipped onto her belly and up onto all fours before crawling away. He gripped her left leg and dragged her back.

'Stay still, will ya?'

Tears poured down her face as her arms collapsed from under her and her face landed on the soft moss. 'Please, let me go. I'll go straight home, I promise,' she begged.

He stood up, gave Evelyn a kick in the ribs and told her to be on her way.

'Just remember, Evie, I'm always watching.'

34

———

The chill deepened as the afternoon crept into early evening, frost marching along the edges of the windscreen as Ziggy pulled up outside HQ. It had been a long day, one of revelations and dead ends, and yet he felt no closer to finding the kill site. Without it, the prosecution's case would crumble before it even started. It wasn't just vital – it was everything.

Professor Sue Grey's call had been, in her usual way, thorough and academic, peppered with fragments of interest, but ultimately frustrating. The plant debris recovered from one of the victims – found tangled in her hair and clinging to her skin – had been traced to North Yorkshire. But that was as close as she could pinpoint. The fragments were maddeningly generic, their DNA a whisper of British soil, a murmur of vegetation, but nothing more. Nothing, that is, except for the cotton grass.

Cotton grass. That single thread had limited the search, though not by much. Professor Grey had explained it in clinical detail: 'Common cotton grass,' she'd said, her voice laced with the certainty of expertise, 'is a keystone species in the restoration of moorland ecosystems. The Moors for the Future Partnership has propagated over one hundred and ninety thousand plants, cultivated from the Dark Peak special site of interest, to repair areas eroded by time and misuse. It stabilises the peat and encourages biodiversity – essentially, it acts as a kind of silent architect for the moors.'

Her words painted an image as vivid as it was haunting – rolling moors studded with ghostly tufts of cotton grass swaying in the relentless wind, a landscape both bleak and alive with secrets. Ziggy couldn't shake the dual thought: was the killer drawn to the moors for their solitude, their isolation? Or was it something more deliberate? A connection hidden amongst the heather and mist? From what they knew about the link to Evelyn Shaw, was it another tie-in – or a coincidence? He didn't finish that thought as he pulled up at home and headed inside. He took a beer from the fridge, made himself a Pot Noodle and headed upstairs to his home office. As he closed the door, he glanced around the room, which was basically a duplicate of the incident room back at the station. Except here he had the space to pace the floor, mutter to himself and scribble on the wall if need be. He took a swig from the bottle and grabbed a marker pen. On the flip-chart pad, he wrote what he now knew about the victims and added Evelyn Shaw's connections to the case wall.

How the hell did Hawthorne and Shaw know each other?

It was the one question that had been going around his head since the revelation at the cemetery. He felt certain that if they had met previously, surely, she would remember? She would have had to mention it as a conflict of interest. A character like that isn't easy to forget. He thought back to what Sadie had uncovered when she'd done a little digging. There had been two years missing. Is that when they had met? Or was it later? Where was she for those two years? What happened to the brother? He made a note to ask Sadie to follow up on it tomorrow as he shifted his thoughts back to what was in front of him. He clicked open his emails and refreshed to see if anything had landed since he'd left the office.

The full forensic botany report from Professor Grey was sat waiting for him. He printed it off and sat down, with his feet on the desk, to take a good look through it. As he flicked onto the second page, his eyes were drawn to an image of a yew tree. Dr Grey hadn't mentioned that on their call. He carried on reading and discovered that as well as pollen from cotton grass that littered the moors, seeds from yew trees were also found consistently across all the victims. It could, of course, be trace evidence. Picked up by someone or something else that had brushed past a tree.

What was significant about the yew tree? Something about a past case was niggling at his brain. He closed his eyes and chewed his bottom lip.

'Graveyards!' he exclaimed, sitting up. He ran downstairs to Ben's bedroom and took the Woodland Trust book he'd given him from his son's shelf. Finding *yew tree* in the index, his memory proved correct: yew trees often grow on their own and are commonly found in cemeteries.

Reaching for his phone, he brought up Sadie's number and dialled.

'Sorry to bother you,' he said as he headed downstairs and grabbed his jacket. 'I think I've found a potential kill site, or at least a definite point of interest that needs exploring.'

'Really? What? No, don't tell me over the phone. I'll meet you at HQ.'

Ziggy raced outside to his car and threw his phone onto the passenger seat and headed back to work, hoping that his instincts were right.

Once he was there, he ran up the stairs into the conference room. Sadie was already there.

'I've seen it,' she said. 'The yew-tree connection?'

'Yes, and the cotton grass. Can you remember seeing any trees at Helmsley?'

'There were trees, definitely, but I couldn't tell you what type.'

Ziggy grabbed the landline and dialled the number to the closest police station. He briefly explained to the officer in charge what he was looking for and replaced the handset.

'He's sending someone to take a look. Let's wait for him to confirm before we alert anyone else. While we wait, I've been thinking about the Evelyn Shaw connection, Sadie. Something just isn't adding up.'

'Me too. Could we talk to her, do you think?'

Ziggy chewed his bottom lip before replying. 'I'm not sure we'd get anywhere. If I'm being completely honest with you, I can't get a handle on her at all. I'm usually good at reading people, but she leaves me scratching my head.'

'In what way?'

'It's hard to pinpoint. She can be overly emotional, as we've discussed before, but at times, she's very cold. Hard-faced, doesn't give anything away. It's as though a wall goes up and that's it – no one is getting in.'

'Hmm, I think I know what you mean, though I've had minimal interactions with her. Are you mistaking coldness for professionalism, maybe?'

'Perhaps, in other circumstances, I'd put it down to personality, but there's no denying the Helmsley connection to Hawthorne and that concerns me.'

'One would be a coincidence, but three? It's hard to walk away from that.'

'Certainly, puts me in a catch-twenty-two position. Do we let her continue working with us, or confront her with what we know?'

Sadie was quiet for a while. 'I'm not sure, boss.'

'And the poor girl that died in the fire. Based on the new knowledge we have, there will need to be a case review, but let's focus on what's in front of us for the time being.'

Ziggy let silence fill the room whilst he thought over his options. Eventually, he spoke. 'I'm not going to say anything to her just yet. She's our in with Hawthorne. We need her. I'll carry on remote viewing the interviews she holds with him, see if anything comes up, and in the meantime, can you see what the other numbers relate to? Pull that young PC in – Fyre, is it? – he seems keen.' He turned back to Sadie. 'And let's find out what happened to the brother too.'

'Sure thing—' Sadie was interrupted by the phone ringing.

Ziggy answered, nodded his head, thanked the officer and hung up. 'A line of yew trees separates the graveyard from the nearby housing estate. Let's get PolSA and Forensics out there as soon as possible.'

35

Thursday, 16 October 2003

It had been late by the time Ziggy had arrived at home. He hadn't slept much, and after an early breakfast with Rachel and Ben, he checked his emails. He'd received an alarming incident report from the prison governor in relation to the last visit between Hawthorne and Evelyn. It had earned Hawthorne another stint in isolation. It surprised him that Evelyn hadn't called him afterwards or even mentioned it yesterday at their meeting. He hoped she was OK and guessed he would find out soon enough. This may explain her odd behaviour, he thought.

Whilst the searches took place over in Helmsley, he'd arrived at HMP Wakefield earlier than Evelyn to make sure he was in situ ahead of the session. Ziggy didn't want either Evelyn or Hawthorne to know he was watching and listening. He wasn't trying to catch her out, more hoping to connect the dots. Adjusting the headphones and tweaking the volume, the detective watched closely as Evelyn set up the room before Hawthorne was brought in. She didn't appear to be injured after her last run-in with Hawthorne as she leant over the over the table and moved the jug of water closer to her side. Evelyn took her seat and flicked through her notepad whilst she waited for the prisoner to be brought to her. Would the previous incident make her more cautious with her questioning? Ziggy wondered. He had hoped that Evelyn would pick up exactly where they had left off. Where did Hawthorne hold the women? Whilst the rest of the case was building nicely, if they could gain more accurate information about the kill site, it would advance the case rapidly.

The interview-room door opened, and he saw Evelyn tense. Hawthorne's demeanour was slow, measured. His face was blank, and his eyes were dead.

Evelyn dived straight in once the usual wellbeing checks had taken place.

'You mentioned holding the women?'

Hawthorne had other ideas. With his head on his chest and a dead-eyed blank stare, Hawthorne slipped into his role. 'He swore to himself that he'd never do it again. He felt he had the control he needed. He knew he could become dormant, so to speak.'

Evelyn said nothing, and Ziggy sighed with frustration, but was equally enthralled as to where the killer was going with this. Did Hawthorne have his own agenda? Ziggy wondered where Evelyn's thoughts were.

Hawthorne continued. 'It was all about a state of mind. But the dormant state also gave him time to reflect.'

'Dormant? Does that mean you, the killer, stopped?' Evelyn asked.

'For a while. To review, reflect.'

'Reflect in what way?'

'The quality of his work.'

In the viewing booth, Ziggy felt his flesh crawl. Hawthorne was completely devoid of emotion. It was all delivered in a monotone. If Evelyn felt the same, she didn't show it.

'What can you tell me about the modus operandi of this sadist?'

'It was simple. That was the beauty of his work. She could be studying at the library, for example. Perhaps taking coffee with a friend. Simplicity was the key to his success.'

'So, there was no pattern or routine? All his victims were random, with no connection to each other?'

'Perhaps that's something you should ask the police.'

Hawthorne lifted his head and stared directly at Evelyn. 'But you'd know all about that, wouldn't you?'

Ziggy watched as Evelyn shuffled in her seat. He hoped that she wouldn't wind up the interview. He was as interested in her side of the conversation as much as he was Hawthorne's.

'I work closely with the police, yes. But you know that already,' she replied.

'It must be exhausting working so closely with someone who doesn't really trust you.'

Evelyn's eyes narrowed.

Huh? thought Ziggy. 'Where is he going with this?' he muttered out loud.

'What do you mean by that?' Evelyn asked, crossing and uncrossing her legs.

Ziggy watched as Hawthorne smirked, as if amused by her naivety. 'DI Thornes, of course. Don't you find it frustrating? How he keeps you at arm's length? How he double-checks your every insight?' Hawthorne paused, clearly watching for her reaction. 'You have to wonder if he truly respects your expertise, or if he's just using you as a convenient tool.'

Evelyn tried to brush it off. 'I have no reason to believe DI Thornes doesn't trust me. We have a professional relationship based on mutual respect.'

Hawthorne raised an eyebrow, and Ziggy realised he was watching a master manipulator at play. 'Oh, really? Then why does he ask for a second opinion on your profiles so often? Or is it just a coincidence that he consults his own sources after every one of your reports?'

Ziggy saw a brief flicker of doubt cross Evelyn's face. Was she remembering the moments when Ziggy seemed to second-guess her conclusions, particularly in recent days, as her behaviour had become more erratic.

Hawthorne seemingly also sensed her brief moment of weakness and pressed harder. Ziggy wondered how far she would let him go.

'I mean, it makes sense, doesn't it? Given your background,' he continued with a hint of false sympathy. 'You've... let's say, been through things that might affect your objectivity. Perhaps Thornes is worried about your mental state. Perhaps he's even questioning your ability to stay impartial on this case.'

Ziggy froze. There was no way that Hawthorne could know he was there, much less that those were his exact thoughts.

'I'm not sure this is entirely relevant to our conversation, James.'

'Let's just pretend it is. Indulge me.'

'I think we're done here.' Evelyn waved for the guard, and Ziggy closed his eyes, willing her to continue.

'Come on, Evelyn,' Ziggy muttered behind the glass. 'Sit back down. He might reveal more than you think.'

'Now, now, Doc, let's start again, shall we? Go on, ask me your questions. I'll behave, I promise.'

Ziggy watched with bated breath as Evelyn hesitated at the door. She waved the guard away and returned to her seat. Ziggy let out a sigh of relief. She rearranged her notes, took a deep breath and continued.

'Talk to me about the trophies that the sadist took from the victims.'

Ziggy stared at Hawthorne, waiting for him to switch to his alternate ego. He was surprised when he continued in his normal voice.

'Trophies? What does that mean?'

'Items that you— the sadist took from the victims. What were they?'

'Oh, you mean like underwear, that kind of thing?'

'Perhaps.'

'Oh, come on now, Dr Shaw.' Hawthorne leant forward. 'Out with it. What's really on your mind? Ask me the real question that you want answered. Don't dance around it.'

Evelyn hesitated again. Ziggy could practically see the cogs clicking over. He silently begged her not to mention the eyes. He wanted to hold that back for as long as it took for the evidence to be processed. Ziggy was grateful when, instead, she changed the subject entirely.

'We've touched on your childhood briefly in past conversations. I'd like to go back there, if that's OK with you?'

Hawthorne sat back in his chair, a sulky look crossing his face momentarily. 'What do you want to know?'

'Tell me about your relationship with your father. I know you said you were quite close, but what about the times when you weren't so close? Perhaps when you were in trouble for something, however minor. What did punishment look like? Was he strict?'

Hawthorne brought his hand up to his face, held his chin and let a finger rest on his cheek. He looked deep in thought. 'Strict. I suppose it depends on your understanding of strict, doesn't it? What may seem strict to you – a belt over the backside for skipping school, for example – but to someone who is regularly physically beaten, it may be... tame.'

'Which were you?'

'Ha.' Hawthorne dropped his hands back to the table. 'I'm not willing to share that information.'

Evelyn closed her eyes. Ziggy thought she'd given up, but instead she changed the question again. 'How was school?'

Hawthorne placed his hands flat on the table and shot back instantly. 'Lonely.'

From the booth, it was hard to see where she was going with this line of questioning, but Ziggy had no choice but to trust her. He had hoped that she would try to entice the alternate into being, but that didn't seem to be her strategy. Then again, how did you summon a monster?'

'You had no friends?'

'I *chose* to have no friends – there's a difference.'

'Why was that?'

'It was easier.'

'What was easier?'

'Life. I knew ultimately that I wouldn't need them.'

'Don't we all need someone at some point? A friend, a partner?'

'A lover?' Hawthorne's voice had dropped, along with his chin. The monster was back.

Ziggy could see that the change wasn't lost on Evelyn.

'Did you have lovers?' she continued without skipping a beat.

'Did you?' came the chilling reply.

'Of course. We all take lovers at some point in our lives,' she said candidly.

Hawthorne suddenly leant forward. 'We're not so different, you and I, are we, Dr Shaw? You've always been a shadow too, haven't you? Hiding in plain sight, carrying secrets no one else can understand.'

Ziggy stopped breathing. Where was this going?

When she didn't respond, Hawthorne continued. 'Your father was a man of order, wasn't he? A disciplinarian. You ask about punishment, but your father taught you about control, didn't he? About keeping secrets, keeping things quiet?'

Ziggy watched as Evelyn gave up any sense of composure and banged on the window for the guard. As the door opened, Hawthorne continued.

'Did he keep your brother quiet too, Evie?' he shouted, but Evelyn was gone. Ziggy stayed in the booth, still able to hear Hawthorne as he was dragged along the corridor.

'The numbers aren't for them, Evie. They're for you. Have you figured it out yet? Or do I have to spell it out to you like when you were younger?'

Ziggy's posture sagged as he took in what had just happened. How the hell did Hawthorne know all that?

36

With the revelation from Hawthorne ringing in his ears, Ziggy headed into HQ.

Like when you were younger.

He had to look at the big picture. A theory had been developing in his mind, and he was keen to test it out. He was very aware that they still didn't have a kill site. After SOCOs had cleared out James Hawthorne's flat, they'd found nothing that pointed towards it being the place where other victims had either been taken or killed. As it stood, they had the weird lab underneath the storage unit and a video showing some kind of chamber that didn't match anything else. He'd reached out to every contact, intelligence source – covert or otherwise – to try to shore up his sketchy theory even though it wasn't yet fully formed. It was outlandish, and he knew that, but it was more than they had had in recent days. He needed to test it out, so he rang ahead and let Sadie know he was heading in.

The office was a hive of activity when he arrived. He greeted Nick, Sadie and Angela with a distracted hello before heading to the conference room. He was stopped just before he had a chance to take off his coat.

'Boss, how's it going?' asked an eager Sadie as she held the door open for him.

'Yeah, good. Just been watching Evelyn interview Hawthorne.'

'Oh wow, how was that?'

'Interesting, to say the least. Look, can we have a quick catch-up ahead of the team briefing later? I have a theory that I want to test out before I share it with the wider team. Fancy sticking around whilst I run it past Mike Gladstone? You can let me know how your inspectors' exam studying is going too.'

'Sure, I'll get the coffees.' He headed to the incident room and then his desk, collecting the various folders and evidence that he needed.

As he returned to the conference room, Mike appeared at the door.

'Ziggy, how's it going?'

'Good, thanks. At least I think I'm on the right path but wanted to sense check it with you.'

'Great, let's hear it.'

Sadie returned with the brews and took a seat alongside Mike.

Ziggy ran through everything they had so far, plus the new information he had uncovered.

He started with what he believed to be his strongest point. 'I believe we are closing in on the kill site, or multiple sites for the Shadow Killer. I also believe that we are looking at more than one killer.' He paused and could see Sadie was intrigued. 'Let me explain.'

Ziggy pulled a photograph from the file. The enlarged crime scene image showed the underground laboratory that had been discovered in the storage unit. 'It's a stretch, but not completely impossible to believe that this was created by one person. The cavity itself has been there for years, albeit unused. The whole storage facility is built on a site that used to be an MOT and car-servicing unit. The pit wasn't completely filled in for reasons unknown, but someone with the plans for the building could have identified it.'

Ziggy took a sip of coffee. With no objections so far, he carried on. 'James Hawthorne had the plans, or at least the architectural firm he worked for had them. They designed the storage unit and submitted the building application.' He scrabbled around for the next image. 'This shows the dismantled construction of the frame that held the victims found in the castle basement ruins.' The image showed several lengths of wood and steel, along with rope, bindings and metalwork. 'Again, though it's possible for one person to construct this, it's not beyond the realm of possibility that Hawthorne had help. To fasten the girls the way he did, it's a stretch of anyone's imagination to conceive how he could do it on his own. In a nutshell, I don't think Hawthorne was working alone.

'I also think there is a third site, where the victims were taken, tortured and killed. Again, possibly underground.'

Sadie sat back and stared at Ziggy. As she blinked rapidly, he could practically see the cogs turning as she thought it through. 'Jeez, that's quite a turn.' She sat forward, pushing her sleeves up her arms. 'Any suggestions as to who the accomplice could be?'

Ziggy slowly shook his head. 'That's where I'm struggling and need more intelligence.' He turned to Gladstone. 'I need more resources. We are covering physical search areas, and I want to extend it to potentially the moors and another search of castle grounds.'

'Just tell me what you need and it's yours.'

'CCTV, re-interviewing witnesses, and any sources you may have that we're not privy to at present.'

'Consider it done,' Mike said.

'What about Evelyn Shaw? Did you dig anything up on her?' Sadie asked.

Ziggy gave a slight smile and a twist of his lips. Before he could speak, Mike interjected.

'What's this about Dr Shaw?'

'I've been looking into Dr Shaw's background. Call it a copper's instinct, but I went to the prison and watched the last interview with Hawthorne. Based on that, along with a few other "incidents", I just had an uncomfortable feeling about her.'

'Me too,' Sadie chipped in.

'I had the inkling that the two knew each other, or that at least Hawthorne knew *her* in some way. I did a bit of digging, and I believe that Evelyn Shaw first met James Hawthorne at a children's home.'

'Really?' Sadie couldn't stop herself from reacting to the new information.

'Yes. Hawthorne was there for a short period, and at the same time as Evelyn was on placement there.'

'Did they meet?'

'It's hard to know. The physical records are missing, but from the information I could find, it's highly likely.'

'Still, that's what? Twenty years ago?' queried Sadie.

'That's what I thought initially, but years later – sixteen to be exact – Evelyn started full-time with the prison service just when the whole system was going through a massive reform. Private firms were given contracts to deal with the overcrowding issue, and guess which firm they used in Yorkshire?'

'The same one that James Hawthorne worked for?'

'Exactly. Now it's a stretch, I'll give you that, but again, it's possible. I need to do some final fact-checking, but there is definitely a connection.'

'Of course, this is all circumstantial at best,' Gladstone said.

'I agree. Let's now look at the forensics. Forensic botany found seeds from yew trees on the victims, but this is likely to be trace evidence, i.e. someone else picked it up and it brushed onto them that at some point. There are yew trees at the cemetery in Helmsley – Sadie and I were there the other day and discovered that Evelyn's parents are buried there...' He took another quick sip of his coffee. 'Secondly, Professor Grey's report identified cotton grass as well – a specific type that had been planted by the Moors for the Future Partnership. Evelyn's parents owned a smallholding in and around the same area. It was found on the torso and hair of the victims – again, trace evidence.'

Mike stood up. 'What are you saying here, Ziggy? That Shaw is his accomplice?'

Ziggy shrugged his shoulders. 'Right now, I'm not ruling anything out. Accomplice, partner? Who knows, which is why I need more people to throw at this.'

'This is a significant breakthrough. Yes, absolutely we'll make all resources available to you. Consider it done,' said Gladstone, placing his phone to his ear as he walked out of the room to make the necessary calls.

Sadie stood with her hands on her hips. 'That's pretty mind-blowing stuff, boss. Do you really think that's possible?'

'I'm not jumping to conclusions, Sadie. We need to exhaust everything before we make any firm conclusions.'

'What do you want me to do?'

'Can you pull together an all-disciplines meeting? Use the biggest room – the media room will do. Make sure and all the top brass are there. We'll use it as a chance to update the whole team and take the next steps.'

'Are you going to bring Evelyn in?'

'Not yet. Let's get some solid evidence first. I'm heading over to her office now for a catch-up. Let me know when the big meeting has been arranged.'

Sadie turned and walked away.

'Oh and, Sadie, do me a favour?'

'Sure,' she said.

'Keep an eye on Gladstone? He seemed a bit overexcited!'

'You can't make demands on me like this, Vernon,' Evelyn said as she hung up the phone.

She'd left the prison with every intention of finding the nearest wine bar and getting slowly, deliciously drunk – sod the time of day. Her ribs were aching from the table incident the other day, and her nerves were shot. She intended to quit the case. To walk away. No one could blame her. She'd only gone for the session today to see how she truly felt. Every instinct screamed within her not to return. She hated herself for being so stubborn in wanting to see a job through, but after today, she was well and truly done.

She threw her phone onto the passenger seat and put her foot down. Some imagined drama had caused Vernon to call her. Of course it was urgent, of course it was. Everything with Vernon was urgent. He had no awareness of what might be happening in Evelyn's world. She was just expected to drop everything and jump. It infuriated her that she should respond as she did. That she couldn't just switch that side of her life off completely. Detach herself emotionally and physically, but the fact was, she couldn't. She'd turned her back on him for years, and yet she was still under his spell.

She slammed the car door and stormed down the littered path. She threw the front door open.

'Vernon!'

Making her way into the basement, dodging the debris on the stairs, she rounded into the living room to find him sat in his gamer's chair, grinning.

She was apoplectic. 'What the hell, Vernon? You said—'

Her sentence was cut short as a hand reached over her shoulder and clamped itself over her mouth from behind. Shocked, she tried to fight her way free, but whoever was holding her was strong. Vernon stood and walked towards her, slowly.

She looked down at his hands to see what he was waving at her – a syringe, full of God knows what. She tried to scream, but the hand held her tighter.

'Not so superior now, are you, Evie?' Vernon said with a supercilious grin on his face. He stood so close to her that she could smell his foul breath. She used her eyes to plead with her brother, but it was futile. Vernon clearly had a mission. Evelyn kicked out with all her strength and clipped Vernon on his leg.

'You bitch,' he roared and plunged the needle into her neck. She struggled, and the hand loosened its grip. Taking her chance, she bit the hand and heard a yelp from behind as the hand released her.

'What have you... done?' Evelyn stammered as she stumbled forward. Vernon caught her before she hit the floor. She looked up at him, confused.

'What, what... are you doing?' Her words were slurred, and she felt drunk. 'Wass... happening tooo... me.'

'You'll be fine, just a little something to make you compliant.' Vernon laughed as he placed her slowly on the floor and squatted beside her, his burgeoning stomach poking out from under his T-shirt. 'You're going to feel a little drowsy for a while, that's all.'

Evelyn tried to talk, but her mouth stubbornly refused to comply. She tried turning her head, and although she had the sensation of moving it, her view didn't change. She tried lifting her legs and moving her arms. The same sensation. She was trapped in her own body. Her thoughts became confused and muddled as she closed her eyes and prayed that whatever was about to happen would be over soon.

37

———

Ziggy had tried calling Evelyn several times but had had no luck. He hoped that turning up unannounced at her office wouldn't spook her too much. As he climbed the steep stairs of the Victorian building, his mind ran through what he wanted to say. He'd make out it was just a catch-up on the case, where they were at and what other information they needed Evelyn to discuss with Hawthorne.

Nice and casual, thought Ziggy as he pushed open the reception door.

The receptionist greeted him with a warm smile. 'Can I help you?'

'Yes. I don't have an appointment, but I was hoping Dr Shaw was available?'

The receptionist looked quizzically at Ziggy. 'I'm sorry, but Dr Shaw is off sick. Can I take a message?'

Trying not to show his surprise too much, Ziggy shook his head and casually made his excuses to leave. 'Sick? Sorry to hear that. I'll try her at home.' He turned and left. Sick? Really? Perhaps the table incident, compounded by the session earlier today, had impacted her more than anyone had realised.

He headed back to his car and called Angela to get Evelyn's home address. It was a short distance to her apartment. Knocking on her door, he waited a few minutes and knocked again. Still no answer. It was perfectly possible that she was staying with a friend or taking some time away – Ziggy wouldn't blame her –but his gut told him otherwise. After several minutes with no response, he was about to knock on next door's apartment when his mobile rang noisily in his pocket. It was Sadie.

'Boss, you need to get back here ASAP,' she said as soon as he answered.

'Why? What's happened?'

'Just get back here, now!'

He shot through the back roads of Leeds as though his tail were on fire, abandoned his car in the car park and shot upstairs. Sadie was waiting for him.

'You are not going to believe this,' she said, leading him to the media room. As she pushed open the double door, Ziggy saw that the room was full and Mike Gladstone was standing behind the podium, pointing to the screen behind him.

'... and it's for this reason we believe that Dr Evelyn Shaw is an accomplice in the Shadow Killer's gruesome murders.'

'What the hell?' Ziggy was stunned. What the hell was Gladstone doing? That wasn't what he had said at all. He looked around the room. The volume increased as colleagues conferred with one another. He spotted a row of seats filled with top brass from the Met and NCS.

He had to make a choice. Either call out Gladstone on his bullshit and stop the shit-show that was taking place in front of him or defer to professional integrity and allow the meeting to conclude. It wasn't even a choice.

He coughed, bringing all eyes in his direction. 'Actually, that's not quite correct.'

Everyone turned and he felt a thousand eyes staring at him. Ziggy shut Gladstone down with one hard look. 'I want to clarify that Dr Shaw is *not* currently a suspect and therefore shouldn't be treated as such. At the most, she is a person of interest,' Ziggy said as he approached the front of the room, all the while staring at Gladstone.

Silence descended on the room, everyone poised to see who would make the next move. Gladstone walked down the steps and left the stage. Ziggy turned to the gathered professionals.

'DS Bates has the day's actions. If team leads could speak with Sadie separately,' he said. 'Thank you.'

As the various teams filtered out of the room, Ziggy took Gladstone's elbow and marched him to a corner of the room away from potential listeners.

'What. The. Fuck was all that about?' Ziggy snarled through gritted teeth.

'It was the update that the teams had been waiting for whilst you disappeared. I'm beginning to—'

'Disappeared? You knew damn well where I was going and why.'

'We had no idea what time you were due back, and I felt it was important to clarify where our thoughts are.'

Ziggy closed his eyes and took several deep breaths.

'Even if I could justify what you had just said, I wouldn't. That is not what I am pissed off about and you know it.'

Gladstone shifted from foot to foot.

'At no point have I ever confirmed that Shaw is Hawthorne's accomplice.'

'But you said— It's obvious, isn't it? All the evidence—'

'Nothing is obvious, nothing. And without concrete evidence, we don't jump to conclusions.' Ziggy turned and started to walk away, then turned back abruptly. 'Why was I seconded to the National Crime Squad?'

'What?' Gladstone, who had appeared relieved at Ziggy's apparent departure, stumbled over his response at the detective's unexpected return.

'Answer me: why was I seconded to the NCS?'

'Because of your solve rate, because you think outside the box, because you're the best detective in the North of England.'

'Why then do you feel a need to interfere? To take my theories and present them as fact?'

'I didn't, I just thought I—'

'Do you know what? I don't care what you think. You have just potentially undermined the progress of this entire investigation.'

'I don't think...'

'And that's the point, isn't it? You didn't think. I will now have to undo any damage that you may have caused by sharing intelligence that has no factual evidence to back it up.'

'There was fact. You just caught the tail end of it. I've been an NCS agent for twenty years, DI Thornes. I know what I am doing.'

'I sincerely doubt that,' Ziggy spat as he walked away.

38

'I'm sorry to bother you, Ms Hawthorne. I'm sure you're tired of speaking to police by now.'

'Not at all, DI Thornes. If it helps the victims in some way, then I don't mind.'

Ziggy had left the office and proceeded with the plans he had made for the day despite his simmering resentment against Gladstone. After Mike's performance, he was more committed than ever to proving Hawthorne had an accomplice. And finding Evelyn. He was sitting in the living room of Alison Hawthorne, James's sister and, to Ziggy's knowledge, his only living relative.

'If we could go back to the childhood that yourself and James shared. Is there anything that stands out to you that may help our investigation?'

'I'm not sure what you mean, Inspector. In what way?'

Ziggy had never been one for skirting around an issue, so he came straight out with it. 'There was a period of time when your brother was placed in a children's home. Can you tell me why that was?'

Ziggy noticed Alison had a habit of twisting her thumbs

around each other, but at the mention of the home, she stopped.

'It was a long time ago... Let me think.'

'Of course.' Ziggy took a sip of the weak tea that Alison had made for him when he had first arrived. It was now lukewarm, so he returned it to the coaster on the coffee table.

'I think you're talking about the time when Dad was due to travel to the Far East with his work.'

'Was that usual, that James would be placed into the care system while your father was away?'

'Oh no, not at all.' Alison stood and took a photograph frame from the mantlepiece. She passed it to Ziggy. It showed the family of four stood on the steps of a hotel in what looked like a foreign country. The children had their eyes screwed up against the sun, and he spotted palm trees in the background. He smiled and passed it back.

'We were on holiday in Spain there. Torremolinos, I seem to remember. All the waiters made such a fuss of us. Blonde and blue-eyed little cherubs that we were.'

Ziggy wasn't sure that was how he would interpret the picture, but he let her continue.

'James loved to travel. I was certain he would do more of it when he left school, but by then, he'd caught the design bug and was focused on university.'

Ziggy wasn't sure whether to interrupt, as she seemed to be going off-track, but after thirty-odd years in the job, he knew that people often let vital details slip into the conversation, so he stayed quiet.

'Once he went to university, we more or less lost touch.' Alison looked wistfully out of the window. After a few moments, Ziggy coughed, bringing her attention back to the room.

'Sorry, was lost in a world of my own there.' She looked down at his mug. 'Would you like a fresh cup of tea?'

'No, no, thank you. You were telling me about your childhood?'

'Oh yes. So, Dad was travelling overseas and this particular trip was going to be longer than any others. I can't remember the exact details, but I suppose that's not important.'

Ziggy smiled and shook his head.

'James had been particularly difficult that year. The usual teenage angst – bunking off school and that kind of thing. He was caught stealing from the chemist on the high street a couple of times.'

You don't get placed into care for stealing from the high street, Ziggy thought. 'Was there anything else, Alison? Any violent or disturbing behaviour?'

'Violent? Disturbing?'

Ziggy thought her reaction strange, considering what her brother was finally arrested for, but again, he remained silent.

'Oh, yes, there had been an incident with the family cat, Tiddles,' she said nervously.

Ziggy's eyebrows shot up. *Bingo*. 'What happened there?'

Alison looked down at her hands and started twisting her thumbs rapidly. 'Poor Tiddles. She wasn't that old. We thought at first she had run away. Three days I pounded the streets shouting for her. I made posters and Mum helped me put them up around the neighbourhood.'

She sniffed so loudly that Ziggy thought she was about to cry.

'Sorry, it still upsets me.'

'Just take your time. It's fine.'

'Anyway, we thought she'd run away, but one day, when

Mum was cleaning James's bedroom, she found her. She was in a box under his bed. Dead. Without her head.' Tears sprang forth, and Ziggy wished Sadie were here; he was useless in these situations.

He spoke softly. 'It must have been very distressing for you.'

'Oh, I was heartbroken,' Alison said, taking a tissue from the box on the table.

'And that's why social services became involved?' Ziggy asked after what he considered a suitable amount of time.

'That, and his reaction when he came back from school and Mum confronted him.'

'He didn't take too kindly to being caught?'

'That's an understatement. He went crazy. Punching walls, breaking things in the house. I'd never seen or heard him act that way before.'

'How did your mum cope with that? She must have been scared.'

'She was. We both were, and, of course, Dad was at work, so she was left to deal with it on her own.'

'What did she do?'

'There wasn't much she could do. She shouted at him, but he was much bigger than her, and she told me later that she was worried he would turn his violence on her. In the end, after he'd smashed the place up, she gave him an ultimatum.'

'What was that?'

'Either apologise for what he'd done or get out of the house.'

'He chose to leave?' Ziggy guessed. He had a feeling he knew how this story ended.

'He did. When Dad got back from his trip, the police had picked James up, but Mum refused to have him in the house, so he was placed into temporary care. Dad knew he would be going away again – to the Far East, as I mentioned – so it was a solution that suited everyone.'

'Alison, can you remember when this was?'

'Now, let me think. He was about fifteen at the time, so let me work that out... 1970? Or thereabouts, anyway.'

Which fitted exactly with what Ziggy had already uncovered. 'You've been most helpful, Alison. Thank you for your time. If anything else comes to mind, here's my number. Call me directly.'

They said their goodbyes and Ziggy sat in his car for a moment before pulling away. Something Alison Hawthorne had said didn't sit right with him, but for the life of him, he couldn't work out what it was.

39

Ziggy had been reluctant to escalate Evelyn's disappearance. They'd ruled out all the places that they knew Evelyn may be at and nothing had to come light. Given her close connection to the case and Hawthorne's seemingly inside knowledge of her past, Dr Evelyn Shaw was officially a high-risk missing person. An all-ports alert had been actioned, and search teams were tracing her last known movements through CCTV and ANPR cameras.

The pace at which Sadie worked never ceased to amaze Ziggy. He watched for a couple of minutes as she executed several actions in one breath. He felt loathe to interrupt her flow, but he needed her help.

'DS Bates, can I have a word?' he said, calling her over.

Sadie stopped what she was doing and made her way across the office. 'Boss?'

'You have an incredible work ethic, Sadie. I don't know any other officer – detective or otherwise – that can continually maintain the pace you do. You deserve that inspector badge.'

Sadie raised her eyebrows. He wasn't known for giving

out compliments, much to Ziggy's shame. 'I don't know what to say... Thank you, I think.'

'You're very welcome. I don't say it often enough, but, on behalf of the entire force, we appreciate you.'

She stopped walking and sighed. 'What do you want?'

'Now, Bates, would I be so transparent?'

'Yes. The infamous "Ziggy ask". What do you want?' She laughed, taking his not-so-subtle approach in good spirits, as he knew she would.

They had walked to the quadrant where they usually worked as they chatted, and Ziggy now held a chair for her to sit on. Nick and Angela were working the incident room. Once they were sat down, Ziggy delivered his ask. 'Evelyn Shaw.'

'Yes, we're waiting to hear but—'

'No, I wanted to ask you something. Has anyone managed to trace an address for the brother? What was he called? Vernon?'

'That's right,' she said, 'but you knew that. What's going on, Ziggy?'

'Take a look at this.' Ziggy turned to his computer and logged on to the internet. He tapped in a web address and a rudimentary weblog loaded slowly. Ziggy navigated to a page and sat back to let Sadie read the contents.

'"TruthUnSocial – a real-time platform for real people, telling it like it is." What's that supposed to mean?'

'Scroll down,' Ziggy instructed. 'Third paragraph.'

Sadie used the mouse to pinpoint where Ziggy wanted her to look and read the paragraph out loud.

'Eminent psychologist Dr Evelyn Shaw has a few things to say about our police force. 'Their incompetence to take a serial killer to trial without all the evidence they need is a fact that we –

the public, and the payer of their wages – are not supposed to be privy to.'

I can confirm that I have exclusive access to insider information about how slack the lead detective, who you may be familiar with from his previous cases, namely a Detective Inspector Andrew Thornes, is. He is yet to pinpoint not only a kill site but also in speaking with the one victim that survived. Incompetence of the highest order, wouldn't you agree?'

The blog rounded off by inviting readers to leave comments. Sadie quickly ran through some of the hundreds that were already there, her revulsion at the vitriol, directed not just at the police force in general but towards Ziggy in particular, clear on her face.

'Wow. That's harsh – and worrying. Who's feeding this to them? Where are they getting this from? Not Evelyn, surely?'

Ziggy unfurled a piece of paper and placed it in front of Sadie. It contained a name and an address. 'Fancy a trip out?'

'Too bloody right,' she replied, taking her coat from the back of her chair.

As they hit the inner ring road and headed toward Belle Isle, Sadie quizzed Ziggy about what he knew.

'Dare I ask how you traced that blog back to this address?'

'Probably best you don't, to be honest,' Ziggy replied. 'I thought it would be some random person with a grudge against the police.'

'And you're sure it's Evelyn's brother?'

'One hundred per cent,' Ziggy said as he turned down a side street and pulled over to the kerb.

'Holy crap. Do you think she's here?' Sadie looked out of the window at the back-to-back terraced house that they were sitting in front of. The windows were filthy, with net curtains that hung in tatters from a wonky curtain pole. The front door was a mishmash of multicoloured MDF panels and batons of wood holding them in place.

A couple of dirt bikes roared past noisily, narrowly missing the wing mirror of Ziggy's BMW. A cluster of youths passed the car on the opposite side, hurling abuse at the bikers whilst drinking from beer cans and kicking a ball between them. They looked like they had an average age of twelve.

Ziggy looked out of the passenger window. 'I doubt it, but I'm hoping the brother can throw some light on where she might be.'

'Do we need backup?' asked Sadie half-jokingly.

'Nah, it'll be fine. He's probably some geek that hides in a dark basement, tapping away at his keyboard. He's more than likely playing *Call of Duty* and munching on Wotsits.'

'Not stereotyping at all there, boss,' chided Sadie as she reached for the door handle.

'Me? Never.'

40

———

They picked their way around the dog faeces on the garden path and Ziggy knocked on the front door. It echoed back, and Ziggy turned to Sadie hesitantly.

'This is definitely the right address,' he said, though the house sounded empty.

'If he lives in the basement, as you say...'

She didn't get a chance to finish her sentence as the door slowly squeaked open.

'Mr Shaw?' Ziggy enquired.

'Yes?' came the tentative reply.

Both detectives produced their ID documents. If Shaw recognised Ziggy's name, then he showed absolutely no recognition, though he barely glanced at them.

'What's this about?'

'It's in relation to your sister, Evelyn, Mr Shaw.'

'What's happened? Is she OK?'

'If we could step inside, sir, rather than standing on the doorstep?' Ziggy said, looking behind him, where a small crowd had gathered.

Vernon Shaw pushed the door wide and stood back to

let the detectives in. That was no easy feat, between the narrow corridor and Vernon Shaw's substantial gut. The hallway widened slightly to reveal a staircase bereft of carpet. Mr Shaw not-too-gracefully pushed passed the detectives and headed towards what Ziggy assumed was a kitchen, as it seemed to be the source of the stale-food smell that assaulted Ziggy's nostrils. They waited to be invited to follow him, but it became obvious that no invitation was coming, so Ziggy pushed Sadie gently in the back for her to move forward.

As they entered the kitchen, Ziggy saw that every work surface was covered with dirty crockery and cooking equipment. A thick layer of grease covered everything else, and he had to use all his efforts to not gag at the sight of the congealed food.

'I apologise for the state of the place – my housemates are students,' Shaw offered by way of explanation, though he didn't seem to notice that the kettle he had in his hand was devoid of a lid as he filled it with water.

'Can I get you anything to drink?'

Both detectives declined, insisting that they had just had a coffee back at the station.

'Fair enough. What's this about Evie then?'

'Your sister, Evelyn. Have you seen her recently?' Ziggy asked as he and Sadie hovered awkwardly in the kitchen, moving to let Shaw past them as he continued to make himself a drink.

'Haven't seen her for at least a month.'

'Do you keep in regular contact with her?'

'About once a month. Doesn't bother me, but she insists. Brings me a bag of shopping occasionally.'

'Would you say you have a good relationship?'

'What's this about, Inspector?' Shaw turned to Ziggy.

'I'm sorry to have to tell you, but she has been classed as a missing person.'

Shaw stopped his tea-making process and stared at Ziggy. 'Missing? What do you mean?'

'No one has been able to contact her for some time, and we would like to speak to her.'

'But doesn't she work with you lot?'

'She does, which is why we want to speak to her. Do you have any idea where she might be?' Sadie asked.

'If she's not at home or with your lot, then no. We're not that close.'

'Does she have a partner, a boyfriend or girlfriend?' Ziggy asked as Sadie made notes.

Shaw finished making a drink and indicated that he wanted the couple to leave the kitchen. 'Just head down there, then turn left into the sitting room.'

They gratefully did as they were instructed, and Ziggy was thankful that it appeared to be in a much cleaner condition. When they were all seated, Shaw picked up on Ziggy's question.

'No boyfriend that I know of, but I suppose she could have. She's a good-looking woman, after all.'

Ziggy thought that an odd thing for a brother to say about his sister, but he banked it and let it slide for the time being. 'What about friends? Work colleagues?'

'Aren't you her work colleagues?'

Fair point, thought Ziggy. 'I mean, from the office she shares?'

'I don't know about any office.' Shaw shrugged his shoulders and took a noisy slurp of his drink.

Ziggy wasn't known for his patience, so gratefully sat back when Sadie jumped in.

'Mr Shaw, forgive me, but you don't seem overly

concerned that your sister is missing.' She leant forward as she spoke, her forearms resting on her thighs, notebook in hand.

Shaw sighed deeply. 'She used to do it all the time when we were kids.'

Ziggy raised his eyebrows. 'And where would she go?'

'Anywhere. Library, out on the moors, even hid in an old shepherd's hut once.'

'Why would she run away?'

For the first time since they'd arrived, Mr Shaw's face lit up and looked animated, vaguely interested in the conversation. 'Who knows? She could be a little bitch at times. Prissy little mare.'

White spittle had gathered in the corners of Vernon Shaw's mouth, and a salacious grin crept across his fleshy cheeks. Ziggy felt sick to his stomach. He'd met men like Shaw before. The earlier comment now made sense.

Putting his suspicions on hold for the second, Ziggy broached the topic of the blog, hoping that a swift change in direction would knock Shaw off balance.

'What can you tell us about TruthUnSocial?'

An uneasy silence filled the room, and Ziggy watched as Shaw's expression changed from one of smugness to a defensive stare. 'What do you want to know?'

'In a post on there, you mention that you have an inside source.'

Ziggy waited.

'I'm sorry, was there a question in there?'

Shaw's entire demeanour had changed. The laid-back nonchalance had been replaced with an angry grimace. His nostrils flared and his top lip had curled into an ugly snarl.

Sadie sat back and looked at Ziggy, raising her eyebrows, but Ziggy pushed on.

He spoke slowly and deliberately. 'Did Evelyn supply you with information for you to write that blog post?'

Nothing could be heard except the whistling from Shaw's nostrils as he continued to breathe deeply. 'What did you say your name was?'

'I'm DI Thornes, and this is my colleague DS Bates.'

'Thornes. As in Andrew "Ziggy" Thornes?' Shaw slapped his forehead. 'Of course. How stupid of me not to make the connection.'

Ziggy shifted uncomfortably as Shaw heaved his substantial frame out of the armchair he was sitting in. 'I'd like you to leave now,' he said as he shuffled past them both and opened the door to the sitting room. Sadie stood, but Ziggy waved her to sit back down. She did so, but not before throwing a glare at Ziggy.

Still seated, Ziggy turned to face the door. 'Mr Shaw, it's clear from your blog that whilst you boast of having inside information, the actual blog content contains nothing but conjecture and speculation. I can understand the public frustration at the enquiry not being as far along as they'd hope, but honestly? Who's to say we're not?'

Sadie looked at Ziggy, who wasn't particularly known for giving speeches. But she would also know that he didn't make statements without there being a reason behind it.

Shaw fortunately wasn't aware of this and had stopped his slow shuffle into the hallway. He turned and stared at Ziggy.

'What are you saying?' Shaw clearly couldn't help but be drawn in on a potential exclusive.

'Tell me where your sister is, Mr Shaw, and I'll give you something that you can share with your readers.' He heard Sadie's sharp intake of breath at the side of him. He continued reeling Shaw in. 'Something that isn't in the public domain. Something that you can really get your teeth into.'

'Such as?' Shaw lifted his chin as if challenging Ziggy.

'Shall we sit back down?' Ziggy motioned to the armchair that Shaw had previously occupied.

Twenty minutes later, Ziggy had the information he needed, and Shaw had been fed a pack of inconsequential, liberal untruths.

41

Friday, *17 October 2003*

Throw.

Had Alternate scared her? Hawthorne had no way of knowing, but he was disappointed that Evelyn hadn't shown any sense that he'd got to her.

Throw.

He was certain that Alternate would have behaved.

Throw.

After all, he hadn't really said anything.

Throw.

Had he?

His cell door rattled, and his PO summoned him. 'Visitor,' he said without fanfare.

Finally, Hawthorne thought. Hawthorne stood and followed him through the maze of doors. As they reached the usual interview room, Hawthorne allowed himself to be fastened to the eye-loop bolt on the table and waited.

He raised his eyebrows when he saw that instead of Dr Evelyn Shaw, it was Detective Inspector Thornes with Hawthorne's own brief. Interesting. He hadn't been prepared for this.

'James how are you?' asked the detective.

James sat back and looked between the detective and his solicitor before settling his gaze on Ziggy. 'You look tired, Inspector.'

'I am a little. Thank you for your concern.'

'Oh, I'm not concerned, Inspector. It was just an observation.'

'And you? How are you, James?'

'I'm well, thank you,' Hawthorne replied. He stared at Thornes, trying to work out why he was here and if it had anything to do with Evelyn's absence.

'You're probably wondering why I'm here,' Thornes said after a moment of silence.

'It's like you can read my mind, Inspector.' Hawthorne smiled and squinted with suspicion.

'As I'm sure you're aware from meetings with your solicitor, we're in the midst of preparing for your trial. As such, I have a couple of questions.'

Hawthorne looked at his solicitor. This wasn't how the process was done. What had changed? His solicitor nodded, giving Hawthorne permission to answer the questions. Not that he needed it, but Hawthorne had to admit, curiosity had got the better of him.

'Your solicitor has copies of the evidence that I'm about to put before you. Due to the urgent nature of our enquiries, I have the authority to present this to you directly.'

Hawthorne remained silent as he watched Ziggy pull several papers and a map from a folder in front of him, along with a host of photographs. A sheet of paper was pushed across the table.

'James, we believe that we have worked out the codes that you left on the victims.'

Carved, Inspector, carved.

'... and that they are OS coordinates for areas in the North Yorkshire moors.'

He still saw no reason to speak. What did Thornes want? A round of an applause?

'Can you confirm that is correct?'

'I thought you had it all figured out, Inspector. You tell me.'

'They are coordinates and we currently have search teams checking each of the locations. There is one area that I, we, are particularly interested in.'

'And that is?'

Ziggy opened up a map of the Yorkshire moors. It had been enlarged and an area circled in red. 'What can you tell us about this area here?'

James leant forward with his hands in his lap and peered at the map. 'What do you want to know?'

'Why this area? We can work out the other places, but this one in particular interests us.'

James traced his finger along the line that Ziggy was pointing at.

If Ziggy hadn't been party to Evelyn's earlier interviews with Hawthorne, he might have wondered what the hell was going on.

Hawthorne's chin dropped to his chest, and when he

next spoke, it was in a deep, gravelly tone that made his solicitor sit up and stare.

'What the hell?' he stuttered.

Ziggy placed a hand on the solicitor's arm to stop him from speaking any further.

'Wait,' he counselled quietly.

A couple of minutes passed before Hawthorne spoke. 'Have you been there, Inspector? I think not, or you wouldn't be asking.'

'Not as yet, but I will. What can you tell me about it?'

'Is this to do with the good doctor?'

'You tell me,' Ziggy ventured, hoping that the direct question wouldn't cause the monster to disappear.

It was one hell of an experience to watch the emergence of a monster from behind a screen, an entirely different one to meet it face to face. The atmosphere was now charged with a febrile electricity that Ziggy could sense silently crackling. He hardly dared to breathe, praying that the alternate would engage with him.

'They were useless at planning. That was always left to me,' Hawthorne said.

Ziggy tapped the map. 'Is this something to do with it?'

Hawthorne ignored the question. 'They thought they knew better. That was the problem.' He laughed. An empty, hollow sound. 'That and their greed.'

Ziggy stopped trying to control the conversation and allowed Hawthorne to carry on.

'It was always one more, just one more. I told them, enough.' He crossed his legs, leaning over to the other side. 'Enough, I said. I'm done.' He paused. 'Tell me, who worked out the code? Was it you?'

Ziggy smiled, deferring the answer.

'I bet it was. You are heralded as some kind of local Sherlock Holmes, aren't you? A poor man's Sherlock, anyway.'

Ziggy let the insult slide.

'You know the coordinates, but what about the rest of it, Inspector?'

Ziggy shrugged his shoulders noncommittally, though his patience was starting to wear thin.

'Ah, I don't believe you have,' Hawthorne said, with a hint of surprise in his voice. 'Well, well, well. Maybe you're not the great Sherlock after all.' He laughed, and it echoed around the room.

'Let me bring your attention back to the map, James. What will we find here?'

'What do you think you will find there, Inspector?'

The continuing use of the word *inspector* was starting to grate on Ziggy's nerves. He remained silent, in part to work out how to rephrase the question, but also in the hope that Hawthorne would give him something, anything, that would help.

'Do you have any further questions for my client, DI Thornes?' Hawthorne's brief asked after no one spoke for a few moments.

Ziggy chewed his lip and looked at Hawthorne, silently acknowledging that the whole conversation had been fairly useless. He rubbed the bridge of his nose and shook his head. Standing, he knocked on the interview-room window to summon the guard. 'No, I'm done here.'

'Giving up so easily, Inspector?' Hawthorne said as he was taken from the room.

Ziggy noted that the alternate had disappeared at the same time as Ziggy had given up hope of getting anything constructive out of the serial killer. He stood aside to let the solicitor follow his client.

Hawthorne shouted back over his shoulder. 'They tell me Evelyn didn't give up quite so easily, Inspector. Apparently, she put up quite the fight.'

Momentarily stunned, it took a second or two for Ziggy to process the information that had been hurled at him.

'Where is she, Hawthorne? Tell me!'

'Ask *them*!'

42

<hr>

'What the hell does that mean?' Ziggy said to an empty car as he headed back to HQ. He'd taken a chance that Hawthorne would answer him directly and it had backfired. But he hadn't expected the introduction of the possibility that there were more than *two* people involved in Hawthorne's plans. The mention of 'they' and 'them' had been a sideswipe, he had to be honest. He rang Gladstone on his way back to the office.

'Ziggy, look. I'm sorry—'

'Forget it,' Ziggy said, never one to dwell on things. 'We've got more important issues to worry about. Where are you?'

'I'm in the incident room.'

'Great, I'm headed in and I have updates. I've just spoken to Hawthorne.' Ziggy's phone beeped to alert him to another incoming call. Sadie's name flashed up. 'Can you let Sadie know I'm on my way? I'll be there in five minutes.'

The call ended and Ziggy thought about the incident with Mike Gladstone the previous day. In the grand scheme of things, he guessed it didn't really matter, as he'd managed to clarify with the team where they saw Dr Evelyn Shaw in the investigation, and now that she was missing, it changed the course of the investigation anyway. Ziggy brushed it off, parked in his usual place and headed upstairs.

Sadie was waiting for him. 'I have updates on the searches. No sign of Evelyn Shaw yet though.'

'OK. I have updates too. Let's get as many as we can into the conference room.'

Sadie rounded everyone up, and ten minutes later, the conference room was packed. As soon as Ziggy had everyone's attention, he began.

'I've just been to HMP Wakefield and where I spoke with James Hawthorne. I had hoped to maybe get some information on the whereabouts of Dr Evelyn Shaw. No such luck. Not directly, anyway. I believe we have an update from the searches?' He turned to Sadie.

'We do. No sign of Dr Shaw yet, though either. The search of her apartment turned up her passport, wallet and, from what we can see, she hasn't taken any clothes. There was nothing at her office to indicate she was planning on going anywhere. For example, her desk diary had appointments for the next couple of weeks.'

'The receptionist said she was off sick?' Ziggy queried.

'Yes,' Sadie said. 'She had phoned in sick that day and her appointments had been rescheduled.'

'OK, anything else?'

'Yes. The churchyard has been searched and there was no evidence of a kill site or otherwise. The old couple we met did say that there had been recent visitors to the Shaw grave, but they couldn't say who it was. We have descriptions, but they don't match anyone that we're aware of so far.'

'And the site on the moors?'

'That's been a bit slower, and the team are still there. National Trust are there too, checking that the areas we want to look at are not under conservation restrictions.'

'Right. Good work. From my enquiries, Hawthorne has hinted that we may be looking at potentially *two* other people that facilitated the murders. I know this comes as no surprise after the briefing from yesterday.' Ziggy looked at Gladstone, before turning back to the room. 'I still don't consider Dr Shaw a suspect. Hawthorne again hinted that "they" – whoever "they" might be – had Dr Shaw, and that she hadn't gone willingly.' Ziggy looked around at the assembled officers. 'I'm not saying we shouldn't act on the information, of course, we should, but I am also very aware that we are working with a narcissistic psychopath with manipulative tendencies.'

Knowing nods went around the room.

'What next then?' Nick asked.

'We keep going. Let's double down on all the brilliant work you've all done so far. Keep pushing, keep looking, keep asking those difficult questions. Support your colleagues. We need to throw everything we've got into finding Dr Shaw. I can't help but think that will be the key to all of this.'

The team dispersed, but Ziggy noticed Gladstone hung back. When the room was empty, he walked over to Ziggy with his hands in his pockets.

'The pace of the investigation seems to be gathering?' he asked.

'Absolutely.' Ziggy knew Gladstone would be relaying updates to the powers that be, and he wasn't about to give an inch. 'We are this close' – Ziggy pinched his thumb and finger together – 'to finding Dr Shaw and solving this whole thing. Trust me.'

'Oh, I do, DI Thornes. I do.'

Ziggy started to collect his notes together to return to his desk when Gladstone spoke again. 'I heard just before the meeting started that Claire Strickland, the survivor, is in a position to be interviewed.'

Ziggy signed in at the entrance to the guarded ICU where Claire Strickland was being cared for. With Sadie at his side, they followed the doctor into a family room.

'I'm sure it goes without saying, but Claire has been through a horrendous ordeal and is left with life-changing injuries. These are physical as well as mental, though I must say that her resilience so far has been admirable.'

'That's good to hear – the resilience, I mean. Is she talking?'

'Yes, she's sat up in bed and can speak, but quite slowly and she has some temporary short-term memory issues, so she may repeat herself, but she can communicate well.'

'Is there anything else we need to be aware of?'

'Just take it steady. She has terrible night terrors and is seeing a psychiatrist, but she insisted on talking to you.' The doctor stood and opened the door. 'I'll introduce you, if that's OK, and then I'll leave you to it.'

They took the short walk to the next hospital room. The first thing Ziggy noticed was how cold the room was, but then he saw that the window was wide open. He glanced at the bed and saw a frail figure laid under a sheet that was half on, half off, with one painfully thin leg poking out.

Claire's head was resting against the pillow, barely making a dent in the cover. She wore a neck brace and below that he saw a pretty pink nightgown. She was looking off into the middle distance as they cautiously approached the bedside.

'Claire,' said the doctor. 'This is Detective Inspector Thornes and Detective Sergeant Bates. They'd like to speak with you, if that's OK?'

Claire nodded, so the officers pulled up some plastic seats and sat at the end of the bed so that Claire could see them easily. The doctor left them to it.

'That was all a bit formal, wasn't it?' Sadie said, smiling gently at Claire. 'I'm Sadie, and this is Ziggy.'

Claire returned the smile. 'That's much easier to remember. Thank you.' She turned to Ziggy. 'I'm so tired, but I need this man caught. Where do you want me to start?'

43

'I suppose we start by asking how you are,' Ziggy said. 'If that's not a daft question?'

'No, not at all. I appreciate my situation is quite unique.'

Ziggy noticed that when Claire spoke, it was very deliberate, as if she was trying to remember the right words.

Sadie sat forward a little. 'I'm going to be taking notes whilst Ziggy asks questions. If at any point you feel distressed, tired, or you no longer want to continue, you just have to say. It's not like you may have seen on TV – we won't hassle you for answers. Just work at your own pace. Is that OK?'

Claire nodded. 'I want to tell you all I can whilst I can remember. Strange, I can't remember my own birthday, but I can recall that day entirely.'

Ziggy smiled his thanks at Sadie and Claire. 'Shall we start at the beginning, Claire. What can you tell us about that day?'

Claire took a deep breath and closed her eyes.

'It had been quite normal. I'd headed into university, as usual. I had two lectures that day, but I also wanted to take a couple of books out of the library.' She paused, taking a few deep breaths. 'I left at around six p.m. and walked towards the Headrow to catch my bus home. As I walked along Calverley Street, I noticed a trail of what I thought was discarded shopping items, like a few tins and a loaf of bread. I don't know, it just looked odd, so I walked into the alley, and that's when he struck.'

'How do you know it was a man?' Ziggy asked.

'I caught sight of him as I fell to the ground. I remember thinking "Who are you?" as I fell.'

'Where did he hit you?'

'I think he was going for the back of my head, but I had twisted when I heard a noise, so he struck my temple.'

Ziggy looked at Claire's face, and even now, you could still see the faint yellowing of the bruise at her temple.

'Then what happened?'

'I remember being picked up, like physically picked up from the ground, and being held in his arms. Then van doors opened and I was thrown in.'

'Did you see the van?'

'I don't recall the outside of the van, but I can describe the inside.'

'OK, let's come back to that.' Ziggy nodded at Sadie, who made a note. 'Can you remember how the doors opened? Did he open them himself?'

Claire was silent for a while. She opened her eyes and looked at Ziggy. 'I'm sorry, I don't know. I can't remember.'

Sadie interjected. 'Claire, you have absolutely nothing to apologise for – believe me.'

Claire thanked Sadie and turned back to Ziggy. 'I was in the van for quite a while. I think he thought I was unconscious, but I wasn't.'

'You're incredibly brave, Claire. I'm not sure I would have been quite so alert.'

'I knew I was fighting for my life...'

Full of admiration, Ziggy encouraged Claire to continue. When she spoke next, it was with a quiver in the back of her throat, and she had to stop frequently for sips of water. Ziggy was cautious that they were pushing her too far, but Claire insisted on continuing.

'I don't know exactly where I was, but it was dark, like pitch black – at least at first, anyway. I was trying to listen for sounds, but everything was dulled, like my senses were muffled by cotton wool. It was inside, I'm sure of that. Claire reached over to her bedside and took a sip of water. 'I was briefly in cold air – I could feel the breeze on my face. The ground was hard, like compacted soil. There was a chamber of some sort.'

'Chamber?' Ziggy asked. 'What kind of chamber?'

'Like, erm... dark, old-fashioned, like historical, dungeon like. I'm not making sense, am I?'

'You're doing brilliantly,' Ziggy reassured. 'Were you on your own?'

Claire was silent for a while, thinking. 'Others had been there. I don't remember seeing anyone else. I just got the sense that I wasn't the first.'

Ziggy tried not to let his eagerness show on his face. He didn't want Claire to be discouraged from sharing. He wanted to focus on her experience before facing the fact that others may have been killed in the same space. It was imperative he tried to find the location of the building they were being held in. His brain scrambled to frame his next question.

'What else can you remember about the location? Anything that may give us a hint as to where it was?'

Claire took another drink and looked thoughtful.

'I know this sounds a bit random, but I heard sheep.'

Ziggy looked at Sadie, who was already on her feet and dialling a number. 'On it,' she said, leaving the room.

Ziggy looked at Claire and went on to explain that what she'd said tied in with other information they had.

'You're doing really great, Claire. Thank you. Let's leave the location for now until we hear from Sadie. What can you tell me about the person that took you? You said it was a man?'

'Yes, definitely, though I only saw him twice. The first time was when he took me, and the second time was when he came to kill me.' Claire didn't falter or pause as she continued. 'I knew that's what he'd taken me for, to kill me. When I saw what I believed to be a cage, I knew for sure.' Silent tears started to slide down Claire's cheeks. He passed her a tissue from the bedside cabinet.

Claire's left hand subconsciously traced along the dressings on her arms and across her chest as she spoke. 'I don't know why I wasn't drugged. I didn't eat any of the food, maybe that's why.'

'The food, how did it get given to you?'

'It was brought in by someone, though I never saw their face. It wasn't the person that had taken me though.'

'How can you be so certain if you didn't see their face?'

'They were wearing what looked like a leather all-in-one suit, and from the outline, they were definitely female.'

44

____

As Ziggy joined the A170 through Hambleton towards Helmsley, his mind went back to the video he had watched earlier in the investigation. He had been certain that the figure in the gimp suit had been a man, but had that been unconscious bias? Had he assumed it was a man simply because of the graphic sexual nature of the content? It was a rare occurrence when he doubted himself, but of course, everyone was fallible. He'd passed the new information onto Digital Forensics, querying whether the figure could have been male or female. While he waited for clarification, he headed to the final search coordinates on the North Yorkshire Moors. He felt the shot of adrenaline surge through his veins as he approached the search teams and pulled up behind the mobile crime scene unit. Peter, the lead search officer, was talking with a woman with a clipboard. Ziggy walked over and greeted Peter, who introduced him to Holly Gudan from the National Trust.

'Holly was just saying that they regularly have to patrol close to where we are searching, due to dirt bikes and four-by-four vehicles running riot and causing damage to protected moorland,' said Peter.

Ziggy tucked his hands further into his pockets. 'Yeah, I've heard it was becoming a real issue. Does it affect where we are searching?'

'Thankfully not,' Peter said. 'Holly has just cleared it for the team to go and disturb some of the moorland and brush so we can get below the surface.'

'Yes, that's right,' said Holly, taking a sheet of paper from her clipboard and passing it to Peter. 'A team member will be nearby if you have any questions, but I'm heading home.'

Ziggy didn't blame her. Though the views were stunning, the air was bitterly cold. As Ziggy and Peter said their goodbyes, their breath hung in the air. Ziggy stamped his feet and smacked his hands together, regretting his decision to leave without gloves.

'Shall we get started?' Ziggy asked.

'Sure, I'll brief the team and set out the cordon.'

Peter walked away and several officers in full barrier suits gathered around Peter and the map that Holly had given them. There was little Ziggy could do now other than wait. He found a relatively sheltered spot and checked his phone. No missed calls.

Claire had said that she was certain she had been out in the open at some point. From what they had discovered on the OS map, along with the information about Evelyn's childhood, he was convinced that this would lead them somewhere.

It had to, surely? They were well overdue a break in the case, weren't they? As he watched the officers' cordon off the search area, he went over the first conversation that he'd watched with Hawthorne and Evelyn. Hawthorne had mentioned the moors then, hadn't he? What was it he had said? '*Do loud noises scare you?*' It had spooked Evelyn. Ziggy remembered that she had been really prickly and defensive.

Why would that bother her?

Loud noises.

Ziggy scratched his neck and quickly shoved his hand back in his pocket. His mind travelled further back to the very first time he'd met Hawthorne on his own. At the time, Ziggy hadn't thought their conversation to be useful, but now he wondered. What had he said?

'Something about hideous buildings...' Ziggy muttered out loud, squinting his eyes as he pictured the scene.

'*The answers are closer than you think, Inspector.*'

'Shit!' said Ziggy. 'We're looking in the wrong place.' He stood upright and pushed himself away from the stone wall he had been leaning against, and dialled Sadie.

'We've got it wrong,' he said without introduction.

'What do you mean?' she asked.

'I think we've missed somewhere. Do you remember that Evelyn and Hawthorne previously met at Hopegood Children's Home?

'Yes,'

'Where is it? Or where was it?'

'Offhand, I'm not sure, but I can find out. Do you think it's important? Of course, you do.'

'I think we've fallen for Hawthorne's manipulations. Find me that address and I'll head straight there.'

'But what about the moors?'

'They're still going ahead. I'm sure they'll find nothing, but we have to search.'

'I'll get the address to you,' she said, ending the call abruptly.

Ziggy hoped he was right. There was a lot riding on it – not least, Evelyn's life.

Ziggy had just left the motorway when his phone rang.

'Sadie?'

'The children's home building used to be a school, Springhead Park for Girls in Rothwell.'

'Rothwell?'

'Yep, it's at the back of Rothwell Park.'

'Is it still in use?'

'Yes, but it's a business premises now.'

'What kind of business?'

'Cook, Hibbet and Hill – sounds like a solicitor's. Hang on.'

Ziggy could hear the tapping of a keyboard.

'Holy shit, boss – it's a firm of architects.'

'Get a search warrant and a team down there – I don't care who. I'll meet you there.'

Ziggy did something he very rarely did and placed the blue beacon on the bonnet of his BMW.

As he pulled up behind Sadie's car in the architects' car park, he hoped his instincts were right.

'Have you got the warrant?' he asked.

'Not yet. It took longer than I thought. was in a meeting. Nick will bring it down. I thought you could catch me up with your thoughts?'

Ziggy quickly ran through where his head was at, and he had never been more grateful to see Nick's Fiesta pull off the main road into the car park, just as he had finished.

'I can't see it,' said Sadie. 'Not that I doubt you, boss,' she said quickly. 'But look at it. It's just a square building by a busy road. It doesn't look like there's an underground dungeon, or sheep, for that matter.'

Ziggy hated to admit it, but Sadie was right. He saw a

questioning look on Nick's face as he joined them and Sadie brought him up to speed.

'It's got to be worth a try, hasn't it?' Ziggy said.

'Suppose so – we've nothing to lose at this stage,' Nick replied.

The officers headed to the entrance of the business premises. He pushed the external buzzer and, after announcing themselves, the voice on the intercom let them in. Ziggy, Sadie and Nick stood in reception, gazing at their surroundings. Various blueprints were framed and on the walls alongside photographs of buildings taking shape, from breaking ground to the completed project. The middle door opened, and a gentleman appeared.

'Good morning. I'm Mick Hibbet, one of the partners. How can we help you?'

Ziggy took the search warrant from Nick and showed it to Mr Hibbet. 'We have reason to believe that the premises may be involved in a recent crime, and as such, we would like to search the area.'

Mick Hibbet screwed his face up and appeared to begin to laugh, but the look Ziggy gave him fizzled that out right away. 'You are welcome, of course, but I doubt you will find what you're looking for, whatever it might be.'

'Can you tell me if there's a cellar or a basement?' Ziggy asked.

'Yes, there is. It's this way, but I'll warn you now it's quite damp and very cold down there. We have a humidifier constantly running.' Hibbet turned and led them to a door that was barely disguised behind a water cooler and magazine rack. Once they had been moved, Hibbet unlocked the door and took them down a set of steep stone steps.

Straightaway, Ziggy could smell the damp, and he knew immediately this wasn't the right place. He carried on, embarrassed to have put everyone to so much trouble and to have taken their attention away from the primary investigation. As they reached the lower floor, Hibbet pulled on a piece of string and the solitary light bulb threw a warm glow into the empty space.

'Yeah, this isn't right,' Ziggy conceded. The small party turned and headed back up the stairs. 'Is there anywhere else? Any outbuildings, for example? I see you back onto Springhead Park – is there anywhere nearby that used to be a barn or maybe an abandoned building?'

Hibbet shook his head. 'Not that I'm aware of. I can ask my colleagues, but if there was, I feel we would know about it. Part of our business is to find those kinds of sites for clients and cost out the reclamation and rebuild costs.'

By now, they were all stood back in the entrance way. Hibbet disappeared into the office and Ziggy turned to Sadie and Nick.

'Sorry about this – seems I let Hawthorne get to me.'

'No, don't be daft. It was worth checking.'

As they waited, Ziggy took a closer look at the maps on the wall. He followed the photographs of a development that he was certain was near their location, but he couldn't quite place it in his mind. A huge open park that he knew Ben loved to play football in. In fact, he had a picture in his mind of a picnic he had taken there with Ben and Rachel in the summer. He scoured along the progress timeline until he came to the name.

'Temple Newsam, of course,' he muttered.

Sadie joined him.

'Before and after photographs, good idea,' she said. 'Imagine if we did that?'

Ziggy turned to her, completely ignoring her comment. 'Temple Newsam – is it far from here?'

'It's in Halton, or Colton... I can never remember which one. Near Crossgates anyway. About twenty minutes or so by car.'

'There's a farm there, isn't there?'

'A rare-breeds farm, yes... Oh, I see what you're getting at. Farm, sheep, old building?'

He moved his gaze to find the final photograph of the building process, to see what they had been working on but couldn't see a completed project. Hibbet came out of the office.

'I've checked, and we can't think of anywhere nearby—'

Ziggy interrupted him. 'What work did you do at Temple Newsam?'

'Oh that. Bit of a nightmare project, to be honest. We're still waiting to complete. We stood the building firm down at the back end of last year and we're yet to restart. That's the problem with listed buildings – nothing is ever straight-forward.'

'But the work? Where were you building?'

'It was the approach to the Little Temple. Certain areas are closed off to the public due to their age and fragility. We were working on the lower side, near the sheep enclosure. It's a part of a new heritage—'

Ziggy felt the familiar shot of adrenaline. 'What were you working on, exactly?'

'It's a new walkway and footpath with an information centre.'

'Why did the building stop?'

'There was a problem with groundworks. We were in the middle of prep when a cavity opened. We had to stop as the fault line was potentially an unused pit seam – though I seriously doubt it and we argued strongly against it. Anyway, it's all gone legal, and we're now wrapped in so much red tape, it will be years before we can restart.'

Ziggy looked at Sadie and Nick, thanked Mr Hibbet and left the office.

'Nick, can you head back to HQ and update the team? Sadie, can you divert Peter and the search teams to Temple Newsam? And I'll speak to Gladstone about getting someone at the top to speak to Leeds City Council.'

45

Ziggy hated being wrong. He didn't hesitate to admit when he was wrong, and he had been colossally wrong in his previous guess. What mattered now was getting it right, and he felt the pressure. He'd spoken with Gladstone, and as if by magic, all red tape had faded away and a crime scene search team and forensic unit were heading to Temple Newsam. When Ziggy got there, he was directed to the route that was usually for disabled cars that led to the lower lakes. He didn't really know his way around that well, so he was glad when he pulled up there that a few familiar faces were there but the whole scene looked like chaos.

Irfan Mohammed, lead crime scene investigator, was waiting for him.

'Mr Thornes, a lovely day for it,' the ever-cheerful man said as they shook hands. Ziggy saw that beneath the white coveralls; Irfan was suitably dressed in several woolly jumpers and long wellington socks.

'Have you started yet?'

'No, we're waiting for one of the Temple Newsam groundkeepers to direct us. It's a huge site.'

Ziggy headed off, with Irfan following. 'It's something or somewhere near a farm, or towards the Little Temple.'

'Perhaps you should tell the search team as well?' Irfan suggested.

'Who's managing the scene?" asked Ziggy.

'That's just it, there *is* no scene. Not yet anyway.'

Realising that he was ten steps ahead of everyone else, literally and figuratively, he slowed down and let Irfan catch up. 'Let's get some organisation here, shall we?' He looked around him and caught the attention of PC Danny Fyre, who was stood at the entrance to the park.

'Fyre,' Ziggy called. Several people stopped and looked at him. Ziggy shook his head and approached the young officer. 'You really need to change your name,' he said, only half joking. 'What's happened so far.'

PC Fyre shifted from foot to foot in his bulky high-vis coat. 'We've closed the footpath to the general public and created an outer cordon. He indicated with his hand and pointed to the blue-and-white tape that had been attached to the wall and a post further up. 'A couple of search officers have headed into the farm, but I'm not sure how far they've got.'

'What about the scene log?' Ziggy asked.

'Yes, it's here.' Fyre pulled a clipboard from underneath his coat and passed it over. Ziggy and Irfan signed in and returned it.

'Great job – keep it up.' Ziggy headed along the footpath. A farm worker approached him.

'I've just directed a group down past the sheep and goats. If you go under the bridge and turn left, carry on and follow the path round. There's a closed-off area. You'll see your colleagues waiting there.'

Ziggy thanked them and followed the instructions. He

walked along the cobbled path, looking around him as he went. Memories of being here with Ben came flooding back as he remembered feeding grain to the goats by the fence. A small enclosure held sheep and rams, all grazing on the rough ground. Sure, enough as he rounded the corner, a group of SOCO's were gathered together waiting for instructions.

Ziggy approached them and addressed the crowd. 'To be a hundred per cent honest with you, I'm not sure what we're looking for. Possibly a barn or some kind of storage or outbuilding.' Chatter rose as he spoke. 'I know, I know. It all sounds a bit odd and free flowing, but this case has been anything but straightforward. Spread out – there has to be something near here.'

The small crowd split up and headed off in different directions in pairs. Ziggy looked around him. 'What's that, there?' he said to no one in particular, pointing to what looked like a small, covered feeding shed. He walked towards it as he spoke. From where he stood, it didn't look anywhere near big enough to be hiding anything other than cattle feed. He waved to a couple of SOCOs and shouted them over. He hadn't yet donned a barrier suit, and as such, didn't get too close. 'Can you take a look over there, please?'

Nods all round. He turned round and mimed climbing into a barrier suit to PC Fyre, who was watching from the edge of the footpath, hoping that he understood. It seemed to work, as within minutes, the lad was breathless at his side with the requested PPE.

'DS Bates has just arrived too. I've told her to suit up and will direct her down here.'

Ziggy thanked Fyre and went to the rest of the SOCOs.

'Anything?' he asked. They were prodding and poking around the ramshackle structure.

'Nothing – are you sure this is right?'

Sadie joined them. 'It's further round,' she said, leading the way over the field. 'Claire said she could hear sheep, and that she thought she was on the moors, right?'

Ziggy was pacing alongside her. 'You know this area well then?'

'Course – grew up here, didn't I? There's a small track that leads up to the Little Temple. That's where the information centre was going to be built, but they had to clear some ground first.'

Ziggy was fit, but he was struggling to keep up with Sadie when she stopped abruptly. 'It's here.'

They had crossed a bridge and to the left-hand side was an abandoned building site. Orange tape waved in the slight wind. Building sand lay unused but covered with the prints of various birds and wild animals. Rocks and rubble lay on the ground, though it looked as though at some point, concrete had been poured into early foundations.

'This is where I had in my head, but I could be wrong?' said Sadie.

They walked further into the site. A pair of steel barriers stopped them from going any further.

'Now what's through here, do you suppose?' Ziggy asked, jiggling the padlock that held the gates closed. He stepped back, debating whether he could climb over them but decided against it. 'Can we get something to remove this padlock?' He fiddled with the hook and realised that it wasn't actually locked at all, just held together to make it look that way. 'No need.' He pulled it apart, loosened the chain and opened the gates. By now, the team of SOCOs and search officers had joined them.

Procedure would dictate that Ziggy should take a step back and allow them to take over, but he'd be damned if he would do that. He'd been to enough crime scenes to know the score, and as such, he walked through the gates and looked around him.

He walked tentatively forward and noticed that the ground beneath him changed texture under foot. What had been solid ground became loose. He stamped his foot. It sounded hollow underneath. Others had heard it also and started to do the same. Ziggy walked on ahead and kicked away some forest and field detritus to reveal a panel of MDF, which he kicked to one side. 'What is going on here?' he said to himself. As he picked it up, he could see it was some kind of hatch that led to some kind of narrow shaft that headed downwards. He could see a flight of steps had been fashioned into the side. He got down on his hands and knees and took a closer look. It looked like a long decorator's ladder had been bolted to the side. He tentatively pushed it with his gloved hand, and dirt fell away from the wall. There was no way he was going down there without a safety harness, a headlight and a life insurance policy, he thought. He stood and turned to the search team.

'I think we'll need your expertise to explore that,' he said.

'That may be something, but it's not where the girls were held,' Sadie said, breaking Ziggy's excitement. 'Claire mentioned nothing about going down any steps. And she was adamant it was a barn or similar.'

'We don't know for sure that Claire wasn't drugged. She may have gaps that she's not aware of.'

'But she didn't fall asleep in a van and wake up on a medieval torture device,' said Sadie.

'But she did say that she was taken somewhere to be killed.'

46

———————

Behind them, a member of SOCO coughed by way of interruption. 'Shall we take a look?'

Looking suitably shame-faced at delaying the team, Ziggy and Sadie took a step to one side and let them start to plan their descent.

While the detectives stood and waited, Ziggy ran his latest hypothesis past Sadie.

'It's hard to picture cages down there, but Claire seemed adamant. Where else could it be?'

'Hmm,' Sadie sighed. 'I was trying to work out under what circumstances anyone would have steel cages, you know like an old-fashioned circus for animals, or a zoo. A building site didn't spring to mind at all.'

'I agree. Could she have got it wrong?'

'What else could it have been?'

'Cage fighting?'

'No, that doesn't fit, I don't think. The storage unit in Selby perhaps?' Ziggy mused.

'There wasn't any mention of cages by the search team,

plus how and why would he have taken her to Selby then out to here?'

'Harder to trace? Which is also why I think we're looking for two or more people.'

'Warehouses use cages to hold and move stock.'

'True,' replied Ziggy. 'How are building supplies sto—'

A shout came from the cavity below, breaking off their conversation.

'Sir!' came the call from the SOCO that had been the first down. 'You need to see this.'

Ziggy walked over to the hole and peered down. 'What is it?'

'There's a tunnel here.' Irfan's cheery faced appeared below him. 'Come take a look.'

Ziggy gingerly stepped on the ladders that had been rigged up and slowly descended to join Irfan and his team. He blinked rapidly until his eyes became accustomed to the dark.

'That is unbelievable,' he breathed.

Stretching before him was an underground tunnel. He walked forward, careful where he stepped but looking closely at the walls around him. Small bricks created an arch and walls of the ancient tunnel. The air was damp, understandably, but the floor was solid and the roof above them, although aged, looked as solid as any he'd seen.

'Tunnels were used in the olden days to transport food from one side of a house to other,' Irfan piped up. 'Or to hide criminals.'

Ziggy knew nothing of the history of Temple Newsam, but he guessed it could be possible. An acrid stench assaulted his nostrils. The unmistakeable smell of blood. He placed a hand underneath his nose. Breathing as shallow as he could, he walked forward.

'It wasn't a cage,' he said, pointing to the steel bars that barred the way. 'It's a gate.' He walked further on, ignoring Irfan's cries that they hadn't searched that far down yet, his stomach churning. He knew instinctively that they were in the right place. To his left, the wall dipped back, creating what looked like a recess, but on closer inspection, he saw that there was a doorway. He lifted the timber strut that was laid vertically across, held in place by two huge gantries on either side. The heavy door creaked open as its hinges groaned under the weight. Screwing his eyes up in the dark to try to figure out what was in there, he hesitantly stepped forward. The ground underneath his feet was solid, but there was a lot of debris. The stench was foul. He shouted to Irfan to get one of the team to bring him a torch. Taking it from the SOCO's hand, Ziggy pointed it into the room.

Dirt clung to ancient bricks, cracks in the brickwork allowed damp, stale water to drip through. As he scanned the walls, he saw hooks and chains, ankle locks and arm braces. As he directed the beam of the torch into the centre of the room, he saw a monstrous contraption. A prickling ran across the back of Ziggy's neck. Some kind of torture device, the one he'd previously seen on a video, dominated the floor space. He approached carefully. Leather straps, stained a reddish brown, hung down, and Ziggy didn't dare to think who or what hellish action they'd seen. Spots of the same reddish brown were spattered all over the bed of the device and along the floor. He followed a trail and saw that it led to the wall. He walked over, and with a sharp intake of breath, he had to step away.

A bed of nails had been strung up on the wall. He noticed that it wasn't entirely secure, and yet every foreboding nail that protruded was coated in blood.

'Jesus Christ,' he gasped. Emotion threatened to overwhelm him. He took a deep breath and forced himself to move on. He stopped as his foot hit something solid. He adjusted his torch and looked down. An anvil sat protruding from the table's edge.

He'd seen enough. He instructed Irfan and his team to take over as he hurried back into the clean, innocent air. He gasped as he carefully placed his barrier suit in a waiting evidence bag, along with the shoe covers he'd pulled on before climbing down.

'Wow, that bad?' Sadie – who had waited at the top for him – asked.

Ziggy swallowed several times to try to get rid of the taste of bile he had in his mouth. 'We've found our kill site.' He leant against a nearby tree, catching his breath.

'It's hell on earth, it really is.'

'Definitely the kill site?'

'I would say so, yes. There's a device down there that wouldn't look out of place in the Tower of London.'

'Jesus, that sounds grim.'

'*Grim* isn't the word for it, Sadie. It's absolute hell. I can't even bring myself to think of what the poor victims suffered at Hawthorne's hands.'

'What about the cages?'

Ziggy straightened up and walked over to the entrance of the site again. 'It isn't a cage. Claire must have been drugged or has a false memory. There's a gate with steel bars – I think that's what she saw.'

'Shit. What now?'

'I guess we wait for Irfan to do his thing, and we take it from there.'

'No Evelyn then?'

'Didn't look like it.'

The two detectives were joined by PC Fyre.

'Sir, Agent Gladstone has asked you to call him.'

'No problem, thanks for letting me know. Did he say what it was about?'

'They've found Evelyn Shaw on the moors just outside Helmsley. She's alive.'

47

Evelyn gasped, desperately dragging clean, fresh air into her lungs. She clung to the search officer that had discovered her, a mixture of relief, shame and joy pulsing through her veins. She had thought she would never see daylight again. Never draw breath in the outside world again. She believed she had been condemned to remain underground, to die slowly in the box that had encased her for the last she didn't know how many hours. She sipped the water that the paramedic gave her whilst reluctantly surrendering herself to the ministrations of his colleague, flinching every time she was touched. Yes, she could hear. Yes, she could understand them. Yes, she knew where she was. Yes, she knew who they were.

A familiar face appeared her in peripheral vision, so she turned away from the volley of questions and looked pleadingly into his eyes.

'Please, Ziggy, let me explain,' she croaked, tiny fragments of dirt still trapped in her throat. She coughed loudly, spat out the phlegm and drank more water. She doubted she would ever taste anything other than gritty, inedible soil ever again.

'Evelyn, there's nothing to explain. Just focus on what the medics are saying. There will be plenty of time for talking later.' Ziggy squatted down at the side of her and gently touched her arm.

It took everything that Evelyn had not to withdraw from what she knew to be a kind gesture. 'I didn't know. You have to believe me,' she pleaded, eyes searching his face to see if he had worked out the truth.

'I know, I know.' He said not sure what Evelyn was reacting to. 'I'll be back in a minute – I just need to speak to the team. OK?'

Reluctantly, she nodded. Of course there was the wider team who would now know. Despite being grateful to be alive, she felt a deep sense of shame at the thought of everyone knowing. She so desperately wanted to see everything that had happened through a positive lens.

For everything, a reason.

She had always believed in that. She had told her patients that when they finally opened up to her. They had called her a miracle worker when she had opened their eyes to the trauma that they may have suffered in childhood, suggesting that it was that which had made them the way they were. They had thanked her profusely for helping them to release the inner demon that had driven them to commit such horrific acts. But what was the reason for the acts that had been committed by others against her? What had she ever done in her life that would provoke someone to act against her? All she had ever tried to do was pacify, play peacemaker, healer, advisor. She had tried to always lead with love, despite – no, *in spite* – of what had been done to her.

And now this.

Where was the positive she could take from this?

Or perhaps there weren't any positives. Perhaps her guiding philosophy of everything happening for a reason was complete bullshit, and she believed in the wrong thing. And now everyone knew.

Leaving Evelyn to the ambulance crew, he walked across the moorland, approaching Peter from the search team who had opted to stay behind as they were uncovering the crate.

'In there,' Peter pointed out.

Ziggy looked at the wooden crate in disbelief. 'What do you mean?'

'Exactly what I said. She was in the foetal position. Scrunched up as tight as a newborn baby and covered in dirt.'

'Buried alive?' Ziggy confirmed, visibly shuddering.

'Yep,' Peter replied as SOCOs joined them to tag the evidence and take photographs of the scene. Peter went on to explain that the original location where they had been digging hadn't revealed anything, so he'd asked for the canine unit to be sent to help search such a vast area. 'Turns out we weren't too far off the mark, about fifty feet or so. One of the dogs suddenly sat down and refused to move. His handler told us that was the Brutus's "tell", so we moved in and had barely scraped the surface under the peat when we hit the crate.'

'Jesus,' said Ziggy. 'Good old Brutus.'

'Oh, he got a treat for being a good boy.'

Ziggy smiled and looked around him. The team were each doing their thing, so he walked back over to the waiting ambulance and climbed inside. 'OK if I ask the patient a few questions?'

'If Doctor Shaw feels up to it, but any sign of distress and I'll step in,' the paramedic warned.

Ziggy looked at Evelyn, who nodded her consent.

'Silly question, I guess, but how are you feeling?'

'Shaken, shell-shocked, grateful,' Evelyn said, momentarily removing the oxygen mask so she could speak.

'What can you tell me about what happened? Can you give me a name?'

Evelyn let out a laugh that came out as a fractured cackle. 'I can do better than that. I can give you two.'

Ziggy held his breath as Evelyn took a few breaths of oxygen. Tears started to slowly trickle down her face, and her next breath turned into a sob. 'I've been so stupid, Ziggy.'

'I'm quite sure you haven't, Evelyn. I actually think you're being incredibly brave.'

'No, in the past, I mean. I've been so stupid. I should have seen it straightaway. I can't believe it was staring at me, and I completely ignored it.'

Ziggy hated to break her off from her wandering thoughts, but he needed those names. He was about to ask again when his mobile phone buzzed in his pocket. Sadie. He faltered for a moment, trying to rapidly weigh up what to do. They had the kill site. They would be bagging the evidence. What he needed were names. He rejected Sadie's call.

'I need the names, Evelyn. Who did this to you?'

'Vernon,' she said in a small, childlike voice. 'Vernon did this to me.'

Ziggy stared at her. 'Vernon? Your brother, Vernon?'

Tears came again. 'Yes.'

Ziggy thought back to the overweight, heaving bulk of a man who had been breathless as he had walked them to his front door. It seemed impossible that he could have entrapped his sister, somehow got her to curl up inside a wooden crate that looked like it had come from a fruit-and-veg stall in Leeds market, dug a hole and dropped it with his sister inside before covering it up. Who was the second person?

'Vernon, and who else? You said you had two names.'

'Alison.'

———

48

'Alison? As in Alison Hawthorne? James Hawthorne's sister?' Ziggy stared at Evelyn.

The paramedic stepped back into the rear of the ambulance as the various machines monitoring Evelyn started to beep.

'Sorry, Inspector, I'm going to have to ask you to leave.'

Reluctantly, Ziggy stepped out of the rear of the vehicle. Walking away from the busyness of the scene to take on board what Evelyn had just said, he dug his mobile phone out of his pocket and dialled Sadie, who had remained at the Temple Newsam site.

'Sorry, I didn't answer before. Was it urgent?'

'No, it's fine. What's going on?' she asked.

'Did we keep tabs on Alison Hawthorne?' he asked without preamble.

'I'm not sure, boss. Why?'

'Evelyn has named Alison as the person that did this to her.'

'What?'

'Not just that, but she's also implicated her own brother.'

'Vernon?'

Ziggy's phone buzzed and beeped against his ear. 'I have to go, Sadie – I've got another call coming in.'

The lines switched as sounds of HQ buzzed in Ziggy's ear.

'You were right,' Angela said after they'd briefly exchanged greetings. 'It is a woman in the video.'

'Hell. Right, remind me of the address for Alison Hawthorne, and also send uniform to head over to Vernon Shaw's address. If they could ask him to go with them to the station for now to help with enquiries, I'll speak to him when I get there.'

'Where are you going?'

'I'm heading over to Alison's.'

'Do you need backup?'

Ziggy hesitated. It was a good question. Would she know they had uncovered her involvement in the murders? 'Yeah but ask them to approach silently. I'll liaise with them when I get there.'

'Address coming across now, boss,' Angela said.

Ziggy's phoned buzzed once again against his ear. He thanked Angela and took a look at the screen. He hadn't been able to remember the house number, though he remembered it was in Helmsley. He felt a shiver of excitement as all the pieces of the complicated puzzle were slowly falling into place.

Once Ziggy pulled up along the pavement, he took a minute to look at the house he'd previously been in but hadn't taken much notice of. It looked like an old cottage, the middle one in a row of three. A neatly kept garden, with a stone path that led to the front door. Ivy covered part of one wall, and some kind of climbing rose was trailing over the door. From the outside, it looked like the quintessential English cottage.

A car in front of him flashed its lights. Ziggy recognised the person sat in the front seat as the lead of the task force team he had requested. No doubt a larger team were waiting around the corner. Ziggy left his car and headed to sit alongside Karl, the covert officer, in his car.

'What's the craic then?' Karl asked in his thick Liverpudlian accent. He was a heavy-set man that you wouldn't want to meet in an alleyway at night.

Ziggy wanted to exercise all caution before approaching the suspected kidnapper. He had no idea how Alison would react.

He ran through everything with Karl, finishing off by stressing that caution was the keyword. It was agreed that Ziggy would knock on the door and speak with Alison. If he felt there was a need to alert Karl and his team, he would call using codeword *bank,* at which point, the team would enter. Ziggy highly doubted they would be needed, and he stressed this, but it was better safe than sorry.

Having agreed the next steps, Ziggy left the car and headed to the door. Karl had assured him that Alison was home; she had returned from a brief shopping trip while he had been sitting there.

A brisk rap on the door, and a few minutes later, it opened slightly with the chain still attached. Ziggy pulled his ID from his wallet.

'Hi, Alison? It's Andrew Thornes from West Yorkshire Police.' He held his ID up to the small gap. 'We've met before, if you remember. I was wondering if we could have a chat?'

Slowly, the chain slipped back, and the door opened fully.

Alison Hawthorne clearly hadn't been expecting anyone. She was wearing a tracksuit that looked two sizes too small, with food stains down the front. At some point, it had been velour, but it was old and worn with threadbare patches. The same orange stains that were down the front of her top were also around her face. The image was a far cry from the matronly appearance Alison had presented on his last visit.

'Would you mind if I came in, Alison?'

'What's this about? Is it James? Is he OK?'

'He's fine, don't worry, but yes, it is about James.'

'Suppose you'd better come in then,' she said, holding the door wide.

Ziggy stepped inside and followed Alison into the living room. This time, he really took in his surroundings. The large-screen TV was playing a quiz show, and a lap table was sitting to one side, holding what Ziggy suspected was the source of Alison's orange stains – a bowl of tomato soup. 'I'm sorry for interrupting your lunch,' he said, trying to think of the last time he'd sat down and eaten a meal. His stomach rumbled loudly, much to his embarrassment.

'Sounds like you need a meal, Inspector. Can I get you a drink?'

'That would be lovely, thank you. Tea with milk,' he said, grateful for the offer, before remembering the mug of coloured water she'd made him last time. Still, it was more than he'd had since leaving the house that morning.

Alison left the room and Ziggy looked around. It was a decent size; enough room for a settee and two chairs, though he noticed only one of the chairs seemed to have any wear and tear – the one where Alison sat. There were a few photographs on the wall above the dated marble fireplace, so he stood up to take a closer look. A couple of them were taken in a garden, two children stood in shorts and T-shirts, arms around each other grinning the self-conscious grin of children with gaps in the front teeth. The other was the photograph of the family of four on holiday that he'd seen the last time he was there. They looked happy. Who knew what horrors lay underneath.

'Ah, I see you're looking at the family photos again?' Alison returned with a tray carrying two mugs of tea and a plate of biscuits. She placed it on the coffee table in the centre of the room and sat down. Ziggy returned to his seat.

'Is that you and James?' he asked of the photo where the two children were arm in arm. He thanked her for the tea and took a ginger biscuit.

'It is, in happier times, of course.'

'Yes, you look like you were close as youngsters?'

'We were. James always needed a guiding hand. Thankfully, he had me for that.'

'Not your parents?'

'I'm sure you know our family history, Inspector Thornes. That's not why you're here, isn't it?'

'Please, call me Andrew, and it's kind of is why I want to speak to you.'

'I'm an open book, Andrew. You can ask me anything.'

Taking his time to frame his next question carefully, Ziggy helped himself to another biscuit and took a sip of his tea. 'What can you tell me about Hopegood Children's Home?'

49

Alison tipped her head to one side. 'We've already spoken about that, Inspector. What else would you like to know?'

He noticed that Alison's thumbs were rapidly twisting around each other. 'Did you visit James while he was in there?'

'Oh no,' Alison said, smiling. 'My parents would never allow it.'

Ziggy pointed to the picture on the mantlepiece. 'That photograph, the one where you have your arms around each other?'

Alison stood up and took it in her hands. 'Yes, happier times.'

'Hmm,' said Ziggy. 'Forgive me for asking this, but what's the age difference between yourself and James?'

'There are a number of years between us, Inspector.'

'And in that picture,' Ziggy nodded towards the frame she was still holding. 'Which one is James?' The young children were dressed identically and of a similar size with the same short haircut that Alison still wore a version of today.

'That's me on the right.' She turned the frame around and pointed.

'So, you would have been around twelve years old here?'

'I would guess so, yes.' Alison stood and replaced the picture back in its place. 'Why do you want to know?'

Ziggy replaced his mug on the coffee table. 'If you're twelve in that photograph, that would make you five years older than James.' He watched her face flush red. 'And if that's the case, James can't have been in Hopegood Children's Home.'

Alison's thumbs were frantically rotating. Ziggy was alert to any sudden movements and stood slowly. 'Alison, it wasn't James in Hopegood, was it? It was you.'

Alison didn't speak; the only movement were her thumbs.

'I need you to come to the station with me, Alison.' He reached forward to take her by the elbow when she suddenly shot up and lashed out at him. He heard a rip and felt a burning sensation in his arm. Blood started to leak through a tear in his coat. He saw the glint of a knife as he let go of her elbow and pushed her away. She swiped forward, catching his hand as she did so. He yelled out, reached for his phone and barked the codeword into the receiver.

Alison had managed to scramble away as Ziggy nursed his wounds but was stopped abruptly by Karl, who had led the charge into the house. As she fell to her knees, with her hands cuffed behind her, Ziggy walked over.

'Alison Hawthorne, I am arresting you on suspicion of kidnap and murder..'

It was mid-afternoon by the time Ziggy made it back to HQ via Accident and Emergency at St James's Hospital. He was nursing a heavily bandaged hand and arm. Thankfully, the cuts had been relatively superficial, allowing him to continue tying up the loose ends. The next piece of the puzzle was Vernon Shaw. He'd already had his house searched, and the results were waiting for him.

On returning to HQ, Ziggy sat with the assembled team and brought everyone up to date. There were incredulous looks around the room, and gasps of disbelief as the whole sorry story unfolded.

'I don't know how she managed to conceal her lies and involvement for so long,' Sadie said after meeting had broken up.

'Me neither,' Ziggy echoed, grabbing the search report for Vernon Shaw from his desk. 'Shall we go chat with our friend and find out what he has to say?'

Entering Interview Room Two, the coldest one available, Ziggy formally introduced himself and Sadie before beginning the tape recorder.

'Sorry to have kept you waiting, Mr Shaw, and thank you for agreeing to help us.'

'It's no big deal – I've been looked after. Is this about Evelyn? Have they found her?'

'Evelyn has been found. She's somewhat bruised, but she's fine.'

Vernon smiled.

'You must be relieved?' Ziggy asked.

'Well, of course. She's my sister after all.'

'When we met previously at your house, we discussed your blog, TruthUnSocial?'

'Right?'

'What is it that you do for a living, Vernon?'

'For a job, you mean?'

'Yes, that's what I'm asking. Is the blog a source of income?'

'Not really. I'm a freelance journalist. I earn money writing articles and features for newspapers and magazines.'

'That's interesting. Does it generate a full-time income?"

Vernon screwed his face up. 'Where is this going, Inspector?'

'I was just wondering how you could afford the fort-four-inch-flat screen TV that was in your living room?'

'That's none of your business,' Vernon said indignantly.

'Or the complex IT system that's set up in your basement?'

Ziggy watched as Vernon blustered and tried to form a sentence.

'You see, we've had a search team going over your property while you're here. What do you think they found?'

'You... you can't do that.'

'We can and we have,' said Ziggy. 'Let's leave that for the minute.' Ziggy took a brown folder from Sadie. 'How do you know Alison and James Hawthorne, Vernon?'

Ziggy watched as Vernon's face crumbled, and tears started to pour down his cheeks unchecked.

When he didn't reply, Ziggy pulled several pieces of paper from the folder. 'We have recovered an interesting email exchange between you and Alison Hawthorne.' He spread the pages out before him and started to read from one.

'"The next one is lined up. Make sure it's all working by the end of next month."

What is she referring to, Vernon?'

Vernon said nothing.

'And again here: "Two of the same cameras and around twenty of the Sony disks as last time."'

'Nothing to say? Shall I tell you what I think? I think Alison Hawthorne reached out to you via your blog. I think she asked you to supply her with IT equipment. I think you became friends when you both realised that you had simi-lar... specific tastes and preferences.' Ziggy looked from the email printouts to Vernon's face. 'Am I on the right lines?'

Still, Vernon didn't speak, so Ziggy continued. 'I think you became friends. Maybe she showed you the kindness that had been missing in your life.'

Fresh tears.

'And as a result, she dragged you into a web that you couldn't get out of.'

Once again, Vernon wiped his face. 'It wasn't like that. You're making it sound like she used me.'

'Didn't she use you? From where I'm sat, it looks very much to me like you were a means to an end. Are you telling me it was different?'

'Yes!' Vernon snapped. 'Alison understood me. She didn't mind about my weight, or where I lived. She didn't care that I don't have a job. She even said that I was a free spirit. She admired that I could do what I wanted.' Vernon was indig-nant, and Ziggy could tell he'd touched a nerve.

'What did she want in exchange for her friendship? The IT and camera equipment?'

Vernon looked down at his hands. 'It wasn't an exchange; it was a business deal. And I volunteered.'

'Volunteered to what?'

'To help, all right.' The resigned tone in Vernon's voice told Ziggy all he needed to know.

'Did you offer to help Alison and her brother James on the basis that you could watch the videos?'

A tiny squeak left Vernon's mouth.

'I'm sorry, what was that?'

'Yes, all right. *Yes!*' Vernon shouted the last word and slammed his hand on the table, making Sadie jump.

'Did you talk with her about Evelyn?' Ziggy knew he had. There was an entire email chain detailing their earlier lives. 'What did you tell her about your childhood?'

'Just growing up on the moors and that.'

'And what? Growing up on the moors, *and what*?'

'The games we'd play.' He shifted uncomfortably in his seat and wiped his hand across his forehead. 'It's warm in here,' he complained.

'What kind of games, Vernon?'

'Kids' stuff, you know.'

'Hide and seek? Tag? That kind of thing?'

Vernon nodded enthusiastically. 'Yeah, yeah.'

'Doctors and nurses?' Ziggy asked. The atmosphere in the room changed in an instant. What had so far, in Ziggy's opinion been fairly gentle questioning, had suddenly taken a dark turn, and Ziggy saw it reflected in Vernon's face.

'I think I've answered enough questions now. I want a solicitor.'

'Vernon, you're not under arrest. You're helping with our enquiries. Why would you need a solicitor?'

'That, the doctors-and-nurses thing, the way you said it. I didn't like it.'

Completely throwing protocol out of the window, Ziggy pressed Vernon harder. His tone being one of steel. 'Too close to the truth, was it, Vernon? It might have been an innocent game to Evelyn, but you had a much more sinister goal in mind, didn't you?' He enjoyed watching the man opposite him squirm. 'How far did it go, Vernon? How far before Evelyn screamed? How far before she ran and you chased after her?'

Vernon suddenly moved and placed his hands over his ears. He started to chant incoherently to drown out the words. Ziggy carried on relentlessly.

'And just like you manipulated Evelyn, Alison did the same to you. You let her manipulate you into taking part. You set up the video and cameras. You watched from your disgusting little den, didn't you?' Spittle flew from Ziggy's mouth as his voice grew louder, and words came spilling out. 'You disgusting piece of shit. We've searched your premises, Vernon. We've found your sordid little stash. You're the scum of the earth and you'll be spending a long time in solitary confinement. Do you know why? Do you know what happens to the likes of you in prison?'

Sadie stepped in, grabbing Ziggy's shoulder and pulling him back. She hit stop on the recording equipment and opened the interview-room door. 'Escort Mr Shaw back to his cell,' she instructed the waiting custody officer.

Once Vernon had left the room, she sat at the side of Ziggy as he composed himself.

'I'm not going to apologise,' he said.

50

Saturday, 18 October 2003

Ziggy sat in front of James Hawthorne and tried not to convey the utter disgust he felt for the man.

'When did it start?'

'With Alison? I'm not sure, after her time in Hopegood, I think.'

'You were five years old!'

Hawthorne laughed. 'Yes, I guess you're right. Gosh, that is young, isn't it?'

'How did it start, this "partnership"?' Ziggy used the only term he could think of.

'I wanted to know how she'd killed the cat. That was seriously impressive, how she took the head off so cleanly. Once she'd shared that, there was no holding back. We had a place where we'd take animals to conduct experiments. She claimed she wanted to be a vet, so it was all perfectly normal.'

'*Normal* isn't the word I'd use. When did it escalate?'

Hawthorne smiled. 'To people, women? I'm not sure. I told Evelyn the truth – I started watching first of all, and it just went from there. After the first one, Alison contacted me. She'd read it in the news and just knew it was me.'

'And she was right?'

'Of course she knew.'

'Yet she never said anything?'

'Why would she? And she was the perfect partner. Did everything I asked and then some.'

This time, Hawthorne wasn't talking with his head on his chest or with the dark look in his eye. Quite the opposite. He was sitting upright, looking Ziggy directly in the face with a sly grin and a twinkle in his eye. The alternate was nowhere to be seen – if he ever existed at all.

'How involved was she?'

'In the killing? After the first one, it was all her.'

'But you sourced the victim?'

'Sourced!' He laughed. 'Yes, I guess you could say that.'

'You lured them into a side street, hit them over the head and dragged them into the back of your van?'

'Correct on all counts.'

'Then what? Where did you take them? Straight to the underground tunnel?'

'Yes. Alison would meet me, and together we'd take them to their resting place. Well, I use the term "resting" very loosely.'

Ziggy was sickened by the dark humour, but he didn't show it. 'And then Alison would what?'

'Depended on her mood, I suppose. Sometimes she'd have me tie them to the wall so she could punish them. Occasionally she'd use the rack. It all depended on her mood.'

'When would you play your part?'

'Afterwards.'

'How did you move them from the tunnel?'

'Same way as we took them in. We'd carry them in the dead of night.'

'And take them to the storage unit?'

'The laboratory, I think you're referring to.'

Ziggy didn't answer. He was long past caring about semantics.

'But yes, I would. Then I'd... experiment.'

'Why the eyes? Why did you remove them?'

'Oh, come on, Inspector, didn't you learn anything from the good doctor? I didn't want them to see what I was doing to them, of course.'

Bile rose into Ziggy's throat. He forced it back down.

'Vernon Shaw, how did he become part it?'

'Alison set all that up. She told me about it and though I warned her not to include anyone else, she got greedy. When we'd committed the final spree, she got carried away. We wanted to divert your attention away from her. Looks like she failed.'

'You were the one that got caught, though,' Ziggy said.

'Unfortunate. Though, now you have her DNA, I'm sure you'll solve a few other outstanding cases.'

'I think we're done here,' Ziggy said, waving the guard in.

He stood and looked at Hawthorne. Words failed him. He doubted they would ever know the true extent of their despicable crimes, and Ziggy wasn't sure if he ever wanted to.

The media room was once again full, but this time Ziggy was on stage. It had been twenty-four hours since the arrests of Alison Hawthorne and Vernon Shaw. The team had worked nonstop to ensure the evidence against them both had passed the charge threshold for the Crown Prosecution Service. While they waited for the charges to come through, Ziggy wanted to run over the entire case with the full team.

'Although we know James Hawthorne to be the serial killer responsible for the deaths of Madeline Wadham, Janine Morley, Julia Newbury, Isobel Harmer, Belinda Riley and the attempted murder of Claire Strickland, we were correct in suspecting that he wasn't alone in his actions. His sister, Alison Shaw, was an equally willing participant. She aided and abetted Hawthorne in all his crimes. We know from the evidence we recovered from both Vernon Shaw's home address and that of Alison Hawthorne, they started an email conversation after the Hawthorne's first victim. She discovered him via his online blog and although she initially coerced him into helping her locate the recording equipment and cameras and various bits of software, she soon established that Vernon had similar "tastes" to that of her and her brother.' Ziggy took a sip of water. 'When it was established that Doctor Evelyn Shaw would be working with us to help understand Hawthorne and uncover the kill site, it unknowingly played right into the hands of the Hawthornes. Alison chose to use Vernon, taking advantage of his willingness to make friends, and fed her brother information that was then used to inform Evelyn's visits with Hawthorne.'

Ziggy looked around the room. 'I know this case has impacted all of you on some level, but your hard work and diligence have paid off. I have no doubt that CPS will come back with a positive charging decision. Once we have that, I know you will remain committed as we prepare for trial.'

Ziggy thanked everyone that had assembled and headed back to the conference room that had become a second home to him in recent weeks. Mike Gladstone was standing, waiting for him.

'Thought you'd be in the media room?' Ziggy said as he started to pull all the loose sheets of paper together into a pile.

'Ha, not this time,' Mike said with his hands in his pockets. 'I wanted to wait here and make sure I was the first to congratulate you on a case well run.'

'It's not over until the fat lady sings, as they say – or at least until a guilty verdict is reached.'

'We'll need you to head to HQ in London at some point. We'd like you to comment on any lessons learnt during this investigation that may be of use to the wider force.'

Ziggy smiled. 'Sure. If you think it would help, I'd be happy to.'

'That's not all,' Mike said, leaning against the wall.

"Oh yeah?' Ziggy said as he carried on clearing up paperwork.

'We'd like to make you a permanent offer.'

Ziggy stopped and looked at Mike. 'What does that mean?'

'It means we'd like you full-time at the National Crime Squad. We figure a mix of lecturing, leading investigations, working with the best in the country – perhaps the world – to solve complex serial murder investigations.'

Ziggy took a deep breath. 'Would it mean relocating?'

'Perhaps, but I'm sure we could work something out if that wasn't an option for you.'

'It's not an option. I have a son, an ex-wife, so...'

'We could look at a case-by-case basis, but look, let's have the meeting at London HQ and talk about options?'

On principle, Ziggy couldn't see any harm in having a conversation, though admittedly, it would be hard to leave the team of Sadie, Nick and Angela behind. 'Can I think about it?'

Mike came over and patted Ziggy on the shoulder. 'Of course you can. Let me know in a day or two.'

Ziggy headed home, finally. He knew he had long days ahead of him as they prepared for trial, but now he had a lot of thinking to do.

Did he want to join the NCS on a permanent basis? Sure, he'd revelled in the melting away of red tape and the speed at which processes could take place, but what about the camaraderie of his team? Would he be a lone wolf? Could he handle the pressure? He was two years away from retiring on a decent pension. Did he want to spend his last two years under an incredible amount of pressure?

And what did he know about lecturing? Aside from lecturing Ben to clean his room, he had no experience.

Ziggy showered and changed into comfortable clothes. Taking a beer from the fridge, he put some classical music on the record player and slouched down on his faux leather sofa. As his thoughts continued to spiral, he heard his mobile phone ringing upstairs. Placing his beer down, he jogged upstairs and retrieved it from his bedside cabinet.

'Sadie?'

'Boss, haven't disturbed you, have I?'

'No, not all. Was just thinking a few things over. Anything wrong?'

'No, actually it's nice to call you with some news of my own.'

Ziggy was intrigued. 'Oh right, go on then.'

'I didn't like to mention it cause we were up to our necks in the investigation, but I attended the final panel interview as part of the inspector exam.'

Ziggy froze and immediately felt guilty. He had known it was on the cards, and he had promised to help Sadie with her revision. 'Well, I don't know where you found the time, and I am also incredibly sorry if I've added to your stress pile.

'Ha, not at all Ziggy. Hastings actually mentored me through it.'

'And do you have the result?'

'Yes... I passed!'

'Sadie, that's awesome! I wouldn't have expected anything less. Bloody well done.'

'Thank you, I'm so relieved. Thank you for being such a great role model.'

'Get lost. You can't look at me as a role model, or heaven help us all.' He laughed. He was genuinely pleased for Sadie. She had worked so hard over all the years he had known her, and no one deserved it more. 'So, what next then, Ms Detective Inspector?'

'Well, that's the not-so-good news.'

Ziggy held his breath. 'Go on.'

'There are no opening at Leeds, or even in Yorkshire for a DI, so I've put in for a transfer.'

Ziggy was silent for a minute or two as he gave it some thought. 'Ah, that's not good. I'd be sorry to lose you. You're an integral part of the team, but I always knew there would be no holding you back.'

Ziggy imagined Sadie's beaming face and felt intensely proud of his work wife.

There would be more time for celebrations later. For now, they had to focus on bringing the case against the Hawthornes and Vernon Shaw to its inevitable conclusion.

51

———————

Prison informant Mark sat in front of Ziggy as he attempted to tie up all the loose ends.

'Mark, when you sat and spoke with my colleague a couple of days ago, you mentioned that Hawthorne had "let one get away". What did you take that to mean?'

'Oh, that some lucky cow had escaped. His meaning was clear, and he wasn't happy about it.'

'Did he give you any more details, like where or when it took place?'

'He didn't give me a name, if that's what you mean. He told me it was near Temple Newsam, close to the farm, if that helps?'

'That's really helpful,' said Ziggy. Sadie was sat alongside him making notes. It was something they would look into to see if they could locate the victim, if they'd even reported the incident.

'Did he say when, give you a timeframe at all?'

'It was summer, I know that much. He told me the girl was wearing low-cut shorts with a thong showing over the top.'

Ziggy closed his eyes. He didn't know much about women's fashion, but he knew it was a trend he'd seen around town.

'That trend's been around for a while,' Sadie said. 'Can you give us anything more specific?'

'Erm, not really. Let me think.' Mark tapped his fingers on the table, then clicked his fingers. 'Oh, wait a second... When was the Carling Festival held at Temple Newsam, and it all went tits up? It must have been that year, cos he said there were too many bodies around anyway.'

'August 2000.' Sadie nodded the affirmative.

'That's a brilliant detail, Mark. Thank you for that,' Ziggy said.

'No worries, man. I mean, I know you've got the bastard, but anything to make the charges stick, right?'

Establishing that the inmate had nothing more to tell them, the two detectives thanked Mark again and signalled for the prison officer to take him back to his cell. They collected their equipment together and headed to the exit of the prison.

'The question we need to ask ourselves is how far back does he go?' Ziggy said.

'Is Alison talking?'

'No. She's gone "no comment", which is fine. The search of her home gave us more evidence, which is currently being processed, though we'll have no problem tying stuff back to her. Fingerprints and DNA are everywhere, on both sites.'

It was unusual for killers to spread their territory as far and as wide as the Hawthornes had. Transporting their victims from the torture and kill site at Temple Newsam to the deposition site at Helmsley would have taken some coordinating. It had been easier when James Hawthorne was active, as it meant he could do the bulk of the work. Subduing the victim, before taking them to Temple Newsam where Alison would be waiting to administer whatever torturous act she felt like. Once she had finished, and James had ended their lives, the bodies were disposed of – how many aside from the five they knew about was pretty much anyone's guess, and all missing-persons cases were being revisited.

When Vernon had been brought onboard to start the viewing and remote recording, the stakes had been raised.

Ziggy could only imagine the glee that Alison must have felt when she made the connection between Vernon and her brother's new psychologist, Dr Evelyn Shaw. That was when Alison had to get rid of the five victims James hadn't yet disposed of, including the poor survivor, Claire. According to Vernon, Alison had bribed him into driving the van and moving the bodies to Helmsley, where she (not James) had created the macabre display of bodies. Whether they would have used Helmsley as the deposition site if it hadn't had been for the connection to Evelyn Shaw, they would never know.

'It's a long time to hold a grudge, isn't it?' Sadie said as they climbed into Ziggy's car.

'Alison's grudge against Evelyn, you mean?'

'Yes. I mean, what, thirty years?'

'Something like that.'

Before Alison had appointed a solicitor, she had talked freely. She had confirmed Ziggy's suspicion that it was her and not James who had been at Hopegood Children's Home. The incident with the family cat had been at her hands, though James had helped, and that's when the evil folie à deux had been formed. The whole story wouldn't have been uncovered if it hadn't been for an overeager student, Evelyn Shaw 'poking her nose in', Alison had said with much venom. Her stay at the home at been extended by another six months whilst she underwent additional therapy.

'Have you spoken to Evelyn since she was discharged from hospital?'

'I have, but I'm calling around later today to see how she's doing.'

'How was she?'

'On the surface she seemed OK, but who knows what's going on underneath. She mentioned that she's been talking to her own psychologist about it all.'

'And she had no idea that Vernon was being used by the Hawthornes?'

'No clue. She kept infrequent contact with him over the years out of some kind of misplaced loyalty until recently when Vernon had tracked her down. She'd never heard of his blog, so all that was bullshit made up by him.'

'Wow,' Sadie said as they pulled up outside of HQ. They made their way up to the incident room, which was still a hive of activity as various team members worked relentlessly to prepare for court and make sure all the loose ends were tied up.

They walked over to their quadrant and updated Angela and Nick with the information from the prison inmate.

'I'll update MisPer,' Angela said. 'It helps that we have a date. That festival always happens on the August bank holiday.'

'Thanks to Sadie. Did you go to the festival?' Ziggy asked.

'I did, with Mac. It was brilliant. We saw Oasis, which Mac was thrilled about, but for me it was all about Stereophonics. Best live band I've ever seen.'

Nick had been drinking his tea and dunking his biscuits as Sadie spoke. 'I went as well.'

Three heads turned and stared at him. Nick was the oldest member of the team, and perhaps mistakenly viewed as somewhat of an old-timer.

'You did?' Angela said, her voice rising at the end in surprise.

'All right – no need to sound so surprised. My nephew wanted to see Oasis, so we got there just before they came on stage and left immediately afterwards. Far too much bare skin on show for me.'

The others laughed, each picturing Nick's face.

Ziggy pushed his chair back. 'Right, I'm heading off to see Evelyn. Anything comes up, let me know.'

52

Ziggy had visited Evelyn whilst she was still in hospital, recovering from her ordeal. She was bruised and shaken but had remained positive overall. He was now heading to her apartment in the hopes of adding to her earlier statement.

When she opened the door, she was dressed in leisure wear. At first, he thought he may have woken her, but she insisted he hadn't.

'Coffee?' she asked after they'd greeted each other.

'That would be lovely, thank you. Here, I brought some pastries as well.' After three weeks of irregular eating due to the long hours the investigation had demanded, Ziggy was craving sugar and carbs. When he'd passed the bakery on his way here, he hadn't been able to resist.

'Fancy,' Evelyn said, taking them off him and pulling plates from the cupboard. 'Make yourself at home.'

He sat on the L-shaped sofa, sinking into the cushions. 'How have you been?' He asked as Evelyn carried everything over. He still had a thick bandage around his hand, though the cut in his arm hadn't needed anything more than a few Steri-strips.

Evelyn nodded towards his hand. 'How's it healing?'

'It's OK, I guess. She must have secreted the knife down the side of the chair when she made a brew. Completely took me by surprise.'

Evelyn shook her head. 'Evil personified.'

'We were just saying that she held that grudge for a long time.'

'Yeah, she was definitely still bitter and ranting at me about it as I was being drugged.'

'Can you tell me about that? Of course we have your initial statement, but as much detail as you can remember would be really helpful.'

'I can't believe I fell for it, to be honest. From both of them, all of them.'

'You can't beat yourself up, Evelyn. These were evil beyond measure.' He paused, remembering that one of those people was Evelyn's brother. 'Sorry, but you know what I mean.'

'I do, and I am being hard on myself, I know... But it's funny. If anyone ever asked me, I would always say I had a happy childhood. People imagine it to be idyllic, growing up in a small market town with God's own county on your doorstep, but in reality, it was hell on earth.' She reached forward and took a tissue from the box on the coffee table.

'Are you OK?' Ziggy asked as he worked his way through another apple Danish.

She waved him away. 'I'm fine. Honestly, this is good. I'm letting go of the horror that's plagued me for years, thanks to all this. Where was I? Oh, yes. I mean, some of it is typical and probably explains why Vernon turned out the way he did. Mum was an alcoholic; Dad was the same. Vernon was allowed to run wild, and I was his first victim.' She took a sip of coffee. She shuddered.

Ziggy briefly wondered if she needed more time. He asked her so.

'I need you to understand, Ziggy. I know much of this will come out in court, anyway, but I want you to hear it first.'

'Well, stop if it gets too much.'

Reassured, Evelyn continued. 'I can't remember how young I was when he began abusing me. He told me it was "normal", what brothers and sisters did.' She shuddered again. 'The worst of it is, I think Mum knew about it and did nothing.' She was shredding the tissue as she spoke. 'Anyway, after our parents passed, we were left to our own devices. Vernon expected me to carry on with the cooking and cleaning as I had done for years. I'd left school at this point, and for two years, I did his bidding. I don't know why, before you ask. Misplaced loyalty? He was the only family I had. I really don't know.'

Evelyn sighed deeply and gazed off into the middle distance. 'He would tell me he'd visited their grave and that they had spoken to him. Telling him that I had been a bad girl and needed to be punished. I put up with it, and then one day, it was like someone had flicked a switch. He'd left for work, a labouring job, and I packed the only bits I had and ran.'

'Where did you go?'

'Leeds.' She laughed. 'I thought the streets would be paved with gold, Ziggy. Turns out, they weren't.'

'Chewing gum and fag ends, maybe,' laughed Ziggy.

'Yes. Anyway, I reached out to a homeless charity and through them I eventually found a flat and registered for college.'

Ziggy knew that she had brushed over much of the detail. Pulling yourself up by your bootstraps at a critical time of life wouldn't have been easy. Ziggy knew that but completely respected her decision to not share the final details.

Evelyn continued. 'I tried to put it all behind me, but he found me. I was heartbroken at first, and emotionally, I went right back to that place inside me that was subservient and eager to please. But I was determined not to allow him to undo all the good work I'd done, on myself and in my studies, so we came to an agreement.'

'Did that involve money?' Ziggy queried.

Evelyn smiled. 'Exactly. I paid his bills and rent, along with an occasional bag of shopping. In return, he kept out of my life.'

'So, when he contacted you to ask for more money, you weren't surprised?'

'Not at all. I went to his disgusting house. They were waiting for me, and the next thing I know, I felt a small scratch in my neck. When I woke up, I was tied up and being forced into some kind of crate – the one you found me in.'

'Where were you when you woke?'

'In the back of a van. The smell will never leave me, I'm sure. I can't even describe it, Ziggy.' She took several deep breaths.

'Do you want to stop? We can talk about something else if you like?' Not that he wanted to, but he had a care for her wellbeing.

'There isn't much to add to it, really. I heard the two of them discussing the best way to "get rid of me", and I was convinced I was going to die. As soon as they realised I was awake, she drugged me again. Next thing I know, my mouth was full of dirt and everything was pitch black.'

She sat back and nursed her mug of coffee to her chest. 'What's happening at your end?' she asked.

'We're pushing hard to get everything tied up. There are more victims out there that we haven't yet reached.'

'My God, that's awful. What about a public appeal?'

'To be honest, it is something we've considered and I'm talking to my boss when I get back. We have a long road ahead to prosecution, but I'm determined to bring justice for those that have been victim to these people.'

53

———————

Some weeks later

'Have you reached a verdict upon which at least ten of you agree?' the clerk asked.

'Yes,' the foreman replied.

'Do you find the defendant, James Hawthorne, guilty or not guilty of the murder of Madeline Wadham, Janine Morley, Julia Newbury, Isobel Harmer and Belinda Riley?'

'Guilty.'

'Do you find the defendant, James Hawthorne, guilty or not guilty of the kidnap and attempted murder of Claire Strickland?

'Guilty.'

Ziggy had to hold himself back from punching the air. Instead, he and Sadie gripped each other's hands.

The judge spoke. 'Would the defendant please rise?'

There was shuffling and muttering in the court as Hawthorne came to his feet, cuffed.

'Mr Hawthorne, you have stood in this courtroom for the past few weeks and at no point have you shown any remorse for your heinous actions. We have heard from a forensic psychologist and various psychiatrists who each have labelled you a psychopath, of having antisocial personality disorder and being a consummate liar who is able to swap and change personalities at a whim. I would go further and say that you are the most despicable human being I have ever had the unfortunate opportunity to meet. We will never truly know how many victims you are responsible for, but one thing I do know is that this city – indeed the entire country – is a much, much safer place with you behind bars for the rest of your natural life. I would like to commend the police and associated agencies for a thorough investigation – exceptionally well run.

'Take the prisoner down.'

As Hawthorne was escorted from the court, he glanced over his shoulder and grinned at Ziggy, who looked away, refusing to give Hawthorne any more of his time.

As they left the court by the front entrance, Ziggy, Sadie, Hastings and Evelyn Shaw gathered around the microphones to address the press. Ziggy spoke first.

'The judge was right; there was only one possible verdict, and James Hawthorne will never be a free man. My team and I have worked extremely hard to reach this conclusion, but this moment isn't mine. It belongs to the victims, and on that, I'll hand over to Doctor Evelyn Shaw.'

Evelyn came forward, chin up, shoulders back, and spoke directly to the media. 'I echo the words of my colleague and would like to take this opportunity to announce that, in conjunction with Victim Support, we have set up a helpline for anyone who feels that they may have been a victim of James Hawthorne. Details are available on…'

Ziggy walked away from the hubbub and waited to one side. Once the press had broken up and Evelyn had managed to prise herself free, they climbed into a waiting cab and headed to the offices of the National Crime Squad in Pimlico, where Mike Gladstone was waiting for them, glass of cheap fizz in hand.

'Got what he deserved,' Mike said after he had passed the glasses around.

'Was never in doubt,' Ziggy joked.

'Alison is up next week, and Vernon Shaw will follow afterwards, I believe?' said. He'd travelled down on the train with Sadie, while Ziggy and Evelyn had been working in London for a couple of weeks as the prosecution ran through several scenarios and worked out their strategy.

'That's the plan,' Ziggy said. 'I'll be heading back up north before then, though. I need my own bed!'

Everyone laughed and turned as the door to the conference room opened and canapés were brought in. Ziggy stayed for a little while before heading outside to grab some fresh air. He was tired of meeting rooms and conferences.

Whilst everyone else congratulated their efforts and slapped each other on the back, he made his way to the pub he'd taken to during his time in the capital. Ordering a pint of Old Speckled Hen, he found a quiet table and people-watched whilst going over everything he had on his mind.

He was glad that Evelyn had started the search for further victims. He knew from their conversations that she needed to find these girls as much as they needed to be found. He had to admit to himself that his case had changed him. He'd delegated way more on this complex case than he had others, and Sadie had handled it effectively whilst he had immersed himself in understanding James Hawthorne. The offer from Mike Gladstone and National Crime Squad was still open to him and he'd had the chance to visit the impressive offices and been given a guided tour of the latest tech and surveillance techniques, which were so far removed from the rudimentary systems used back at Leeds HQ.

Had he changed enough during this investigation to make not just his biggest career change yet, but also a huge life change?

'All right there, boss?' Sadie sidled up alongside him with a pint of her own.

'I think so. Just needed some time, you know?'

'I know, it's been a long case,'

'It has, and a stressful one.'

'You took it in your stride, though. Handled it well.'

'Sadie, have you heard any more about the transfer you mentioned?'

'No, it looks like you're stuck with me a bit longer. Sorry about that.' She laughed, then took a sip of her pint.

'Not necessarily. I have an idea...'

The End

PLEASE LEAVE A REVIEW

I hope you've enjoyed Ziggy's latest outing. If you have then a review would be invaluable. This helps new readers find my books – and also earns you my never-ending thanks! It doesn't need to be long, just a few words are absolutely fine.

- Goodreads
- Amazon

FREE EBOOK

Claim your FREE SHORT STORY, Feel The Fear

Click the link or visit www.catherineyaffe.co.uk

A DI Ziggy Thornes exclusive.

You can also sign up to receive regular updates on the series, exclusive previews of new releases, more short stories and a behind-the-scenes look at the life of an author. All for free!

CATCH UP ON THE SERIES

Book 1 – The Lie She Told

mybook.to/thelieshetold

Book 2 – The Web They Wove

mybook.to/thewebtheywove

Book 3 - When We Deceive

mybook.to/whenwedeceive

Book 4 - Catch Me Twice

mybook.to/catchmetwice

Book 5 - The Shadow Killer

mybook.to/theshadowkiller

COMING SOON JUNE 2026

Book 6 - Deliberate Harm

mybook.to/deliberateharm

ACKNOWLEDGMENTS

Thank you so much for choosing to read this book. In a world that's filled with books you chose mine and I am deeply grateful.

My thanks also go to my wonderful editor Rebecca Millar who in amongst getting married and moving across the world still found time to completely overhaul this book and make it so much better for you, the reader. Thank you, Rebecca, you're an absolute star.

A huge thanks to those prison officers and associates from HMP Wakefield (who shall remain anonymous as requested) that helped me with the research into 'Monster Mansion.' I have used a couple of 'Americanisms' for dramatic purposes so please forgive me!

To my ARC team and Beta readers – thank you for your eagle-eyes and consistency. Though this book has been thoroughly revised and proof-read I apologise for any of those typos that will creep in the minute publish is pressed!

We must never forget the victims of sometimes atrocious acts of violence, and it is why organisations such as Victim Support are so important. A donation has been made to victimsupport.org.uk in acknowledgement of the vital service they provide.

Research for this book wouldn't have been possible if it wasn't for the plethora of knowledge and information available both publicly and privately by professionals that work with offenders to help recidivism and rehabilitation. My thanks go to Professor David Wilson, Dr Sohom Das and Kerry Daynes.

As always, my never-ending gratitude goes to my family, especially Mark who tolerates several iterations of the book before it lands in the hands of the reader. He will always be my first real-world reader (sorry love.)

If you've enjoyed this book, please leave a review. Just a few short words or even a star rating is super helpful to others looking for a dark and twisty read!

Don't forget you can download free books on my website and join my mailing list while you're there so you're the first to hear about any new releases.

Until next time, Cat.